High Tea at
The Beach House Hotel

by

Judith Keim

8

BOOKS BY JUDITH KEIM

THE HARTWELL WOMEN SERIES:
The Talking Tree – 1
Sweet Talk – 2
Straight Talk – 3
Baby Talk – 4
The Hartwell Women – Boxed Set

THE BEACH HOUSE HOTEL SERIES:
Breakfast at The Beach House Hotel – 1
Lunch at The Beach House Hotel – 2
Dinner at The Beach House Hotel – 3
Christmas at The Beach House Hotel – 4
Margaritas at The Beach House Hotel – 5
Dessert at The Beach House Hotel – 6
Coffee at The Beach House Hotel – 7
High Tea at The Beach House Hotel – 8
Nightcaps at The Beach House Hotel – 9
Bubbles at The Beach House Hotel – 10 (2025)

THE FAT FRIDAYS GROUP:
Fat Fridays – 1
Sassy Saturdays – 2
Secret Sundays – 3

THE SALTY KEY INN SERIES:
Finding Me – 1
Finding My Way – 2
Finding Love – 3
Finding Family – 4
The Salty Key Inn Series – Boxed Set

SEASHELL COTTAGE BOOKS:

A Christmas Star
Change of Heart
A Summer of Surprises
A Road Trip to Remember
The Beach Babes

THE CHANDLER HILL INN SERIES:

Going Home – 1
Coming Home – 2
Home at Last – 3
The Chandler Hill Inn Series – Boxed Set

THE DESERT SAGE INN SERIES:

The Desert Flowers – Rose – 1
The Desert Flowers – Lily – 2
The Desert Flowers – Willow – 3
The Desert Flowers – Mistletoe & Holly – 4

SOUL SISTERS AT CEDAR MOUNTAIN LODGE:

Christmas Sisters – Anthology
Christmas Kisses
Christmas Castles
Christmas Stories – Soul Sisters Anthology
Christmas Joy
The Christmas Joy Boxed Set

THE SANDERLING COVE INN SERIES:

Waves of Hope – 1
Sandy Wishes – 2
Salty Kisses – 3

THE LILAC LAKE INN SERIES

Love by Design – 1
Love Between the Lines – 2
Love Under the Stars – 3

OTHER BOOKS:

For more information: www.judithkeim.com

PRAISE FOR JUDITH KEIM'S NOVELS

THE BEACH HOUSE HOTEL SERIES – Books 1 – 10:

"Love the characters in this series. This series was my first introduction to Judith Keim. She is now one of my favorites. Looking forward to reading more of her books."

BREAKFAST AT THE BEACH HOUSE HOTEL – *"An easy, delightful read that offers romance, family relationships, and strong women learning to be stronger. Real life situations filter through the pages. Enjoy!"*

LUNCH AT THE BEACH HOUSE HOTEL – *"This series is such a joy to read. You feel you are actually living with them. Can't wait to read the latest one."*

DINNER AT THE BEACH HOUSE HOTEL – *"A Terrific Read! As usual, Judith Keim did it again. Enjoyed immensely. Continue writing such pleasantly reading books for all of us readers."*

CHRISTMAS AT THE BEACH HOUSE HOTEL – *"Not Just Another Christmas Novel. This is book number four in the series and my introduction to Judith Keim's writing. I wasn't disappointed. The characters are dimensional and engaging. The plot is well crafted and advances at a pleasing pace.*

MARGARITAS AT THE BEACH HOUSE HOTEL – *"Overall, Margaritas at the Beach House Hotel is another wonderful addition to the series. Judith Keim takes the reader on a journey told through the voices of these amazing characters we have all come to love through the years!*

DESSERT AT THE BEACH HOUSE HOTEL – *"It is a heartwarming and beautiful women's fiction as only Judith Keim can do with her wonderful characters, amazing location. and family and friends whose daily lives circle around Ann and Rhonda and The Beach House Hotel.*

COFFEE AT THE BEACH HOUSE HOTEL – "*Great story and characters! A hard to put down book. Lots of things happening, including a kidnapping of a young boy. The beach house hotel is a wonderful hotel run by two women who are best friends. Highly recommend this book.*

THE HARTWELL WOMEN SERIES – Books 1 – 4:

"*This was an EXCELLENT series. When I discovered Judith Keim, I read all of her books back to back. I thoroughly enjoyed the women Keim has written about. They are believable and you want to just jump into their lives and be their friends! I can't wait for any upcoming books!*"

"*I fell into Judith Keim's Hartwell Women series and have read & enjoyed all of her books in every series. Each centers around a strong & interesting woman character and their family interaction. Good reads that leave you wanting more.*"

THE FAT FRIDAYS GROUP – Books 1 – 3:

"*Excellent story line for each character, and an insightful representation of situations which deal with some of the contemporary issues women are faced with today.*"

THE SALTY KEY INN SERIES – Books 1 – 4:

FINDING ME – "*The characters are endearing with the same struggles we all encounter. The setting makes me feel like I am a guest at The Salty Key Inn...relaxed, happy & light-hearted! The men are yummy and the women strong. You can't get better than that! Happy Reading!*"

FINDING MY WAY- "*Loved the family dynamics as well as uncertain emotions of dating and falling in love. Appreciated the morals and strength of parenting throughout. Just couldn't put this book down.*"

FINDING LOVE – "_Judith Keim always puts substance into her books. This book was no different, I learned about PTSD, accepting oneself, there is always going to be problems but stick it out and make it work._
FINDING FAMILY – "_Completing this series is like eating the last chip. Love Judith's writing, and her female characters are always smart, strong, vulnerable to life and love experiences._"

"_This was a refreshing book. Bringing the heart and soul of the family to us._"

THE CHANDLER HILL INN SERIES – Books 1 – 3:

GOING HOME – "_I was completely immersed in this book, with the beautiful descriptive writing, and the authors' way of bringing her characters to life. I felt like I was right inside her story._"
COMING HOME – "_Coming Home was such a wonderful story. The author has such a gift for getting the reader right to the heart of things._"
HOME AT LAST – "_In this wonderful conclusion, to a heartfelt and emotional trilogy set in Oregon's stunning wine country, Judith Keim has tied up the Chandler Hill series with the perfect bow._"

SEASHELL COTTAGE BOOKS:

A CHRISTMAS STAR – "_Love, laughter, sadness, great food, and hope for the future, all in one book. It doesn't get any better than this stunning read._"
CHANGE OF HEART – "_CHANGE OF HEART is the summer read we've all been waiting for. Judith Keim is a master at creating fascinating characters that are simply irresistible. Her stories leave you with a big smile on your face and a heart bursting with love._"
~Kellie Coates Gilbert, author of the popular Sun Valley Series

A SUMMER OF SURPRISES – "Ms. Keim uses this book as an amazing platform to show that with hard emotional work, belief in yourself and love, the scars of abuse can be conquered. It in no way preaches, it's a lovely story with a happy ending."

A ROAD TRIP TO REMEMBER – "The characters are so real that they jump off the page. Such a fun, HAPPY book at the perfect time. It will lift your spirits and even remind you of your own grandmother. Spirited and hopeful Aggie gets a second chance at love and she takes the steering wheel and drives straight for it."

THE BEACH BABES – "Another winner at the pen of Judith Keim. I love the characters and the book just flows. It feels as though you are at the beach with them and are a part of you.

THE DESERT SAGE INN SERIES – Books 1 – 4:

THE DESERT FLOWERS – ROSE – "The Desert Flowers - Rose, "In this first of a series, we see each woman come into her own and view new beginnings even as they must take this tearful journey as they slowly lose a dear friend.

THE DESERT FLOWERS – LILY – "The second book in the Desert Flowers series is just as wonderful as the first. Judith Keim is a brilliant storyteller. Her characters are truly lovely and people that you want to be friends with as soon as you start reading. Judith Keim is not afraid to weave real life conflict and loss into her stories.

THE DESERT FLOWERS – WILLOW – "The feelings of love, joy, happiness, friendship, family and the pain of loss are deeply felt by Willow Sanchez and her two cohorts Rose and Lily. The Desert Flowers met because of their deep feelings for Alec Thurston, a man who touched their lives in different ways."

MISTLETOE AND HOLLY – *"As always, the author never ceases to amaze me. She's able to take characters and bring them to life in such a way that you think you're actually among family. It's a great holiday read. You won't be disappointed."*

THE SANDERLING COVE INN SERIES – Books 1 – 3:

WAVES OF HOPE – *"Such a wonderful story about several families in a beautiful location in Florida. A grandmother requests her three granddaughters to help her by running the family's inn for the summer. Other grandmothers in the area played a part in this plan to find happiness for their grandsons and granddaughters."*
SANDY WISHES – *"Three cousins needing a change and a few of the neighborhood boys from when they were young are back visiting their grandmothers. It is an adventure, a summer of discoveries, and embracing the person they are becoming."*
SALTY KISSES – *"I love this story, as well as the entire series because it's about family, friendship and love. The meddling grandmothers have only the best intentions and want to see their grandchildren find love and happiness. What grandparent wouldn't want that?"*

THE LILAC LAKE INN SERIES – Books 1 – 3:

LOVE BY DESIGN – *"Genie Wittner is planning on selling her beloved Lilac Inn B&B, and keeping a cottage for her three granddaughters, Whitney, the movie star, Dani an architecture, and Taylor a writer. A little mystery, a possible ghost, and romance all make this a great read and the start of a new series."*

LOVE BETWEEN THE LINES – _"Taylor is one of 3 sisters who have inherited a cottage in Lilac Lake from their grandmother. She is an accomplished author who is having some issues getting inspired for her next book. Things only get worse when she receives an email from her new editor with a harsh critique of her last book. She's still fuming when Cooper shows up in town, determined to work together on getting the book ready."_
LOVE UNDER THE STARS – _out June 2024_

High Tea at
The Beach House Hotel

The Beach House Hotel Series – Book 8

Judith Keim

Wild Quail Publishing

High Tea at The Beach House Hotel is a work of fiction. Names, characters, places, public or private institutions, corporations, towns, and incidents are the product of the author's imagination or are used fictitiously. Any resemblance to actual events, locales, or persons, living or dead, is coincidental.

No part of *High Tea at The Beach House Hotel* may be reproduced or transmitted in any form or by any electronic or mechanical means, including information storage and retrieval systems, without permission in writing from the author, except by a reviewer who may quote brief passages in a review. This book may not be resold or uploaded for distribution to others. For permissions contact the author directly via electronic mail:

wildquail.pub@gmail.com
www.judithkeim.com

Published in the United States of America by:

Wild Quail Publishing
PO Box 171332
Boise, ID 83717-1332

Dedication

This book is dedicated to you my faithful readers who love Ann and Rhonda as much as I do.

CHAPTER ONE

ON A BEAUTIFUL SUNDAY MORNING IN EARLY OCTOBER along the Gulf Coast of Florida, Rhonda Grayson, my business partner at The Beach House Hotel, turned to me in our office. "Annie, take a gander at this. Remember the royal wedding we almost had here at the hotel?"

I accepted the sheaf of heavy, creamy stationery she handed me and noticed the engraved coat-of-arms at the top.

I read through the request for a two-week stay at the hotel in late January and sighed. "It's such a busy time, and Hilda Hassel already seems difficult. She's requesting high tea at the hotel every day to keep to her usual routine. Doesn't she realize we're all about relaxing and having a good time, not dressing up during the afternoon for something like that? Let's do some research before we respond to her."

"Smart idea," said Rhonda. "There's something about the way she's demanding things I don't like. Having someone royal in a family doesn't make her a fucking queen."

"Let's not rush things," I said trying to remember the Hassels and the history behind them. Although the monarchy of Bavaria was demolished in the early twentieth century, there had been a succession of pretenders to the throne, and the royal family was well-respected. Joseph and Charlotte Hassel's daughter Katrina had chosen to have a wedding at The Beach House Hotel and then eloped with another man before it could take place. The entire situation had been difficult, especially for Jean-Luc who'd planned an elegant meal and then was told at the last minute that the menu had to be changed to a traditional German *biergarten* one. Sighing loudly, I said, "I don't have a good feeling about this. But if we could expand our European business, it could be a wise move for us."

"This woman says she's Charlotte Hassel's second cousin by marriage. I'm not impressed," grumped Rhonda. "Let's look her up online."

Hilda Hassel was listed as part of the royal family due to her somewhat scandalous marriage to Henrick Hassel, twenty-five years older than she. He died eight years ago, and Hilda was an heiress to his estate. Though rarely seen, she supposedly did some charitable work in his name. No photograph of her was available, only a drawing of what appeared to be a regal-looking woman with a straight nose and fine features. Her husband was a handsome man who'd owned a glass factory. Hassel stemware was well-known for their variety of wine glasses and goblets.

"She says she wants our finest accommodations, but she's not getting either house after the mess with her family," said Rhonda. "Let's give her the Presidential Suite and make her pay a healthy deposit. If she's willing to do that, it will tell us a lot about her."

"Sounds like a plan," I said. "After the family cancelled the wedding at the last minute, I don't want to take any chances on disrupting our reservations schedule for the houses. They bring in a lot of money."

"Okay, let's write her back and see what happens," said Rhonda. "It's almost time to leave. It's going to be fun to go to a Buccaneers game to see Bobby and Sydney."

Tina Mark's nanny, Sydney Harris, had met and fallen in love with Bobby "Bugs" Bailey, a standout football player with the Tampa Bay Buccaneers, here at the hotel when Bobby was sent to our hotel for an attitude check. Success on the football field had turned him into an insufferable jerk. Our job had been to show him how a team works together. One person may shine brighter, but there were other people contributing to that success.

He wanted to get engaged, but Sydney, determined not to be a sports groupie, was holding off until she'd gone through a football season with him. Smart girl. Still, I loved the idea of their being together and counted it as a matchmaking win for me.

"Okay, let's finish up here and get ready for the game," I said. We'd arranged to have Paul, Consuela and Manny's nephew, drive us and our spouses to Tampa's Raymond James Stadium in the hotel limousine. Bobby had reserved seats for all of us in a luxury suite, and my husband, Vaughn, and Rhonda's Will, were especially thrilled.

The game against the Atlanta Falcons was scheduled to start at one o'clock and we wanted to get there early to look around. Sydney had flown into Tampa earlier that week and had agreed to meet us at the gate leading to the luxury boxes.

We left the hotel shortly after eleven. To celebrate, the men and I wore the Buccaneer T-shirts Bobby sent us while Rhonda wore a soft red silk caftan to honor the occasion.

"It's a great day for a game," said Vaughn, putting his arm around me as we took our places in the back of the limo.

"It's been a while since I've been to a sporting event," said Will, sliding onto a seat opposite us. "I'm looking forward to it."

Rhonda climbed into the limo next to Will. "I hope I don't make a fool of myself. I can't help yelling when I'm excited."

"You will be fine," said Will, giving her an affectionate look.

She leaned over and kissed him on the cheek. "Thanks, Will. Ever since we came back from Tahiti, you say the sweetest things."

Vaughn and I exchanged amused glances. The trip to Tahiti had been just what Rhonda wanted for revving up their sex life. It still hadn't worn off though they'd been back for over a month.

After parking the limo in a reserved parking area, we all got out and headed for the gate. I squeezed Vaughn's hand, aware of his excitement. The crowds, the red shirts, and baseball hats with the Buc's logo, helped create a colorful, festive air.

I saw Sydney standing by the gate and felt an unexpected sting to my eyes. She looked content. Short and on the thin side but still shapely, Sydney had reddish-brown hair, light-blue eyes and freckles sprinkled across her nose. She was as nice as she was adorable.

As we got closer, she left the gate and sprinted to greet us.

I hugged her tight, remembering the trauma we'd gone through when her charge, Tina Marks' son, Victor, had been kidnapped. That had made us even closer. After she hugged the four of us and greeted Paul, we showed our tickets to the man at the gate, and Sydney led us up to our luxury suite.

"Bobby's mother, father, and brother are already there," said Sydney. At my unasked question she added, "They seem nice."

As we entered the room reserved for us, I studied the red and brown décor. A young man looked up from the couch where he was sprawled and gave us a little wave.

A gray-haired man in brown Bermuda shorts and wearing a red Buccaneers T-shirt stretched over his belly set down the plate of food he'd been holding and walked over to us. "You must be Ann and Rhonda. Mike Bailey here." He held out his hand. "Guess you whipped my boy into shape."

I smiled and shook his hand. "We came to an understanding, but Bobby is a good kid."

"Yeah, he shaped up nicely," said Rhonda shaking Mike's hand.

While the men were greeting one another, I walked over to the woman sitting in one of the chairs outside.

"Hello, I'm Ann Sanders. I'm assuming you're Bobby's mother."

She stood up and I realized how tall she was. "Hi, I'm Michelle. I'm very proud of my son. Watching him play football is difficult, though, when I see how hard he gets hit." Her blue-eyed gaze roamed over me, and when she saw Vaughn approach, her eyes widened. "I didn't realize ..."

"This is my husband, Vaughn," I said, watching Michelle's cheeks turn bright pink.

"I'm a huge fan," Michelle gushed. "I watched *The Sins of the Children* every day for years because of you. The soap opera isn't the same without you. We all miss the mayor."

"Thanks," said Vaughn. "I may do a couple of cameo spots soon, but my work is mostly in movies now."

Rhonda and Will approached, and I stepped back to give them room and then decided to see what was on the buffet laid out for us.

Sydney came over to me. "I see Michelle is fangirling over Vaughn. She couldn't believe I work for Tina Marks and I know Vaughn Sanders. Seeing her acting this way over Vaughn is almost the same way it is when I'm with Bobby, or "Bugs" as people here call him."

I laughed. "You'll get used to it. How are the two of you doing?"

"It's been great. I've met a lot of Bobby's friends, and they're easy to get along with."

"I'm happy for you," I said, giving her a quick hug.

"Help yourself to some food," said Mike, waving us over. "I told Bobby I wanted plenty of it."

I walked over to the buffet table. A platter of assorted sandwiches, a variety of salads, a chafing dish full of a cheese dip and chips, crackers, and cookies were laid out. Hot trays holding brats with peppers and onions, lasagna, and steaming hot dogs were on another table.

"Ice cream bars and cake come later, after half-time. In addition to the full bar, there's plenty of coffee, tea, sodas, and beer," Mike said, indicating the ice-filled bucket on the bar and the coffee service and plate of doughnuts set up on another table.

"Thank you," I said. "It all looks lovely."

"I work as a fireman in upstate New York, and I always make sure the crew has enough food. Even cook it myself on the nights I'm assigned. I'm pretty good, too."

I studied him and realized though Bobby's height might come from his mother, his broad shoulders and stocky body came from his father.

"Bobby tells me your hotel is first class all the way. I told Michelle that sometime we'll drive down and take a look," said Mike.

"Let us know when, and we'll be pleased to give you lunch or dinner," I said, turning as a young man I assumed was Bobby's brother joined us. Though he was tall, not an ounce of fat thickened his body. He was as handsome as his brother but in a different way, built more like a tennis player. But he had the same rich brown hair and hazel, almost soft-gold eyes.

"This here is Bobby's brother, Rick," said Mike. "He's definitely not a football player. The kid has had asthma all his life. That and football don't mix well."

I nodded sympathetically, wondering how it must feel to be

the star's sickly brother.

"I'm great at poker, though," said Rick, winking at me. "That helped get me through college."

"What did you study?" I asked.

"Yeah, what was it?" said Mike. "Poker, wine, women, what?"

"C'mon, Dad. You know I got a degree in business." He turned to me. "I'm between jobs at the moment, but I'm thinking of moving to Florida. I like it here."

"Florida living is nice," I said. "I grew up in Boston and prefer my lifestyle here."

Rick gave me a thoughtful look. "Good to know."

Vaughn came over and accepted a beer from Mike. I helped myself to a cup of coffee and walked to the outside seats to study the crowd as it was building.

Michelle smiled at me as I sat beside her. "I love seeing the stadium fill. It's fun to watch all the people."

"Have you met parents and families of the other players on the team?" I asked.

"Some," said Michelle. "But I can't always make the games. I'm an ER nurse. But Mike and Rick come as often as they can." She turned to me. "I appreciate what you and Rhonda did for Bobby, and I can't thank you enough. I see such a healthy change in him."

"Sydney has something to do with that, too. She's a lovely girl, not about to be starstruck over a football player, which is the best thing that could happen to Bobby."

"Yes, she seems like a lovely young woman," said Michelle.

Rhonda sat down beside me. "What are you talking about?"

"Bobby," I said. "His mother thinks he's changed a lot."

"He had to," grumbled Rhonda. "But everyone likes him now that we got rid of that cocky attitude of his."

Michelle blinked at Rhonda's bluntness and then laughed.

"I couldn't have said it better."

Sydney joined us while the men stayed inside talking. "I'm getting nervous waiting for the game to start. Bobby sent me all kinds of information about the rules of a football game, and I've tried to learn them, but it still seems a little complicated to me."

"There are things to watch for, but you'll catch on," said Michelle.

"I just don't want to see Bobby get hurt," said Sydney.

"Neither do I," said Michelle. "You can help me cheer him on."

Rhonda and I exchanged glances. It seemed things were working out for Sydney. After having a verbally abusive mother, she deserved a nice relationship with Bobby's mother.

We stood and cheered as the Buccaneers jogged onto the field accompanied by the booming of the cannons firing on the Pirates' Ship at one end of the stadium. I'd watched an occasional football game on television with Vaughn, but being in the stadium, deafened by the roar of approval that greeted the team, I realized what I'd been missing.

At the coin toss, the Buccaneers won and deferred to take possession at the start of the second half, so the Falcons were the first to receive the ball. The kickoff resulted in a touchback, so the ball was given to the Falcons on the twenty-five yard line. They ran three plays, gaining only five yards and then punted the ball to the Bucs. I watched anxiously as Bobby came onto the field as part of the Bucs' offense. With his helmet and shoulder pads, he looked bigger than ever.

Later, when he caught a pass and was running the ball to score, I cheered along with the others, proud of what he'd done for the team.

Time flew by as we watched the game and socialized in the room. Before I was ready, the Buccaneer fans were celebrating a win.

"We're to wait here for Bobby," said Mike. "He'll come up as soon as he can."

Sometime later, Bobby arrived with his hair still wet from a shower. He gazed around the room and went over to Sydney for a hug.

His father clapped him on the back, and smiling, Bobby shook hands with Vaughn, Will, and Paul.

There was an awkward moment when he couldn't seem to decide between a hug or a handshake, then he hugged Rhonda and me. "Thanks for coming."

"Great job," said Rhonda. "Loved how you made mincemeat of the other team."

He laughed. "Glad we won."

We chatted for a few minutes more. Then we left the suite, got into the limo, and headed out of the stadium in a long line of traffic.

"That was great," said Vaughn.

"A lot of fun," I agreed. "Sydney and Bobby are getting along well, and his mother was very kind to her."

"It was a blast, but I hope Drew doesn't play football. I don't blame Michelle for being nervous about Bobby getting hurt. Some of the players were huge," said Rhonda. "Even bigger than Bobby."

"That's what it's all about. Force against force," said Will. "But I agree with you."

Rhonda beamed at him and took hold of Will's hand.

Vaughn rolled his eyes at me, and I held in a laugh.

Rhonda and Will were adorable together. Always had been.

CHAPTER TWO

FALL WAS A BUSY TIME FOR WEDDINGS, AND OVER THE next few weeks, Rhonda and I found ourselves active both as part of the functions and behind the scenes. Lorraine Grace, of Wedding Perfection, did her usual fantastic job as the hotel's wedding planner, but Rhonda and I made a point of greeting those guests as often as we could. Even so, we tried to watch many of the Buccaneers' football games now that we had a special player to root for.

We also kept to a routine of walking on the beach whenever we could. It was a productive way to do some creative thinking about the hotel. Some days we could get by without seeing our nemesis, Brock Goodwin. Now that he was once again president of the neighborhood association, he kept thinking that we should share our business ideas with him, so he'd be the first in the neighborhood to know. As if we would ever do that. He'd use our ideas to find some way to interfere.

On one October day, Rhonda and I walked briskly along the sand in front of the hotel. Some people thought Florida had no seasons, but subtle as it was, there was a change in the weather from summer to fall and into winter. The onshore breeze ruffled the tops of the waves rushing into shore as if announcing that change.

I carried my sandals and met the lacy edge of the water, letting the waves rush over my toes. I looked up at the sky as seagulls and terns circled above, crying out. Behind me, sanderlings and sandpipers scurried by, leaving their footprints behind as tiny reminders they were there.

"Some days are especially beautiful," I murmured, turning and facing The Beach House Hotel. It sat like a pink jewel beside the beach like the lovely gem it was. We'd been lucky to be able to keep the architectural features intact. The Spanish influence of the tiled roof and decorative features were stunning.

My self-satisfaction was interrupted by someone calling my name, and I turned as Brock Goodwin approached.

A handsome man in his late sixties, he was not the gentleman he presented himself to be. Several years earlier, he'd tried to force me to stay alone with him at his house on a date I'd foolishly agreed to. I'd felt very threatened by it and had barely escaped what might have become a rape.

"What do you want, Brock?" Rhonda said coming to stand by my side. She had no patience with him.

"I just wanted you to know that I heard you might be thinking of doing some more additions to the property. As president of the neighborhood association, I should be included in their approval. That way there will be no trouble with them later."

"There are no plans," said Rhonda. "And if there were, they would be none of your business."

"We'll see about that," said Brock, giving us a condescending look. "By the way, what's this about Bugs Bailey being a friend of the family. When did all of that happen? Can you get me tickets to a game? Maybe a seat in a luxury box?"

"No fucking way," murmured Rhonda.

I spoke up. "Sorry, we can't be put in that position. It's the same as giving out information about our guests. We can't and won't do that."

Brock shook his head. "You know the hotel is going to fail. I can't wait."

"Don't hold your breath, Brock," warned Rhonda. "If we're in trouble, why do you keep coming to enjoy the amenities we offer? We're doing just fine. In fact, we have royalty coming to the hotel."

Brock's eyes rounded. "Really? I should probably meet them."

I glared at Rhonda and then faced Brock with a forced smile. "Of course, we can't talk about it."

"See you later, Brock," said Rhonda.

I took Rhonda's arm, and we walked away from him before she could blurt out any other news.

"I'm sorry, Annie," said Rhonda. "Brock makes me say things I probably shouldn't, but he makes me so fucking mad."

"I know," I said. "I feel the same way."

"Well then, let's go inside for a cup of coffee and one of Consuela's cinnamon rolls."

My stomach growled. Laughing, we headed back to the hotel.

In November, I received a phone call from Sydney asking if I was still looking for a full-time nanny for Liz's triplets. "I've talked to Tina, and she understands that I want to move to Florida. She recommended that I call you," Sydney explained. "I said I wouldn't become a groupie to Bobby, but he and I want to be together. Neither one of us is happy with a long distance separating us."

"I totally agree," I said thrilled with the prospect of hiring Sydney. "Let's talk to Liz, but we definitely need you. What are your plans for living quarters?"

"Bobby is willing to move to Sabal. It's not that far from Tampa and he can easily drive there when needed."

"Oh, good, because Liz doesn't have room for live-in help

but needs assistance first thing in the morning. Let me speak to her, and I'll call you right back." I hung up the phone and all but danced around the office as I waited to tell Liz the news. She'd met Sydney earlier and liked her.

"Really?" said Liz when I told her the news. "That's fabulous. How soon can she start?"

"I assume right away. If necessary, she can stay with Vaughn and me while she and Bobby find a place to live. Shall I call her back? I can put you in a conference call."

"Perfect," said Liz. "Do it now, because the kids are busy playing, and I don't know how long that will last."

Noah, Emma, and Olivia were now 18 months old and were walking and getting into everything. Liz and her husband, Chad, had turned one of the first-floor rooms in their house into a playroom for the kids, and that worked well for short periods of time.

I immediately called Sydney, and with the three of us on the phone, we were able to take care of details. Elena no longer worked for us, but her cousin, Liana Sousa, was able to work for both Liz and me part-time. Liz's hiring Sydney would mean I could have Liana whenever I needed her without any conflicts with Liz.

We agreed on a start date within a week. Though she was sad to lose Sydney, Tina had found another nanny. With Sydney, Liz, and me ecstatic about the arrangements, I hung up and let out a huge sigh of relief. The Ts, as we sometimes called the triplets, were a handful, and having Sydney work full-time for Liz would be a big help to her. I couldn't wait to tell Rhonda the news.

I went to find Rhonda, following my instincts and heading for Lorraine's office. Rhonda had initiated matchmaking between Lorraine and Arthur Smythe, her daughter's father-in-law, and the romance had blossomed. Rhonda was convinced any contented couple in the hotel family was because of her great skills at bringing people together and only reluctantly accepted that I'd done my part with Sydney and Bobby.

Rhonda was sitting in Lorraine's office grinning like the Cheshire cat when I entered. "Guess what! Arthur and Lorraine are engaged. Look at the gorgeous ring Arthur gave her."

Beautiful," I said as worry dug into me. "What about the business? Are you still going to run Wedding Perfection?"

"Absolutely," said Lorraine, lifting her hand to allow me to inspect the oval yellow diamond on her left hand.

"It's beautiful, but I'm very relieved you're staying with the us."

Oh, yes," said Lorraine. "I told Arthur I would marry him only if he moved here and I was able to keep my business. He'll set up an office here. The thought of marrying a retired exec was terrifying. Besides, Arthur and I are too young to retire."

"I'm delighted for you," I said. "The two of you are great together."

"I told ya," said Rhonda, smiling smugly.

"I've got news," I said, and told them about Sydney coming to Florida to move in with Bobby. "She and Bobby are great together, too," I ended, giving Rhonda a mental jab.

She let out a raucous laugh. "We sure know how to pick them. Right, Annie?"

Smiling, I turned to Lorraine. "Have you set a wedding date?

"That's something I wanted to talk to you about," said Lorraine giving me a worried look. "We're thinking of getting married on New Year's Day and taking a honeymoon following that. No weddings have been booked for that time. Do you think those dates are okay?"

I hugged Lorraine. "We'll make it work. I'm delighted for the two of you."

Rhonda and I left Lorraine's office and went to find a cup of coffee.

Consuela, who handled the breakfast meal, was in the kitchen. She and her husband, Manny, in charge of landscaping and maintenance at the hotel, were more like family than members of the staff. They'd been with Rhonda before we opened the hotel and were strong supporters of us and the hotel. Growing up with a strict grandmother after my parents died in an automobile accident, I thought of them as the parents I wished I'd had.

"'Morning," said Consuela cheerfully as I gave her a hug. "I understand we have an engagement at the hotel."

"All because of me," said Rhonda, accepting a plate with a cinnamon roll from Consuela.

I rolled my eyes, and Consuela laughed.

We took our coffee and treats to the office.

"We're going to have to coordinate times with Lorraine. New Year's Eve is a big night for us," I said. "And we need to find out how long their honeymoon will be."

"We probably should talk to her about pulling one of the hotel staff into her business permanently," said Rhonda. "Any suggestions?"

"Lauren Fletcher at the front desk helped at one of the summer weddings. Let's talk to Lorraine about it. You and I both know that Arthur will demand a lot of her time," I said, thinking how fortunate I was to be married to Vaughn. Between jobs, he was home, and while he was grateful for the way I tried to spend more time with him, he understood when I couldn't.

"Let's wait a day or two and let her celebrate," said Rhonda.

"Good idea." As different as Rhonda and I were, we usually

agreed on most business matters.

"This might be a smart time to ask Bernie to go over staffing issues as we prepare for the upcoming high season," I said. The busiest time of year was December through March.

We called him, and then Rhonda and I headed to his office.

Bernhard Bruner was our general manager. He could be stiff and imposing at times. He'd been affronted at first when Rhonda insisted on calling him Bernie. Much more relaxed now, he and his wife, Annette, continued to be important, beloved people in our hotel family.

We sat in Bernie's office. After going through staffing needs for the next couple of months that included Thanksgiving, Christmas, our annual Christmas Party, and New Year's Eve celebrations, we realized we needed all the help we could get. Gone were the days when Rhonda and I worked in the kitchen or filled in on other functions as needed.

Bernie was amenable to having Lauren switch to Wedding Perfection as long as she agreed to help train a replacement. An image of Rick Bailey flashed in my mind, and I wondered if he'd be interested in working at the hotel. If so, a place to start would be behind the reception desk. I decided to talk to Rhonda about it.

As we walked back to the office, I told her my idea. "He seemed like a nice guy who is eager to move to Florida. He has a business degree and was rattling off football stats like crazy, which tells me he's excellent with numbers. The hotel business might be interesting to him. What do you say?"

"I think it's a great idea," said Rhonda. "I liked him and his family. We need to hire someone like him as long as he makes a firm commitment to stay with us for more than a few months."

"Okay. I'll get his number and call him." We gave each other high fives and moved into the office to start the process of preparing for our annual Christmas party. Dorothy Stern, who'd been a fabulous volunteer for us from the beginning, was already planning on handling the invitation list.

While we were brainstorming, Sydney called to confirm that she'd like to stay at my house for a few days. "Bobby found a house he thought I'd like, but he wants me to see it before making an offer." I heard the excitement in her voice.

"Rhonda and I are thinking of offering his brother, Rick, a job at the hotel," I said. "Do you have a phone number where he can be reached?"

"A job for him? Really? I know Bobby would love that idea. Me, too. Rick's a great guy."

Pleased by her response, I put his telephone number in my cell.

Later, when I called him, Rick was very enthusiastic. "As an elective, I took a course in hotel accounting just to see what it was like. This seems like a perfect opportunity to get to know the business side of it better."

We chatted easily about a starting salary, life in Sabal, and what housing might work. "At the moment, we have an apartment available at the hotel. It was used by someone helping Manny with landscaping, but he and his wife moved, so it's available. If it works out that you want to stay, we can arrange for you to rent it." My heart pinged sadly at the memory of Jax, Mandy, and their baby girl moving out. But moving back to Virginia was a wise option for them.

"That sounds ideal," Rick said. "Thanks. When do you want me to start?"

"As soon as possible. We'll be extra busy with the holiday

activities, and we'd like you to be comfortable with the hotel and your job before they start."

"I'll drive there, so it'll take a couple of days at least. Shall we say five days?"

"Okay, that's a plan. See you then. Thank you."

I hung up and turned to Rhonda with a grin. "We got him. Now, we'll see what he does with this chance to find himself."

"If he's like his brother, he'll come through for us. Honestly, Annie, it's gotta be hard for him to compete with a brother like Bobby who's all about sports."

"Well, he's handsome, bright, and nice. Let's see what happens."

Rhonda grinned. "Lauren isn't going to have any trouble finding time to train him. I just have a feeling something might happen there."

I groaned. "Not another matchmaking scheme. Aren't you satisfied you got Lorraine and Arthur together?"

"You know I have the magic touch," said Rhonda. "And I like doing it."

"Let's give the guy a chance to get here before you start all that."

"Okay. Let's talk bonuses for the staff," said Rhonda. "I think we should give them a very generous one because costs are rising. What do ya say?"

"I agree, but we still buy the staff's kids Christmas toys right? That's the fun part of our annual Christmas party for me. I'll take care of getting names and ages of all the children."

"Deal. I'll take care of the bonus list," said Rhonda. "I can't believe the holidays are almost here. My Willow and Drew are already talking about Christmas. And this year, Angela's three kids will be even more excited, though Bella, like the Ts, is still a little young."

"Unfortunately, a friend told Robbie there's no real Santa

Claus. But I said the spirit of giving is what makes a true Santa Claus. I love the holidays, especially now with my family. My Christmases growing up were not exciting."

"Yeah, I know. We need to find a local magazine to feature us for the holidays," said Rhonda brightening. "I'm going to make a few calls."

"Should we throw a party for foster kids like we did last year? That was fun and gave a lot of them the opportunity to come together with our staff's children for a good time."

"Two birds, one stone. I say go for it," said Rhonda, and I realized how busy we were going to be for the next few months.

The one thing I wanted to do for myself was to spend a couple of days in the city with Vaughn. He still kept a condo there, and Christmas in New York was always special. This year, we might be able to go alone. The thought sent a frisson of excitement through me. A vacation together was long overdue.

Later, Rhonda and I met with Lorraine. She was thrilled with the idea of Lauren being permanently placed on her staff as a full-time employee who would work on several events alongside her. She'd employed a part-time person to help her and, occasionally, Annette stepped in to help. But I knew the happiness that radiated on Lorraine's face was real. No matter his age, Arthur would still be a groom wanting time with his bride.

Satisfied that we'd accomplished a lot. Rhonda and I parted company, and I headed home to my favorite people.

CHAPTER THREE

As I DROVE TOWARD MY HOUSE, I NOTICED VAUGHN AND Robbie shooting baskets in the driveway and pulled into the circular drive in front of the house. I enjoyed seeing them play together. With the weather a bit cooler, they weren't spending as much time on Vaughn's sailboat, *Zephyr*.

I got out of the car and watched a minute as Robbie jumped off the ground trying to sink the basketball into the net. He was tall like my ex-husband, his birth father. And if I wasn't mistaken, he was quite talented. Basketball and swimming were sports I hoped Robbie would keep playing. Football? Not so much after seeing what punishment Bobby went through.

Yapping noises from inside caught my attention, and I hurried to the kitchen door to say hello to our dachshunds, Trudy and Cindy. As they caught sight of me, their tails moved so fast they were a blur as the two dogs wiggled with delight. I couldn't help laughing. They always made me feel treasured by simply coming home.

Vaughn and Robbie stepped into the kitchen behind me. I straightened and turned to them. "How was the game?"

Robbie shrugged. "Okay, I guess."

Vaughn placed a hand on Robbie's shoulder. "It was a close game, and you did fine."

As Robbie knelt on the floor to play with the dogs, Vaughn swept me in his arms. "Glad to see you home."

His lips met mine, and as always, his kisses shot desire through me. I hoped those feelings would never stop.

His broad hands cupped my face, and when we pulled apart, I saw the way his face had flushed and knew he was feeling the same desire.

"What's for dinner?" Robbie asked, and I turned to him, grounded once more. "Grilled shrimp and a salad. Plus, I'll make your favorite cheesy bread too. Hungry?"

"Starving," said Robbie rubbing his stomach.

"If you'd rather not wait, Dad can grill you a hamburger. Would you like that?"

Robbie's smile gave me his answer.

With Robbie growing fast, I knew I couldn't ask him to wait until Vaughn and I were ready to eat. And this was one evening I wanted to relax with a glass of wine and talk with Vaughn about Christmas in New York. He'd just completed a movie, and I had no idea what might come next for him.

Later, Vaughn and I sat on the lanai with Robbie and the dogs. While Robbie played with Trudy and Cindy, Vaughn and I chatted about our days. "I thought it might be nice to plan a little getaway in New York for the Christmas holidays. Would that work with your schedule?"

Vaughn wiggled his eyebrows. "Are you talking about the two of us?"

"Yes. We went with Robbie last year, but I really need some time away. What do you say?"

"That would be great. We didn't get to take a real vacation because of work. This could be a nice break for us."

"We're going to be really busy at the hotel for Christmas, but we'd have time between Thanksgiving and Christmas Day to have a couple of days away. Then, with Lorraine planning a wedding and taking time off, I'll have to help with a couple of events. No weddings, though."

"Yeah, and then high season gets into gear," said Vaughn accustomed to my schedule.

"And if our royal guest, Hilda Hassel, pays her deposit, we'll be busier than ever with high tea at The Beach House Hotel."

"You think she's legit?" asked Vaughn.

"She's real, but we want to see the money before committing to her plans," I said. "She's full of attitude. She might think we're not serious about requiring a deposit, but we are."

After Robbie was tucked in for the night, Vaughn and I sat in bed reading. I glanced at him and recalled how, when we'd first met, he'd made me believe in love again. He was a decent man and an excellent father.

He rolled over and gently took the book from my hands. "Enough with words. I want some action," he said in a teasing voice.

I lifted my arms to him, and he drew me close, we fit together perfectly. It had always been that way, as if our bodies were meant for each other, giving us confidence that we'd each made the right choice.

"Have I told you lately how much I love you?" murmured Vaughn before his lips met mine.

I reveled in the taste of his lips, the manly smell of him. For a man in his fifties, he was healthy and strong and virile. I reacted to his kisses and wanted more. Much more.

Snuggled together, we talked about Liz and the babies, and his daughter, Nell. Six months pregnant, Nell and Clint were bringing their daughter, Bailey, to visit for Thanksgiving. Not only was I fortunate to find Vaughn, but lucky that Nell and I shared genuine love for one another. His son, Ty, was married to June, a lovely woman. Their son was a little older than the triplets. Though we didn't see Ty, June, and their little Bo as often, and I didn't know them as well as I'd like, we enjoyed one another, which was a blessing in any family.

"What would you say if I made a comeback on *The Sins of the Children*? I got a call from the producers, and they are thinking of having the mayor return to town and take over after the acting mayor is killed. The ratings have been slipping, and they've offered to pay me very well."

"I know you enjoyed being on the soap for years, then wanted other opportunities. But if you think you'd like to do it again, I say go for it. It would keep you busy. And as Michelle Bailey said, the show isn't the same without you. As long as you come home to me, I'm okay with it."

Vaughn nuzzled my neck. "I'll always come home to you." His lips traveled to my ear and then he kissed me.

Groaning with pleasure, I melted in his arms.

The next morning, I woke full of eagerness to face the day. Sydney was flying in that afternoon, and I was going to pick her up at the Southwest Florida International Airport after taking a late lunch hour to do some shopping. Some people were under the impression that the seasons stayed the same in Florida. Not true. Even fashionable boots were sometimes worn during winter. I decided to get a couple of holiday dresses, nothing too fancy but different from the familiar ones hanging in my closet. Having grown up with a thrifty grandmother, I'd learned to buy classic clothes that could be worn over and over.

At the hotel, Rhonda greeted me with a smile. "Guess what I discovered this morning." She lifted the paper she'd printed off. "The $5,000 deposit for the Presidential Suite came through on a charge card last night. Looks like we're going to have a royal guest, after all."

"Okay, then after the Christmas and New Year's holidays, we'd better get used to serving high tea. We can make it something new and fancy at The Beach House Hotel. I bet the 'snowbirds' would love it."

"We can even make and freeze some treats ahead of time. And I do love fresh cucumber sandwiches," said Rhonda. "Thanks for the offer to go with you to pick up Sydney, but Willow has a ballet class. I promised I'd watch her if she'd take off those cowboy boots she likes to wear with her ballet outfit."

We laughed. At five, Willow was as strong-willed as her mother. As her godmother, I adored her.

Dorothy Stern arrived. Short, bright, and a fierce opponent of Brock Goodwin's, she'd been with us from the beginning. Looking at her now, I saw the sparkle in Dorothy's eyes behind the thick lenses of the glasses she wore. She was always upbeat.

"'Morning, girls," she chirped. "I'm reporting for duty to help with the Christmas party."

"Great," I said. "Here's a print-out of the list of people who came last year. We need to talk about those we want to add."

"Too bad we're forced to include Brock Goodwin. At the last neighborhood association meeting, he won a vote to pay him a monthly stipend of $1,000." She shook her head. "Of course, no one in the group wants the job and figured it was worth paying him to keep from being appointed to a committee."

"You're still on the board, aren't you?" I asked. Her position on the board had helped us in the past. And now that Brock was freely allowed back on the property, we might need her assistance.

"I'm still there," said Dorothy. "It's the only way I can keep an eye on him."

"Good thing you have strong glasses," said Rhonda. "He's a slippery guy."

Dorothy laughed. "Believe me, I've got his number, and it's a low one."

Our Christmas party for the local community, like our annual spring luncheon, was meant as a PR move for the hotel and as a means to raise money for kids in the foster care system. The staff party, on the other hand, was small and intimate. Organized by Lorraine and her appointed committee made up of people from all departments, it was loads of fun with games and prizes for both parents and kids. In the past, different men took on the role of Santa Clause, but after Bernie had reluctantly agreed to do it one year, he was voted the best and had assumed the role ever since.

Rhonda, Dorothy, and I added names to the Christmas Party invitation list, pondering each one carefully, and then Dorothy went to her small office near us to enter names and addresses into her computerized database. She'd keep us and the department heads apprised of the number of acceptances she received for planning purposes.

I went over the daily financial records while Rhonda started a list of people to contact for PR coverage of our event. I focused more on the numbers while Rhonda handled a lot of the PR for the hotel by contacting local magazines and news outlets with our latest updates.

When it was time for me to leave to do some shopping, , I was ready. I got in the car and headed to Styles, my favorite clothing store. The owner, a lovely woman named Christine, always seemed to know what would look perfect on me.

I entered the shop and stopped, seeing the chaotic scene. Open boxes were everywhere. Christine saw me and grinned. "You're just in time. Our holiday selections have arrived, and you can be among the first to see them, even before they're pressed for display."

I clapped my hands together. "Oh, it's like Christmas."

"What are you looking for? I ordered a few dresses with you in mind," said Christine.

"I need something simple, classic, and wearable for lots of events at the hotel."

Christine led me over to one of the boxes. "Here are some choices you may like. Help

yourself to whatever you want to try on."

Like a kid at Christmas, I lifted out one dress after another, delighting in the colors and styles. I found two in my size and held them up to show Christine. "What do you think?"

She came over to me. "Nice choices. Let's see how they fit on you." She took them from me and led me over to the changing room area.

I waited while she hung the dresses on a hook and smoothed them out. "This one comes in a red that would look pretty on you. Why don't I see if I can find it? In the meantime, do you need any help with these two?"

"No, thanks. I'm fine." I could hardly wait to try them on. They were simple in design, and could be dressed up or down with jewelry or accessories.

I tried on the cap-sleeved sheath and studied myself. I had dark brown, almost black hair that met my shoulders in a soft curl, a style that Liz told me looked good on me. I leaned forward. Was that a gray hair? I straightened and smoothed the dress over my hips and realized that I was a little heavier. But the garment, in the same shade of blue as my eyes, fit nicely. As long as I didn't gain weight, I'd be able to wear it for a long time.

"How are you doing?" Christine asked.

When I stepped out of the dressing room, she gave me a

nod of approval. "Very nice. I've got something fabulous to go with it. Wait there." She left and returned with a beautiful silk scarf in varying shades of blues and greens. "That, nice jewelry, and you're set for almost any occasion."

The dress was pricey, but I decided she was right. This was a smart choice. "Let's see this one on you," said Christine, handing me the red one she'd mentioned.

I tried it on and let out a sigh of disappointment. I couldn't deny it. It barely fit. I caught my lip with my teeth and shook my head. Was this the beginning of middle-age years? I hadn't started menopause yet, but my hips were definitely wider. Even my bust was a tad bigger. I let out a long sigh. Why did men seem to be better-looking as they aged, while women just aged?

I leaned in and studied my face. There were soft laugh lines at the corner of my eyes. That was natural, wasn't it?

"Are you okay in there?" Christine asked.

"I don't know," I answered honestly, not sure.

"That dress runs a little small. Let's try another style," came Christine's comforting voice.

Feeling better, I tried on another simple, fuller style in black. It fit. I stepped out of the dressing room to show Christine.

"Lovely," she said. "Turn around."

I twirled, feeling as if my thoughts were twirling on their own. I was a grandmother and felt every bit of that. I thought of the young women Vaughn worked with and scolded myself for thinking, even for a second, that he might stray like Robert had. What Vaughn and I shared was much deeper, much healthier. I couldn't get on that merry-go-round of needing constant proof that we were okay. He deserved better than that.

I left the store resolved to accept the changes in my body.

It was, after all, just what was covering the spirit inside me. I was young and healthy, loved, and lucky in a life I'd never imagined growing up.

CHAPTER FOUR

KNOWING I WAS PART OF A NEW BEGINNING FOR SYDNEY, I waited in the baggage area of the airport, excited to see her. Rhonda had asked me to pick up a bouquet of flowers to give Sydney. I clutched the pink roses and scanned the crowd walking toward us. When our eyes met, Sydney waved at me and dashed forward.

We hugged, I gave her Rhonda's flowers, and then I said, "Let's get your luggage and head back to my house."

"Could we make a stop along the way? Bobby has a different house for me to look at this afternoon. The real estate agent will meet us there as soon as I call."

"That's not a problem. I'd love to see it with you," I said.

We waited for Sydney's suitcases to show up on the baggage carousel and then we each rolled a bag to my car in the short-term parking garage.

"I've shipped a box to your house, as well," said Sydney. "Things not safe to pack in suitcases."

"No problem. We have plenty of room to store them until you're ready for your move." I gave her an encouraging smile. "You might be lucky enough to like the house Bobby has found. You have no qualms about living with him?"

Sydney shook her head. "No. It will allow us the chance to really get to know each other. I think it's going to be fine, but it's better to find out sooner rather than later. We've talked about it for hours and hours on the phone."

"As you said earlier, living through a football season with Bobby will give you a good idea of how life with him can be."

We got into my car, and Sydney called the real estate agent who agreed to meet us at the address Bobby had given Sydney.

Curious, I drove down I-75 to Sabal and into the neighborhood where the house was that Bobby had chosen. It was located near Rhonda and though lovely, the neighborhood wasn't as exclusive as Rhonda's.

I watched Sydney's eyes round with surprise as we pulled up to a large, two-story white house with a brown-tile roof. "This is really nice," she said.

The agent, who introduced herself as Sunni Bloome, was an attractive blonde who was thrilled that Bobby "Bugs" Bailey had called her. "I told Bobby we'd make this work somehow. He loved the house and thought you would too," she said to Sydney.

"Let's take a look inside," said Sydney in a neutral one, but I could tell she was excited. She waved me forward. "C'mon, Ann. Your opinion is important to me."

We walked through the front entrance into an open area with a fireplace and bookshelves built in on either side of it. The gray wooden floors shone against the cream-color walls. The far facing wall opened to the screened-in lanai and pool, accessed through sliding glass doors. Off to one side was a master suite with plenty of closet space, a huge bathroom with spa tub and large shower with two showerheads, a dressing area off the bath and an office next to the primary suite.

On the other side of the first floor was a kitchen worthy of any chef, with gleaming gray counters, off-white cabinetry, and a small butler's pantry next to a pantry closet. The kitchen bar, part of the center island, could easily hold four stools.

Off the kitchen, sat a nice-size dining room that had a built-in china cabinet.

Sydney turned to me and whispered, "I think I'm in love."

"It's gorgeous," I agreed.

Upstairs, there were four sizeable bedrooms and three baths. "Obviously, the house was built for family and entertaining. Bobby told me you hope to have a large family one day," Sunni said.

Blushing, Sydney said, "We've talked about it, but we're just dating at the moment."

"This house is a wise investment in a fine neighborhood. The price has come down from the original asking price, because of its size and the fact it isn't one floor. So, for a young couple like you, it's a steal."

"It's very nice. How old is it?" I asked, impressed.

"Two years. An exec built it and then was transferred," said Sunni.

"Would you want to change any of the colors?" I asked Sydney.

She shook her head. "Not at the moment." The entire downstairs had off-white walls. Two of the four bedrooms were painted a pretty, light green; one was a sunny yellow, and the other a pale gray.

"The blinds on the windows are all included," said Sunni. "That's a great savings right there. And downstairs, the drapes are included. Another savings."

"I'll talk to Bobby about it, and he'll get back to you," said Sydney. "Thanks for your time."

"Certainly. Be sure and tell him not to wait to place an offer. It's a beautiful home," said Sunni. "Go ahead. I'll lock up. But I'm going to tell Bobby you liked it. Okay?"

Sydney nodded, then followed me out of the house, stopping outside to turn around and study it.

I put my hand on her shoulder. "Well?"

"It seems surreal to even think about living here. It's gorgeous."

"Yes, and if he could get it for a low price, it might be a

smart investment should he ever have to move."

Sydney placed a hand on my arm. "Thank you for coming with me. I was anxious to see what you thought. You know Sabal well, and I respect your opinion. Even if it doesn't work out with Bobby, I'd want it to be a good decision for him."

"That kind of caring proves to me your relationship will work," I said, beaming at her.

When we drove into my driveway, I heard the sound of the dogs barking at our arrival.

Robbie and Vaughn appeared with Trudy and Cindy, and we all took a moment to greet each other before bringing in Sydney's suitcases and placing them in the guest wing.

"This will be your home until you're ready to move in with Bobby. I know you're anxious to talk to him. I'll give you some privacy. If you'd like, invite him to come here for dinner, tomorrow. We'd love to have him."

"Thanks," she said, smiling as she looked out the window of the room to the water view beyond. "This is lovely. And there's the sailboat."

I left her and went to the car for my purchases.

"Been shopping?" Vaughn asked as I carried the dresses into the bedroom.

"Yes. It was an awakening experience," I said and turned to him. "I realize I'm not in my twenties or thirties anymore."

"Thank God. You're perfect just as you are," he said taking the bag from me and sweeping me into his arms.

Tears stung my eyes as I hugged him harder. He was my rock, the one who grounded me.

The next morning, I took Sydney to Liz's house to meet the

Ts for the second time. She wouldn't officially start her job until tomorrow, but she wanted them to get used to seeing her. She'd sold her car in California and was going to rent one for a while until she was ready to buy.

Liz was still in her pajamas when we arrived. She greeted Sydney with a hug. "I'm thrilled you're here. The kids are going to love you, and I feel as if you're a real friend already."

"Where are they?" I asked. "It's unusually quiet."

"They've had breakfast and are watching television in the playroom. If you stay with them, I'll take a quick shower and then show Sydney around."

I led Sydney to the playroom. The three toddlers looked up at us with interest.

"Hi, darlings," I said. "Come say hi."

Noah got up on his feet and toddled over to us, laughing when Sydney plopped down on the floor to greet him.

Emma and Olivia stared at them and then hurried over to us.

"How am I going to be able to tell them apart?" asked Sydney, ruffling Noah's blond hair.

"Noah looks and acts more like a boy with his short haircut. The girls look a lot alike, but Emma's hair has more red color in it than with Noah or Olivia. That strawberry blonde comes from Chad, and I love it on the two girls."

Sydney pulled Noah into her lap. Emma and Olivia stood on either side of her touching her hair. Sydney looked up at me and grinned. "They're adorable."

Olivia tried to crawl into Sydney's lap. Sydney deftly shifted Noah to one side and made room for Olivia. Then Emma crawled on top of her brother and sister. When they all began to fuss, Sydney moved them all off her lap and stood. "Three at once is a challenge, but I'm going to love working here."

Liz entered the room. "Thanks for letting me shower and get dressed. It might seem like such a small thing, but to be able to do it makes a difference to the day." She swooped up Olivia in her arms and kissed her. "Hey, punkin." Then in one continuous movement, she kissed the other two.

Watching how Liz handled her children, I couldn't be prouder. She was affectionate with them, even though I knew how exhausting it was to manage three toddlers.

"Let me show Sydney around," Liz said to me. "And then the three of us can put them down for their morning naps."

"Sure," I said, fortunate for the chance to have the Ts to myself.

I sat with Noah and the girls with a pile of bright-colored, soft building blocks. Though they were too young to actually build something, it was interesting to see what they did with them. Some were cylinders to roll. Others, cubes to stack. While we were playing, I sang one of Liz's favorite tunes to them. I loved music geared for kids.

"Boy, does that bring back memories," said Liz smiling as she and Sydney rejoined us.

Together, the three of us got the kids into their cribs for morning naps. Noah had a room of his own and the girls shared a larger room with a cloth-covered divider between the cribs for privacy. Liz kept the Ts to a strict schedule which made it easier to get them settled.

We went to the kitchen where the baby monitors were set up.

"Ordinarily, this is when I might shower," Liz explained. "Or if I've already done it, this is when I can do things like laundry. With three toddlers, there is dirty laundry constantly. The one thing I've learned is not to try to have everything perfect. Life is full having kids in the house, but it's messy."

"I'm all about being with the kids," said Sydney. "I'll meet you here tomorrow morning at eight, as you requested, and I'll stay with the children until Chad gets home at five."

"Thanks," said Liz, giving Sydney a hug. "And special thanks for stopping by today. Good luck renting a car."

Sydney and I left Liz's house, and then I dropped Sydney off at a car rental place. "Call if there are any problems. See you this afternoon at home in time for dinner with Bobby."

"Thanks for everything," said Sydney. "I'm going to meet him at the house, and then we'll come to yours."

I waved and drove away, pleased by Sydney's flexibility. An important quality for the job of being the Ts' nanny.

As soon as I entered the office at the hotel, Rhonda let out a huge sigh. "Bad news. Lorraine is sick with a flu and the Baker wedding is tomorrow. What are we going to do?"

"I'm sorry to hear that. Looks like you and I are going to put on a wedding. Lorraine keeps meticulous records. We'll just follow her plan."

"This is like the old days where we did everything ourselves," said Rhonda. "I'm glad, though, that the wedding is for an older couple who want a quiet ceremony and an elegant meal." She handed a folder to me.

I studied the notes. Jonathan Baker and his bride, Lucinda, were in their early 60s and had found each other at a singles meeting a year ago. He loved to cook, and they wanted a late afternoon wedding and a fabulous meal. From New Jersey, they were looking forward to a tropical wedding. Lorraine had made a note to keep to tropical flowers.

"Let's make sure Jean-Luc is set for tomorrow. Looks like a guest list of 25 people with Beef Wellington as the main course, with grilled salmon for those who don't eat meat.

Instead of a wedding cake, they want an assortment of pastries served. It looks easy, not like some others."

"Okay," said Rhonda. "But this makes me realize how important it is to get Lauren involved. Let's have her take care of this with our help."

Rhonda called the front desk and asked Lauren to meet us at the office.

She came right away, and I studied her. Of medium height, she was a blonde with a pretty face and bright blue eyes. A little on the heavy side, her curves were appealing, and she carried herself with confidence. Her friendliness was a plus in the hotel business.

"Lorraine is sick," I said. "This is a time for you to handle the event with our help. It's a fairly simple affair that Rhonda and I were going to handle ourselves, but then we thought it a good opportunity for you to supervise us."

"How do you feel about it?" asked Rhonda.

"I'd like to give it a try. Lorraine makes careful notes, so I don't think it will be that hard. The only issue is having someone take over for me at the front desk the day of the ceremony."

Perfect Answer. "We'll talk to Mr. Bruner about it. No worries there."

"According to the notes, you'll need to verify the menu with Jean-Luc and double-check with the housekeeping department to make sure special bottles of both still and bubbling water will be placed in the rooms of the wedding guests, along with the welcome baskets Lucinda chose for them."

"Are the welcome baskets ready?" asked Lauren.

"Let's find out," I said, rising.

We went to Lorraine's office. The room behind it was used for storage. There, sitting on a table were thirteen small, white wicker baskets full of goodies.

"Looks like they're ready," said Rhonda.

"It's important to keep ahead of the game for emergencies like this," I said.

"Yes. I helped make them last week."

"I think you're going to be excellent at handling weddings for Lorraine. Is this something you really want to do? It can be nerve-wracking and requires huge chunks of time."

Lauren gave me a steady look. "I want to do this. Weddings are usually fun. At the moment, I have no plans for one of my own. This gives me the chance to plan for others."

"Oh, but ..." Rhonda began and stopped when she saw my glare.

I knew what she was about to do and wanted to stop any mention of Rick Bailey or any other man for Lauren.

Lauren took a seat at Lorraine's desk and opened her computer to the schedules. "Lorraine showed me how to check for any last-minute changes. But I don't see any for this wedding."

"Let us know how you do with Jean-Luc and the housekeeping department. You'll need the rooms ready for the guests as early as possible tomorrow."

"Yes, I'll take care of it."

"Good job, Lauren. You're going to be fine," said Rhonda.

"We'll let Mr. Bruner know about the change in schedule," I said.

Rhonda and I left Lauren in the wedding planner's office and went to talk to our manager.

Bernie listened to us. "We can handle the change until Rick Bailey gets here. Then we're going to need Lauren to train him. Lorraine told me she thought she'd be back on Monday. She has some kind of nasty flu."

"Thanks, Bernie. The sooner we can get Lauren into the

wedding department position full-time, the better," I said. "And, of course, we always appreciate Annette's assistance. She's already agreed to help more often."

"Yes, I know." A smile lit his usual stern features. "She does such an excellent job."

"Is there anything else you want to talk about?" I asked.

"I did want to ask you about our so-called royal guest. Her deposit has come through, but I don't know much about her personally. Do you have any more details about her other than what you've already told me?"

Rhonda shook her head. "No, but I like the idea of royalty. As long as she pays, I'm okay with it."

A little shiver dashed across my shoulders. The same kind of shiver that had told me the governor's daughter's wedding would be difficult.

"Thought you might like to know, one of the state senators and his wife have just booked one of the houses for Thanksgiving. The family, including a brother, are coming for the long weekend. A last-minute thing, but I was glad to book it after a cancellation."

"I'm anxious to start recouping some of that construction cost," I said. I'd really pushed for building a second house on the property and was eager to prove it a smart decision.

We chatted for a few minutes longer, then Rhonda and I returned to our work.

As we were seated Rhonda said, "I think you'll be pleased. I have a commitment from *Fabulous Food Magazine* to come to Thanksgiving at the hotel and then do an article on it. I asked for a big spread but told them we'd take the best of what they could give us."

"Marvelous!" I exclaimed. "We've needed a boost of this kind for a while. Have you told Jean-Luc yet?"

"I thought we'd do it together. Maybe have lunch in the

kitchen. We haven't done that for a long time."

"Let's go. I'm hungry," I said, liking how things seemed to be working out. We had some busy times ahead, but we were a team.

CHAPTER FIVE

THAT EVENING, WHEN I DROVE INTO MY DRIVEWAY, A silver, low-slung sportscar was sitting behind a yellow jeep. Sydney had rented the jeep, and the sportscar had to belong to Bobby. Things were happening fast for them, but they still wanted to be careful, which I thought was a good sign.

When I went inside the house, all was quiet. Looking out the kitchen window, I saw Vaughn, Bobby, and Robbie down by the boat. Sydney was playing with the dogs on the lawn. Cindy was doing her best to keep up with Trudy as Trudy ran after a ball.

Laughing softly, I went to join them.

"Looks like a beautiful evening," I said to Vaughn as he walked up the slope to meet me. "Are we going for a sail?"

"As a matter of fact, we just got back from a short sail. Bobby wants to learn all he can about it," said Vaughn, embracing me for a kiss.

"Mom?" Robbie tugged on my arm. "I got a gold star in class today for good citizenship."

I turned to him and gave him a high five. "That makes me proud of you."

"Yeah, I know," said Robbie, giving me a wide grin.

Vaughn and I exchanged amused looks and I turned to Bobby. "Welcome. It's nice to see you. I toured the house you're interested in purchasing, and I liked it."

"I put in an offer today. I'm pretty sure we'll get it." He smiled at Sydney. "It's better than renting a condo."

"Oh, yes. And a good investment too if Bobby can get it for

the price he offered." Sydney shook her head. "I can't believe this is happening so fast. I've told Bobby how cute the triplets are. I can't wait to start work."

"I see you've rented a car. Excellent." She'd be independent at our house.

Sydney nodded and grinned. "I wanted something fun to drive to the beach."

Vaughn put his arm around me. "Should we have a swim before dinner? I got some steaks out to grill."

"That would be delightful. It's been a busy day. Lorraine is out sick, and we have a wedding tomorrow. Lauren is going to handle it, but Rhonda and I will back her up."

"Tomorrow, I have a game with New England," said Bobby. "I have tickets for you both, if you can manage."

"How about Robbie and I using them?" Vaughn said, glancing at me.

Robbie's eyes lit up.

"That should be fun," I said, loving how close they were.

Later, sitting around the pool, having cold drinks, the same easy companionship existed between the five of us.

"I talked to Rick, and he's excited about coming here. That's another reason I bought the house. It'll be big enough for the family when they visit."

"Rick is going to be living in an apartment at the hotel until he makes a definite decision about working at the hotel," I said. "Knowing he can stay with you at the house will give him options."

The more I saw of Bobby, the more I liked him. I'm not sure what happened to him to make him difficult when we first met, but that brash, self-entitled man had disappeared. Observing the way he kept looking at Sydney, I had a feeling she'd played a major role in those changes.

"What is your schedule?" I asked Bobby.

"I had a training session this morning. Though we don't have to show up until two hours before kick-off, I'll go back to my apartment tomorrow morning and fix myself a carb-heavy meal before game time at four." He smiled, almost shyly. "Vaughn said I could sleep over tonight. I hope that's okay with you."

"Sure," I said. "Tonight, we'll give you a healthy meal."

"I have steak enough for an army," teased Vaughn, bringing a laugh from all of us.

We got out of the pool and headed inside to change.

That night as I lay next to Vaughn in bed, we talked about Bobby and Sydney and what a nice couple they made.

"Their future looks bright," I said. "But Sydney is wise to step back a bit and stay with us for a while before moving in with him."

"And he has to prove to everyone that he's worth the money he's being paid," said Vaughn. "Enough talk about them. I want you to know that I'm flying to New York on Monday to talk to the producers about returning to the show."

"I think you'll enjoy doing it. You'll still have the option to do some movies, too. Right?"

"Yes, I won't budge on that. But we can set it up in such a way that if an opportunity comes along, it can be handled."

I turned to him and cupped his face in my hands. "Then, I'll be able to say I'm married to a mayor again?"

He laughed before pressing his lips on mine, and all thoughts of mayors disappeared.

The next morning, I stood with Rhonda at the top of the hotel's front stairway to greet Jonathan Baker and his bride,

Lucinda. I was curious to meet them. They seemed like a nice couple on paper.

A car drove into the front circle and pulled to a stop. A gray-haired man got out and hurried around to the front passenger door, opened it, and then opened the back door.

He helped a blonde from the front and then assisted a younger, dark-haired woman out of the back.

The three of them stood by the car as Rhonda and I descended the stairs. The man and the older woman waved at us, while the younger woman, dressed in black, frowned.

"Welcome to The Beach House Hotel," I said.

"You are Jonathan and Lucinda?" Rhonda asked the older couple.

"Yes, we're excited to be here," said the woman. Though we knew she was in her sixties, Lucinda looked much younger, with dyed blond hair styled in a carefree look that didn't quite meet her shoulders. Her hazel eyes sparkled with happiness. Her stylish pants and linen top were a lovely shade of green.

Jonathan grinned at Lucinda and then he shook hands with Rhonda and me. "We're very pleased to be here. Have our other guests started to arrive?"

"Two couples are already here." I turned to the younger woman. "Welcome. And you are?"

"Oh, sorry. My apologies," said Jonathan, putting his arm around the woman. "This is my daughter, Joanne Baker. She's been a great help to me since her mother died."

Joanne straightened and gave me a stiff, prim smile. I recalled Lorraine's notes which warned of tension between Lucinda and Jonathan's daughter.

Rhonda, who'd been chatting with Lucinda, came over to greet Joanne. "Welcome. It's a beautiful weekend for a wedding. You must be excited to be part of the occasion."

"Well, of course, I'm part of the occasion. I'm Jonathan's

daughter," said Joanne in a sharp tone. "Right, Daddy?"

I noticed Lucinda's lips tighten and realized the game Joanne was playing. Jonathan looked uncomfortable, but he said, "Right, sweetie."

Rhonda turned to me and rolled her eyes.

"Let's get you inside and settled in your rooms," I said. I'd let Joanne find out for herself that Jonathan and Lucinda had requested a room away from hers.

"We'll reconfirm with you, Lucinda, about the plans. Rest assured that the dinner is set for tonight. The garden is looking beautiful for a late afternoon wedding and reception."

"I'm sure it will be lovely," Lucinda said smiling. "Lorraine has assured us of that. Where is she?"

"Unfortunately, she's ill," I said. "But Rhonda, Lauren Fletcher, and I have taken over, and there's no need to worry."

"My father is paying for this wedding," said Joanne. "It'd better be everything he wants. I told him it would be easier at home, but Lucinda wanted it here."

"It *is* the bride's choice," I said smoothly, though I wanted to choke Joanne at the pained expression she'd caused to emerge on Lucinda's face.

Rhonda overheard and said, "We always make each wedding special. I'm sure this one will be, too."

At the front desk, I turned Jonathan over to the staff there and said goodbye to Lucinda. "I'll speak with you later. Enjoy your time before the ceremony. I know the wedding brunch tomorrow will be lovely as well, giving you and Jonathan time to relax here for a couple of days afterward."

"Thank you," Lucinda said, looking excited again as she gazed around.

Rhonda and I left them wondering how easy this "easy" wedding was going to be.

In the office, I turned to Rhonda. "We'd better warn Lauren

what the deal is with Joanne. We'll have to work to keep Jonathan's daughter out of the picture as much as possible. She might think she has a say as 'daddy's girl', but Lucinda is the bride."

"Yeah. Doesn't he see how awful his daughter is to his future wife?" groused Rhonda.

"He doesn't want to make waves between them. Did you see the way they look at one another? It's very cute."

"Well, his daughter isn't cute. She's mean," said Rhonda.

Lauren arrived in the office.

"I told Lucinda we'd be in touch," I said. "I think it's best if I introduce you right away so you can tail her and be available for any request she might have."

"Okay. Let's do it now before they get too settled," said Lauren.

"It's best if I don't get involved," said Rhonda. "I can't deal with someone like Joanne without letting her know exactly what I think."

I chuckled. "We know."

We left the office and went to Jonathan and Lucinda's room just as room service was leaving.

Lauren knocked on the door, and Jonathan opened it.

I introduced them and then stood by as Lauren explained what her role was, gave him a card with her cell number, and told both him and Lucinda that she was there to see that every wish of theirs was met."

Listening to her, I knew we'd made the right choice in bringing Lauren on board to help with weddings. She was charming.

Satisfied we'd made a nice impression, we turned to leave.

Joanne arrived looking cross. "Why is my room far away from my father's? I'm stuck on the second floor while his is on the first floor."

"Your father and his bride are in the bridal suite away from everyone else. That's the way it should be," I said. "I'm sorry, but we have no rooms available on the first floor to make a room change for you."

"From your balcony, you'll have a lovely view of the grounds and the Gulf," said Lauren.

Joanne sighed. "I guess it will have to do."

From behind us, the door to Jonathan and Lucinda's room closed.

Joanne studied it and another, longer sigh escaped her.

Lauren and I left to return to the office.

As we walked away, Lauren said, "What was that all about?"

"As Rhonda would say, that was a frickin' disaster averted. I'm sure neither Jonathan nor Lucinda want his daughter barging into the bridal suite or even stepping on their patio uninvited."

"How old do you think Joanne is?" Lauren asked.

"When she's not acting like a two-year-old, she must be in her early 40s. I don't know the story behind her, but it seems Joanne's come to count on her father for all kinds of support and doesn't want Lucinda to upset that."

"I'll keep my eye on her," said Lauren. "I spoke to Lorraine, and she said Lucinda is a wonderful woman who deserves someone like Jonathan. She, too, doesn't like the idea of the daughter interfering."

"Thanks. Have all the gift baskets made it to the proper rooms?" I asked.

She bobbed her head. "I checked out the small dining room and everything looks great there too."

"Perfect. I think I'll take a look at it. See you later."

I left Lauren and went to the small private dining room at one end of the main dining room. It was one of my favorite places. The walls were painted a very pale pink above dark wood wainscoting. The rug was green and pink in a tropical pattern. Crystal wall sconces reflected the light that came through the windows overlooking the beach.

For this event, light-pink, linen tablecloths covered the tables. Linen napkins in a floral pattern sat at each place with crystal goblets and wine glasses. Tropical Fleurs had done a beautiful job with floral centerpieces of roses, green button pompons, pink Asiatic lilies, white alstroemeria, and some eucalyptus to add a touch of green. It was both elegant and informal as requested by Lucinda.

I returned to the office to find it empty and went to the lobby to see if Rhonda was there greeting guests. It might seem a waste of time to some people for Rhonda and me to do this, but a warm welcome often set the stage for a fantastic visit and the spreading of praising words about the hotel.

Rhonda was talking to two women as I approached.

"Hi, Annie. This is Julia Grossman and Heather Withers, friends of Lucinda's. They've arrived early for the wedding. Though they're not staying here, I've suggested they use the lobby and our other facilities while they wait for the festivities to begin."

"Wonderful," I said. "Welcome to The Beach House Hotel."

Julia smiled at me. "The hotel is as special as everyone says. No wonder Lucinda wanted her wedding here."

"I was just asking about Jonathan's daughter," Rhonda said.

Heather shook her head and leaned closer. "Such a trial to Lucinda. Apparently, Jonathan has been paying Joanne to stay with him after Joanne claimed she gave up her job to help him after her mother died. Lucinda will put a stop to that, I'm sure."

"It's a disaster, but like Heather says, Lucinda will take care of that very nicely. While they're here, Jonathan's house is being put on the market with a potential buyer already in line." Julia raised a hand. "But you didn't hear that from me."

Rhonda and I exchanged quick glances.

"Good news," said Rhonda. "Please accept my offer to make yourselves comfortable while you wait."

We walked them over to a comfortable area in the lobby and then headed to our office.

"Lauren is handling the details for the wedding beautifully," I said happily. "The dining room looks beautiful, and the gift baskets have been delivered. We have some time before the wedding itself. I told Lauren we'd help direct guests to the garden."

"Let's go to the staff room and turn on the television," said Rhonda. "The game has already started."

"Since when did you become such a football fan?" I asked, amused.

"Ever since we went to Bobby's football game, I'm a fan of his," Rhonda said. "The luxury suite was pretty cool."

We went to an area beyond the kitchen where we'd built a special room for staff. A couple of couches and overstuffed chairs faced a large television screen placed on the wall. Two tables and chairs were lined up against the opposite wall, and the back wall housed the kitchen equipment. Separate lavatories were tucked behind the kitchen. Pretty simple, but well-furnished and comfortable. Several people were already there watching television. I recognized them as part time staff brought in to handle weddings.

Two men stood and offered us seats on the couch.

Rhonda waved them back into the places. "Thanks anyway."

We pulled over a couple of the kitchen chairs and took our seats amid the group.

I could feel myself tense up as the action took place. As a tight end, Bobby had his work cut out for him. He caught a ball and took off running as fast as he could toward the end zone.

Rhonda and I jumped up and started screaming, "Go, Bobby!" along with everyone else in the room. When he made the touchdown, Rhonda and I hugged.

"He did it!" Rhonda said, jumping up and down. "Our boy did it!"

I couldn't stop laughing for the pure joy of it. I remembered how Rhonda had felt about Bobby at the beginning. Now, she was his biggest cheerleader.

We continued to watch the game. When I had a question about what was going on, a waiter helped me understand. I still had a lot to learn. The game continued. I saw Bobby being tackled helmet to helmet. I and everyone in the room grew still as Bobby lay sprawled on the ground.

I clapped a hand to my heart. "Is he alright?"

The team doctor and others surrounded him, talked to him, then Bobby stood and waved before he was helped off the field.

"That's it for Bugs," said the announcer. "Looks like he might have a concussion. That's the news I'm getting."

Rhonda looked as stricken as I felt. I sent a text to Vaughn and asked him to keep us informed. It was time for Rhonda and me to help with the wedding.

"No wonder Bobby's mother hates seeing her son play football," said Rhonda as we made our way to the lobby. "Did you see the way that guy ran into him? I swear he hit Bobby's head on purpose."

I felt a little sick recalling the sound of their helmets clashing.

As we'd often had to do, Rhonda and I brushed away

personal concerns and faced our guests with pleasant smiles.

Lauren had followed Lorraine's instructions for the wedding guests to gather in the lobby and while we waited for everyone to show up, Rhonda and I chatted with some of them.

Finally, it was time to lead the guests to the side garden. Chairs were lined up on either side of an aisle. The backs of the chairs were covered in white fabric and added a pleasant formality to the occasion. A small white table was placed at the head of their grouping.

The minister hired for the occasion stood behind the beautiful floral arrangement and two candles on the table. Jonathan, looking dapper in tan slacks and a navy blazer, stood smiling next to him. A harpist sitting in the background played music as we helped seat the guests. The musical notes lilted in the air like doves flying above us.

It was a small gathering, which made it nice for the intimate ceremony Jonathan and Lucinda wanted. Two couples from Jonathan's past life were seated on his side next to Joanne. Lucinda's son and daughter-in-law, who arrived early this afternoon, were placed on her side of the aisle along with Heather and Julia. The others were friends of both and were scattered on both sides.

"Nice group," I murmured to Rhonda.

The music changed to Mendelssohn's Wedding March and the low conversation stopped as people stood and turned to face the bride.

Soft gasps of delight were uttered as Lucinda walked toward us wearing an ecru silk ankle-length dress edged with lace. Lace was repeated in the bodice that showed how trim the bride was. Capped sleeves covered toned arms. In her sixties, she was the epitome of a woman who kept in shape, yet still had a welcoming softness about her.

Observing the smile on her face and the loving look she gave to Jonathan, I felt a sting of tears. It was always touching when weddings were full of love and, in this case, second chances.

I followed Lucinda's walk to the improvised altar and happened to glance at Joanne. Her look of displeased resignation was annoying. Lucinda appeared not to notice.

Jonathan stepped forward and drew Lucinda into his arms.

I wasn't the only person sniffling as they hugged each other teary-eyed.

Rhonda and I stayed in the background and watched as we sometimes did. Off to the side, Lauren was waiting to give a signal to waiters and servers to come into the garden with trays of tulip glasses filled with champagne. For those wanting something non-alcoholic, bubbling water was offered.

As I listened to Jonathan and Lucinda exchange their vows of love to one another, my thoughts turned to Vaughn and our beach wedding. It, too, had been a simple ceremony, but very meaningful.

At the appropriate time, clapping began for the bride and groom. Lauren gave the signal, and in moments, four servers stepped into the garden with the trays.

Rhonda and I left the scene and checked on the dining room. As I'd told Rhonda earlier, it was lovely.

Anxious to hear about our football player, we hurried to the office, and I checked my cell phone for messages from Vaughn.

He'd sent: "Bobby has a concussion and will be on NFL concussion protocol for the next few days. He'll be staying at our house and should be fine."

"Whew," said Rhonda. "Glad he's okay. I hate to hear about concussions. He's valuable to the team, and I'm sure they'll take good care of him."

I typed a message to Vaughn. "Thanks. Has he spoken to his mother?" I knew Michelle would be upset.

"Yes. ☺ " came Vaughn's reply.

"Okay, then," said Rhonda. "Back to the wedding, and then I'm going home."

CHAPTER SIX

BERNIE'S WIFE, ANNETTE, WAS STANDING BY THE door to the dining room to make sure people could find their seats. It was a small group, easily managed. But having someone greet them was important to Rhonda and me. We'd learned it was the little touches that made a stay at The Beach House Hotel special.

Four servers stood along the wall ready to spring into action for the three tables of six and one head table for seven.

"Everything is lovely," said Annette to me, before turning and smiling as the first guests from the garden arrived.

"Do you need anything from us?" I asked her.

She shook her head. "Lauren is doing a great job. It was a wise decision to move her into the wedding department. Everyone loves her."

"And you," I quickly added. Annette was a lovely representative for the hotel. Of average height and striking in appearance with graying dark hair and sparkling brown eyes, she had an air of a regal but friendly woman.

Rhonda approached us. "Everything set here?"

Annette and I both nodded.

"Lauren is checking with the kitchen now," said Annette.

"Great, I'm going home," said Rhonda. "Drew has a birthday party to go to, and I promised his friend's mother I'd be there."

"I'm going home too. I want to check on Bobby," I said. "I'm not sure when he's going to be with us, but I want to be ready. I'm still shaking inside at seeing him being led off the field."

"Bernie saw it too. Now that we all have a personal star to root for, even Bernie has become a fan," said Annette, smiling her love for him.

As I drove into my driveway, I was relieved to see Bobby's and Sydney's cars parked outside the garage and Vaughn's automobile inside it. I pulled into the space next to Vaughn's and got out.

Vaughn greeted me outside. "I thought I'd better warn you not to fuss over Bobby. He's furious that he was hurt and had to leave the game. The team lost by one point. I'm holding back and letting Sydney take care of him. I figured it's practice for the two of them."

"Very well. I'm glad you told me because seeing how hard he was hit made me sick to my stomach."

Vaughn drew me to him and hugged me. "He's going to be alright."

"I'm relieved that Robbie likes swimming," I said. "I hope it stays that way."

"I hear you, Mom, but let's not worry about that now, okay?" He lowered his lips to mine, and I felt my body relax as warmth filled me. He always made me feel so loved.

We pulled apart and went inside.

The dogs didn't rush to greet us. When I saw them sitting by the couch on the lanai where Bobby was stretched out, I understood why.

Sydney sat at Bobby's feet. "I'm making sure he doesn't fall into a deep sleep," she said, patting him when Bobby emitted a grunt of displeasure.

"I'm glad to see you, Bobby," I said. "You made a fabulous run for a score. I'm sorry you got hurt."

Bobby looked up at me. "Yeah, thanks. Too bad I couldn't stay in the game."

"Vaughn told me that you've talked to your mother. When you talk to her next, please tell her she's welcome to stay with us anytime."

"Thanks. As soon as I get my house furnished, she and my family can stay there," said Bobby. "Sydney and I are meeting with a designer at Tropical Furnishings on Monday. Syd's already cleared the time with Liz."

"I know several people who've used them, and I think you'll be more than satisfied with their work." I leaned over and picked up the puppy, who gave me licks and then whined to get down as she noticed Trudy snuggled up against Sydney.

"Are the dogs okay here?" I asked.

Bobby gave me a boyish grin. "They're fine."

"Relax, and I'll let you know when dinner is ready. First, I'm going to have a swim and a glass of wine."

"That's a great idea," said Vaughn.

"Where's Robbie?" I asked.

"Next door with Brett. They're working on a computer program," said Vaughn. "He's been invited for dinner, so we don't have to worry about him."

"Nice. Annette and Lauren have the wedding dinner under control, and I can relax."

I went to get into my bathing suit, pleased with the way things were working at the hotel. We paid staff to take care of these details, but Rhonda and I liked to do our share of oversight to maintain the hotel's reputation.

A few minutes later, I floated in the pool staring up at the sky feeling as if I didn't have a care in the world.

"Feels nice, huh," said Vaughn treading water beside me.

"Delightful. But then as much as I love the hotel, I savor my time here with you," I said. Weddings always brought out the romantic in me.

"I like this haven of ours," said Vaughn. "Especially sharing it with you."

He tugged me into his embrace, and laughing, we treaded water together, careful to keep our feet from tangling.

"May I join you in the pool?" Sydney asked.

"Sure, come on in. The water's warm," I said. I liked knowing Sydney was comfortable with us. Aware she'd also be part of Liz's family made her friendship special.

Vaughn and I moved to the steps at the shallow end of the pool to give Sydney space to swim. She swam easily with smooth strokes as she did the crawl. When she came to a stop, she said, "I needed that." She climbed out of the pool and sat on the edge of it, near us.

"I hope you don't mind that I need time off from my job with Liz. I'll make it up to her, I promise."

"No worries. We all have to cooperate in order to make it work." As I spoke, I realized how our "family" had once again grown.

With Thanksgiving approaching, I was ready to greet Vaughn's daughter, Nell, her husband, Clint, and their two-year-old daughter, Bailey. Nell was six months pregnant with a baby boy, and everyone in the family was thrilled for them.

The weekend before Thanksgiving they drove down to Florida from their home outside of Washington, D.C., with a stop in northern Georgia. By the time they arrived in Sabal on Tuesday, Nell admitted she was saying "Are we there yet?" along with Bailey.

I hugged her to me. Nell wasn't one to complain so I knew she must be tired and was still feeling the effects of being trapped inside the car for the long trip.

"Your dad and I are going to baby you while you're here. We want you to rest and relax. It's been too long since you last visited." I smiled at her, as always surprised by how much she and Liz looked alike. It had been startling when we first met.

"I'm glad to be here," said Nell, pulling away so Clint and I could hug and then take Bailey from Vaughn's arms. Named after Nell's mother's family, Bailey was a doll with hazel eyes and butterscotch hair as if she couldn't decide whether to be a blonde or more like Vaughn with dark hair.

"Hi, Bailey. Do you remember me?" I asked. "Your cousins have started to call me GeeGee. You can call me that, too. Would you like that?"

Bailey patted my cheek. "GeeGee, can I have a cookie?"

We all laughed.

"You must be hungry. Come inside, I have some refreshments for you. Vaughn is grilling up some steaks for dinner."

"Delightful," said Nell. "Where's Robbie?"

"He's at school but should be home soon. Sydney, Liz's nanny, has moved out and is staying with her boyfriend nearby. But both of them stop in from time to time. He's bought a house not far from here."

"The boyfriend is Bugs Bailey. Right?" asked Clint.

"Yes. It's a long story, but he's one of the family now. Though his parents will be here for Thanksgiving, we probably won't see much of him. He's finally been allowed back on the team following a concussion."

"Pretty scary," said Nell, grabbing her purse and a diaper bag for Bailey.

"You two women go ahead," said Vaughn. "Clint and I will get the luggage."

I picked up Bailey and led Nell inside the house. We'd kept the dogs in the kitchen so they, in their excitement, wouldn't jump up and scare Bailey.

"Doggie," said Bailey, struggling to get down as Cindy and Trudy barked and wiggled with excitement.

I lowered her to the floor and knelt by her while the dogs sniffed her. "Doggie," she said, patting Trudy on the head and laughing when Cindy bumped into her, making her sit on the floor with them.

"Gentle," I reminded the dogs and they lay beside Bailey who shrieked with glee and patted them.

"How are Trudy and Cindy getting along?" Nell asked. "They're both adorable."

"It's working out well. They're now BFFs," I said, realizing how true it was. Trudy was the leader and Cindy her adoring follower.

"Come. I'll show you to the guest suite. We already have Bailey's crib set up." I recalled the fiasco when I'd taken care of Bailey as a new baby and marveled at how grown-up she seemed. At almost three, she was talking clearly, which was a big help.

As I usually did when Nell and her family came to visit, I had gifts for each of them sitting on the bed. When Bailey saw the big, soft Teddy Bear, she ran toward it.

"Mine?" she asked me.

"Yes, darling, yours," I said, laughing as I handed it to her. She squeezed it as hard as she could.

"New beach towels for Clint and me? How nice," said Nell. "You always make me feel as if I'm coming home, Ann." She hugged me. "I'm glad you and dad found each other."

"Me, too," I said, giving her an extra hug. "You know how much I love you and your family."

"Yes," said Nell. She stood back and rubbed her round stomach. "I wish my mother could know about my life and how happy I am. Part of that happiness is because of you."

"Aw, Nell, that's sweet of you to say." I fought unexpected tears.

The men came in with the luggage and our conversation ended, but I vowed to make plenty of time for Nell this visit even though I knew Thanksgiving was the busiest day of the year for the dining room.

Nell and Clint had just joined Vaughn, Bailey and me on the lanai when Robbie burst into the room. "Hi, Nell!" he said and went to her for a hug. He studied her belly. "You're having another big baby?"

I couldn't hold in my laughter. When Nell had been pregnant with Bailey, I'd had to warn Robbie not to mention big or fat to Nell with the baby growing inside her. This time, Nell was handling the pregnancy better and didn't seem to mind as she hugged her stepbrother.

"Wait until you see how I can sail the boat," Robbie said. He turned to Clint. "You'll come sailing with us, won't you?"

Clint ruffled Robbie's hair. "I wouldn't miss it."

We sat together on the lanai catching up on news, watching Bailey play with the toys we had for her, and being careful to make sure Cindy wasn't being too rough with her. It was cute to see a tug of war between the two of them over a stuffed dog toy.

I glanced over at Vaughn, seeing the fulfilled look on his face. He caught me looking at him and gave me a wink. It was great to have the family together.

"When can I see Liz and the Ts?" asked Nell.

"As you can imagine, it's easiest if you meet at Liz's house. If you're ready, the two of us can go now before dinner."

"I'd love to do that." She turned to Clint. "You don't mind waiting to see them?"

Clint shook his head. "I'll stay here with Bailey and catch up with everyone tomorrow."

"Clint and I'll have a drink while you're gone," said Vaughn. "Robbie can help with Bailey and the dogs."

"Perfect," I said, delighted to have this girl time.

CHAPTER SEVEN

WHEN WE DROVE INTO LIZ'S HOUSE, WE COULD HEAR noise coming from the backyard. We went around the house to the gate. Inside the yard, Liz and Sydney were playing a game of chase the ball with the Ts. Like a pack of puppies, the triplets, laughing and giggling, ran after Sydney and the ball she held out to them.

At the sight, I felt my heart burst with love.

Liz noticed us and shouted, "Hey! Glad to see you." She ran over to us and hugged Nell.

"When did you get here? And where is Bailey? And Clint?"

"Clint and Dad and Robbie are home watching Bailey and the dogs, giving Ann and me a girl break," said Nell.

Liz studied Nell. "You look terrific. Just a few months until your little boy comes."

Nell beamed. "Yes, and I'm feeling well." She chuckled. "Robbie asked if I was having another big baby."

"He can be very cute," said Liz. "Thank God he didn't talk to you about elephants like last time. Come meet Sydney Fletcher and see my babies." The hint of pride in Liz's voice was telling. She'd tried hard to get pregnant and had ended up unexpectedly with three babies at once.

As we walked across the lawn, the triplets stopped and turned to stare at us.

"Come here," Liz said to them, and they made their way to us on strong toddler legs.

Liz swooped one up in her arms. "This is Emma, the youngest."

I picked up Noah. "And this is Noah."

Sydney said, "And this sweetie is Olivia. Hi, I'm Sydney Fletcher."

"Syd, this is my stepsister, Nell Dawson. Her husband, Clint, and daughter, Bailey, are at my parent's house, but you'll meet them tomorrow." Liz smiled at her and turned to us. "The Ts already adore Sydney."

"Nice to meet you, Sydney. You certainly have your hands full," said Nell. "Oh, Liz, the triplets are beautiful and healthy. The pictures you text me don't do them justice. I want to hug each one."

"Thanks. They're pretty cute and are getting to such an interesting age when they can say some words."

"Bailey is talking a lot. She's going to call Ann 'GeeGee' now."

"Oh, good idea to have all the grands calling people the same name," said Liz. "Come inside. I've got some fresh iced-tea or homemade lemonade. We can talk there."

"I'll let the two of you talk while I stay here to help Sydney," I said, giving Nell and Liz a chance to catch up.

After they went inside, I plopped down on the grass and played pattycake games with the Ts. As they were growing, I could see subtle changes in them. Olivia was the leader in quiet games, Noah liked physical games, and Emma was the easiest to please.

"How are things with you and Bobby?" I asked Sydney.

"So far, good," said Sydney. "We've had fun furnishing the house, getting it ready for his parent's visit. Now that Bobby is playing again, he's content. It's important to him."

"You had help from a decorator, didn't you?" I asked.

"Yes, but we've also gone online for bargains, and there are a lot of them in Florida. Bobby and I pretty much agree on money and spending. Neither one of us likes debt."

"That's important. You meant it when you said you two were trying to see where a relationship might lead. You're way ahead of a lot of young couples."

"I never want to live like I did growing up," said Sydney quietly. "It is just one of the ways I want to make changes." She hugged Emma to her and gave her a kiss on the cheek.

My admiration for Sydney grew. I wondered if Bobby knew how lucky he was to be with a down-to-earth, kind, loving person like Syd.

After some time, the children got restless, and we took them inside.

Liz and Nell were sitting at the kitchen table, heads close together talking. They'd been friends from the beginning.

"It's almost time for dinner," said Sydney. "Mind if I give them each a cracker while I begin work on their meal?"

"Not at all," said Liz. "I'll help you in a minute."

Nell stood. "I'd better get back to my family. This is Bailey's cranky time. She'll be fine after she eats."

Liz rose and hugged her. "We'll set up a playtime for all the kids tomorrow afternoon, including Angela's three. Then I'll be on my own for a couple of days while Sydney spends some time with Bobby and his family."

"What's it like going with a football star?" Nell asked Sydney.

"It could be a lot of different things, but for me, it's about keeping Bobby grounded because I'm not going to become a groupie of his. Fortunately, his family doesn't like him acting as if he's unusually special. Between all of us, we make sure he doesn't get out of hand as he did earlier."

"Yes. Rhonda and I met him when we did a favor for a friend of Amelia Swanson's by having him work at the hotel."

Nell gave a nod of approval. "I like it. I can't wait to meet him. Ann said she was throwing a dinner for all of us at the house tomorrow."

"Yes. It should be fun." I'd already worked out an easy menu with Jean-Luc and wouldn't have to cook. Just one advantage of owning a hotel.

The next morning, I checked in with Rhonda and when I heard there was nothing requiring my appearance, I sighed with happiness. Today was for Nell. As a surprise I made an appointment for her at Elena and Troy's spa for a facial and maternity massage. Then I was taking her to lunch with Liz and shopping before the kids' playdate after naps. I couldn't remember the last time I had a day like this.

I went out to the pool and sat with Nell in the sun as we watched Clint in the pool with Bailey. Clint was a nice guy who was proud to be a husband and father. Nell, normally an easygoing person, could be very determined at times, and Clint was the right person to deal with her stubbornness.

"Are you ready to be pampered?" I asked her.

She turned to me with a smile. "It all sounds heavenly. Let's go."

I walked down to the boat to say goodbye to Vaughn and Robbie. Cindy raced toward me wearing her yellow lifejacket. Even though she could swim, we didn't want her ending up in the water without one.

I petted her and she trailed me down to the dock. "See you later," I said to Vaughn. "Nell and I are off to a girl's day."

"Have fun," said Vaughn. "Robbie and I are here to help Clint with Bailey."

I left them feeling pleased about the bond between Vaughn and Clint. It was especially nice when family members got along.

###

The spa that Troy and Elena owned in the center of town was a favorite of mine. The simple tropical look both inside and out set the stage for relaxing. Soft music played as we stepped inside and inhaled the lemony citrus aroma.

Nell and I looked at one another and grinned.

"I'm relaxing already," she said and gave me a quick hug of excitement.

We were led to the changing room and then while we waited for our masseuse, we were offered water with cucumber.

Nell was called to go with her masseur and then a person came for me.

I lay on her table, listened to soft, new age music, and allowed the attendant to work on my face. The Florida sun could be hot and tough on skin. While she worked rubbing in various lotions, I kept my eyes closed and tried not to think of the hotel.

An hour plus later, Nell and I were using the showers and getting ready for lunch with Angela and Liz.

"I'm so relaxed my legs feel as if they can't move," said Nell. "I have to tell Troy how special my maternity massage was. I hope you're still promoting that program at the hotel."

"Yes, we are," I said. 'I love the idea of offering new mothers a getaway. Believe me, Liz used the program as much as she could. It helped her get back in shape."

"I don't even want to know how some movie stars end up looking fantastic after just a couple of weeks," groaned Nell. "My body has never been the same after Bailey, and as Robbie pointed out, this is another big baby."

"You're beautiful, Nell, just the way you are. Angela and Liz, too. Wonderful mothers, beautiful women."

"I can't wait to see them. To think they were college roommates and now best friends living in the same neighborhood. I wish I had that."

"Vaughn and I and the rest of the family would love to have you and Clint move here one day," I said wistfully.

"I would too, but it's not going to happen. At least for a while. Clint is doing well with his job," said Nell. "And I love my job, too."

"I know and that's good," I said, not wanting to push the issue. Maybe someday.

We were to meet for lunch at André's, a French restaurant Nell and I could easily walk to from the spa. Margot and Andre Durand, friends of Jean-Luc, were the owners and provided delicious, authentic French food. The restaurant was located in a little alleyway, along with a silversmith and a dress shop.

As we approached it, we saw Liz and Angela seated at an outdoor table.

Waving, Nell and I hurried forward.

Liz and Angela stood to greet us and we all exchanged hugs.

"This is a real treat," I said and turned to Angela. "Is Rhonda going to be able to join us?"

Angela shook her head. "Willow has a dance recital that Mom couldn't miss. She said she'd join us for the playdate."

"It's nice that Willow has an outlet like dance," I said. Willow was my goddaughter, and I loved her like crazy. Her features were a combination of Will's and Rhonda's, but she had her mother's spirit.

"Yes, Willow tries so hard that it's very cute to see," said Angela. Her son, Evan, was the same age as Willow, which had caused a bit of talk when Rhonda and her daughter were pregnant at the same time.

I became an onlooker as the three young women caught up

with each other's news, but I loved sitting back and listening to it, thrilled that three of my favorite people loved one another. To think I'd lived such a quiet life before I met Rhonda.

We were finishing our desserts when I got a phone call from Vaughn. "Hi, Ann. What do you do for a bee sting? Bailey got stung. It looks red but not too swollen."

I turned away from the others and spoke softly. "Be sure and wash the area with soap and water. Apply an ice pack for twenty minutes and then put on a thin coating of hydrocortisone cream. You'll find that in the medicine cabinet."

"Okay, thanks. Clint wanted me to tell you not to let Nell worry."

"I will, thanks."

"Who was that? And what's wrong?" asked Liz, as three pairs of eyes studied me.

I held up my hand. "No need to worry. Bailey got stung by a bee, but she's going to be fine. Clint doesn't want Nell to worry."

Nell's shoulders slumped. "I should probably go to her."

I put a hand on her arm. "No, Nell. I know how you feel, but this is your time to relax."

"I know, but ..."

"No buts," said Angela. "We're here to have a good time."

"You're right," said Nell. "It's just that I seldom have time to myself like this."

"Let's all enjoy it," I said, satisfied that the look of panic on Nell's face had disappeared.

"Ready to shop?" Liz said grinning.

"Yes," came the answer from all of us. We were going to walk the street looking inside the stores and shops. If we were lucky, we might find a few bargains.

CHAPTER EIGHT

As soon as Nell and I walked into the house, Bailey ran to her mother. "Look! Bad bee," she said, pointing to the sticker on her arm.

Nell swept her up. "What a brave girl. It's all better now."

"Yes, Daddy gave me ice cream," said Bailey. Her impish grin made me chuckle.

Vaughn and Clint met us. "Now that you're here. Clint and I and Robbie and Brett from next door are going to go for a sail."

"Okay, great as long as you're back by five. Dinner is being delivered at six thirty and people will want time to get ready."

"Yes, ma'am," said Vaughn, winking and giving me a kiss.

I laughed, knowing how eager he was to get back on the water. When Vaughn had bought his boat, I wondered if he'd be an owner who never used it, but he enjoyed it as often as he could.

The men and boys left, and Nell and I relaxed while Bailey took a nap. I pulled out a book I'd been reading and settled on a couch on the lanai where both dogs slept. Nell said she was going to lie down in her room, and sitting alone while everyone did their own thing, I found it lovely to be by myself for a while.

I went into the kitchen and quietly set the dining room table for ten. In addition to Vaughn, Nell, Clint, and me, I'd invited Angela and Reggie, and Rhonda and Will. Robbie would be with Brett, and Sydney would be with Liz's kids. Bobby was playing the Green Bay Packers in an away game generally referred to as "The Battle of the Bays."

Satisfied that things were looking nice, I headed back to the lanai.

I stopped in surprise. Bailey was lying on the couch with the dogs.

"Hey, you! What are you doing up?" I asked, pulling her into my arms and sitting with her in my lap.

"I'm awake," she said, smiling at me.

I kissed her cheek. "Okay, but let's let Mommy sleep."

"Okay. GeeGee, I want a cookie."

"Okay, but we have to be very, very quiet. Like a game."

Her eyes lit with excitement, and she put a finger to her lips.

"That's right." I carried her into her room and whispered a story to her. Minutes later, I carried her to the kitchen and set her down at the kitchen table while I got her a sippy cup of milk and a graham cracker. She was close in age to Angela's middle child, Sally Kate, and I couldn't wait to see them play together.

My cell rang. *Vaughn.* "Hi, what's up?" I asked.

"Brett isn't looking too well. I think he's seasick. It's been a rough sail. We're heading back to shore. Poor kid is miserable."

"Oh, dear. Have someone keep an eye on him," I said, imagining how awful Brett must feel.

"Do you mind calling his mother and telling her? Robbie was to stay overnight. It looks like that's not going to happen."

"Can I do anything to help you?" I asked.

"Just be sure his mother is ready for him when we get back. I'm estimating another twenty minutes or so."

"Okay. See you soon." I called Brett's mother and when she heard, she said, "I'll come over as soon as you tell me he's back. Oh, Ann, I hope he didn't ruin the sail for the others."

"This can happen. Don't worry about it," I said. Brett was a trouper, and for him to say he didn't feel well was a big admission from him.

Vaughn and Clint dropped the boys off at the dock and then went to work on washing down the boat while I led Brett up the slope to his mother. The poor kid's pale face had a greenish tinge to it, and I knew how awful he felt.

His mother wrapped her arms around him. "Let's get you home." She turned to me. "Thank Vaughn for letting Brett come for a sail. He loves to do that. I'm sorry it didn't work this time."

"I'll tell Vaughn," I assured her as they walked away. "Feel better soon, Brett." I wrapped my arm around Robbie's shoulder. "How are you feeling?"

"Fine. I want to go with you to see the Ts," said Robbie.

"Okay. Nell and Bailey are ready to go." We went inside and spoke to Nell, who'd just gotten off the phone with Liz. "Everything is a go," she said. "Are you coming too, Robbie?"

He nodded and grinned. "The Ts are great."

After getting Bailey into the car, I realized how easy it was simply to take off without having to worry about wet diapers, forgetting a favorite toy, and other delays that came with a child Bailey's age.

Liz met us at the door and ushered us through the house and into the backyard where Sydney was playing with the Ts.

Bailey started wiggling in Nell's arms, anxious to join them. Nell set her down, and as I watched her run to them, tears stung my eyes. It was a tender moment.

Three pairs of eyes followed Bailey's movements, and then all three triplets got to their feet. Bailey went to hug Olivia and knocked her down.

Sydney talked softly to Bailey, explaining the Ts were still sometimes unsteady on their feet.

Noah came over to Bailey and put his arms around her.

I glanced at Nell and saw the moisture in her eyes. "I think they're going to be close friends."

"I hope so," Nell said. "This is why I'd even consider moving to Florida. Being here with family."

Bailey walked over to the large, purple-plastic climbing tunnel and immediately crawled inside. Emma crawled over to her and followed her.

"How adorable," said Nell to Liz.

Liz grinned. "Something to keep them busy. That, the water table, and the special swing set with three baby swings are worth every penny. Thankfully, their grandparents agree."

Nell put an arm around Liz. "I don't know how you do it."

"I can do it because I have Sydney to help me," Liz said modestly.

I turned as Angela arrived with her three. Evan marched into the yard as if he owned it, followed by Sally Kate, who toddled behind him. Angela followed, holding Isabella.

I went to greet Angela. Rhonda's daughter was like my own and I loved her dearly.

"Hi, Ange," I said, taking the baby from her and kissing her cheek.

"Thanks again for lunch," she said, and twirled around. "How do you like my new outfit?" She'd found a pair of black jeans on sale and a light-weight turquoise sweater that offset her long, dark hair nicely.

"I knew they'd look terrific on you," I said.

"The kids are excited to spend some time here. Where's Mom?" asked Angela.

"She should be here any minute," I said. "Drew took a late nap."

We went over to Liz, Nell, and Sydney, who stood watching Robbie crawling along the grass chasing the Ts. When he stopped and rolled over, the Ts crawled over to him and climbed up on his body their laughter ringing out. Evan and Sally Kate threw themselves down by Robbie, allowing Bailey and the Ts to crawl on them.

"They're like a pile of playful puppies," said Nell grinning.

"Good thing the grass Chad put in can handle it and still be soft for the kids," said Liz. "Chad makes sure it's a safe place for them. No fire ants or anything like it."

"Chad has turned out to be such a great father," I commented. "All three of you young mothers are lucky. It doesn't always happen that way."

"Here she is," said Liz, smiling and waving to Rhonda. They were as close as Angela and I were.

Rhonda swept onto the lawn, holding Drew's hand while Willow, dressed in her favorite ballerina costume and cowboy boots hurried ahead of her and went right to the water table.

"Willow, come say hi to everyone," said Rhonda. "Drew, this is Nell, Liz's sister, and Sydney who babysits for Liz."

Drew half-hid behind Rhonda and lifted his hand in a cute, little wave.

Willow marched over. 'Hi, everyone." She stopped and stared at Sydney. "Who are you?"

Sydney knelt in front of her. "I'm Sydney. Who are you?"

"I'm Willow Grayson, and I'm four and a ballerina. See?" Willow took a flying leap in the air and landed on her feet.

"How marvelous," said Sydney. "I bet you felt like you were flying."

Willow giggled. "Yes. I can sometimes fly." She looked up at Rhonda. "Right, Mommy?"

"I'm sure it feels that way," Rhonda said, playing along. "Please, take Drew's hand and lead him over to the other kids."

Willow grabbed Drew's hand and tugged him away from Rhonda. "C'mon. It'll be fun."

Drew trotted behind Willow.

"They are very cute together," I told Rhonda.

"They can be when Willow isn't bossing Drew around. As shy as he is, he knows what he wants to do and what he doesn't," said Rhonda.

"I'm hoping Bailey is as nice to her younger brother," said Nell. She approached Rhonda and gave her a hug. "It's wonderful to see you."

"It's great to have you back in town for Thanksgiving. When are you going to move here to be part of the family year-round?" Rhonda asked in her usual blunt way.

Nell laughed. "I guess you and Ann have discussed it. Seriously, I'd like to be able to do it, but Clint's work and mine keep us in D.C."

"Well, stranger things can happen. Reggie's father is engaged to Lorraine Grace who handles our weddings and soon he'll be living here. All because of me."

I rolled my eyes. "Rhonda arranged to have them meet and now they're getting married."

"I have a special talent for matchmaking," said Rhonda. "Why if it weren't for me, several couples I know would not now be married."

"Okay, that's going too far," I said, laughing. It was an ongoing contest between us. Rhonda had been a little miffed that I'd claimed success with Sydney and Bobby.

We women continued to chat, interrupted occasionally by the need to handle a situation with one of the kids. I loved having the chance to be together and to see how the kids got along. Robbie led Willow and Evan around while the smaller kids stuck together playing in and around the tunnel.

When fussing began, Sydney handed out crackers and sippy cups full of juice which gave us a little more time before we had to get back to our schedules. Thank God dinner was being catered.

That evening with my guests seated at the dining room table, I gazed at them, my heart filling with love. It had been a day spent with family, a day to treasure.

Later, lying in bed with Vaughn, I told him about my day and the joy of being together.

"We have a wonderful family, both real and adopted from the work you do at the hotel. Your hotel family," said Vaughn. "It makes life interesting."

"And rewarding," I added and then sat up as Robbie came into the room.

"Mom? I don't feel good," he said.

I quickly got out of bed and led him to the bathroom where he proved how sick he felt.

CHAPTER NINE

THE NEXT TWO DAYS WERE MISERABLE FOR BOTH Rhonda and me. What we thought had been Brett's seasickness was a fast-moving flu. Every child from the playdate was sick at one time or another. I worried my apologies to their mothers were not enough. I should've kept Robbie away from them, but he'd told me he felt fine.

Just when the children felt better, I felt sick, and then Rhonda had what turned out to be a 24-hour bug the day before we had a photo shoot with the people from Fabulous Food Magazine. We'd agreed to do an interview with them before they did a series of photos of the behind-the-scenes activity for the hotel's Thanksgiving dinner.

Still feeling off, I called Rhonda. "We're supposed to meet with the reporter from Fabulous Food Magazine at two o'clock. I don't know about you, but I look awful after being sick."

"If you look terrible, you know I look even worse," said Rhonda. "What are we going to do?"

I let out a long sigh. "I hate the thought, but I'll call Chad's mother and ask if she can do makeup for us." Sadie Bowen was all about the local theater. She'd even told the kids that she wouldn't be available to babysit the Ts because she'd be too busy with productions. She had, however, written a wedding song for them which she insisted upon singing at their ceremony and had written a song for the Ts which she put in one of her performances.

"Sadie might be a big help," said Rhonda. "Having The

Beach House Hotel part of their magazine was a coup for us. I'd hate to have to back out at the last minute."

"We can't," I said. "I'll call Sadie and set up an appointment with her."

After I hung up, I drew a deep breath and punched in Sadie's number. We were always polite to one another, but I knew she'd hurt Liz in the past, forcing me to work on my attitude when dealing with her. As it turned out, Sadie was thrilled to be asked.

At one o'clock Rhonda and I sat in our office waiting for Sadie to show up.

"Annie, I've never seen you looking so washed out," said Rhonda. "But then, you usually look beautiful."

I gave her a wan smile. "Sadie can help us both. Are you feeling better?"

"Better than I was a day or two ago," she sighed. "Thankfully, Will hasn't got it."

"Neither have Vaughn or Clint," I said. "Let's hope it stays that way. It's Nell we were worried about, but she's bounced back beautifully. She says it's the fresh air here in Sabal that's helping her."

I looked up as Sadie entered the office. Her long hair was dyed a bright red and her blue eyes were surrounded by a line of dark kohl, exaggerating them. She wore a full knee-length skirt and a peasant blouse that she'd kept open at the neckline to show her cleavage. Her carefree appearance always amused me because her son was as conservative as she was flamboyant.

"We're relieved you're here," said Rhonda.

"Thanks for coming to our rescue," I said.

"Anytime I can put my theater skills to use, I'm happy to

do so," said Sadie. She lifted her large cosmetics bag. "Who's first?"

"I am," said Rhonda. "It's going to take you longer to do me."

Sadie hummed a song as she opened her case and attended to Rhonda. I watched her work, impressed by how easily she applied makeup, added blush, mascara, eyeliner and all the other tricks of the trade to make Rhonda look more refreshed.

"Wow." said Rhonda, gazing at herself in a mirror. "You do nice work."

"Thanks. I must say you look better," said Sadie. She turned to me. "Your turn, Ann."

Fifteen minutes later, I studied myself in the mirror. "You're a true miracle worker, Sadie. How can we ever thank you?"

"I don't do enough with the kids, and this makes me feel better. But, as I told Chad, the theater has kept me independent all these years, and I can't give it up."

"I know how much it means to you," I said, wondering why she couldn't spend even a little bit of time with the Ts. It made me wonder what Chad's childhood had been like living with his single mother. He'd grown into a man who loved our family.

"By the way, I was talking to my theater group about activities in town for the holidays. I think The Beach House Hotel should offer high tea every Sunday for the month of December. It would make a nice holiday gift or treat for the community."

Rhonda and I grinned at each other.

"Great idea," said Rhonda. "We were thinking of trying some out after the New Year, but December is even a better time to do it before our royal guest arrives in late January."

"Royal guest?" Sadie leaned forward. "Who's coming?"

"You know we can't talk about our guests, Sadie," I said. "This one is someone I suspect few have ever heard of."

"Okay, but if you get the chance to introduce me to them, I'd be honored," said Sadie, giving me an air-kiss goodbye.

After she left, Rhonda turned to me. "Sadie did a great job. We look like different people. I'm racing home to change and will be right back."

I'd brought the dress I'd chosen to wear to the office and quickly changed there, relieved to have time to spruce up the space. Then I called Jean-Luc to make sure he'd be ready to meet with the reporter who'd be taking photos.

By the time Rhonda returned to the hotel, we were ready.

The reporter turned out to be an attractive young woman named Chloe Davenport who loved to talk and had an easy way about asking for information.

"As an independent woman, I love the story of how you two got together and made a success of this hotel. What would you tell other women in your similar situation of having your husband leave you after many years of marriage?"

Rhonda glanced at me and back to Chloe. "I'd tell them not to let any rat bastard ruin your life, to begin a new better one."

Chloe laughed. "And you, Ann?"

"I'd tell them to try and think of it as a new beginning. I was lucky because Rhonda wanted me to work with her on building The Beach House Hotel. Not everyone will be that fortunate. But I would encourage them to reach out to other women for support."

"Everyone wants to come to The Beach House Hotel. I can see why. It's elegant yet not stuffy. And I hear the food is delicious. Are you doing anything special for the holidays?"

"Yep. We're serving high tea on Sundays," said Rhonda. "To practice for a certain royal guest's appearance."

I sighed. We'd now be committed to having Hilda Hassel

at the hotel. I'd do my best to ignore the bad feelings I had about it. We had to get through Thanksgiving, Christmas, and New Year's Eve before she was scheduled to arrive.

"High Tea at The Beach House Hotel sounds delightful," exclaimed Chloe. "How do I sign up?"

"We don't have it organized, but I'll make a note to call you when we do, ," I said.

"We'll be advertising it, but it'll be every Sunday around three," said Rhonda, turning away from my warning look. I loved Rhonda's excitement, but we had no idea what was on the ever-changing wedding schedule, and I wasn't sure we could have high tea and a late afternoon wedding at the same time.

"Okay," Chloe said. "Let's discuss your policy of privacy at the hotel. Everyone knows that guests are not allowed to talk about or interfere in any way with others staying at the hotel. It's a policy that has obviously worked for you because your guests include famous people who want their privacy."

"Yes," I said. "It's important to us to be able to provide that sense of privacy. It started with a few high-level government meetings and grew from there."

"How do you keep guests from taking photographs of others?"

"We talk to them at once," said Rhonda. "If it happens again, they're asked to leave. Guests must sign an agreement at check-in time stipulating this."

"It's worked pretty well, and those who want their privacy are understanding as a rule," I added. "But you're here to talk about food."

"Yes," said Chloe. "I ate breakfast here this morning, and the cinnamon rolls were to die for. Tell me about those."

We launched into how those breakfast rolls were a hit from the beginning, how the recipe appeared in New York City media, and how it helped grow our name.

By the time, Chloe was ready for her next interview at the hotel with Jean-Luc, I was exhausted, and by the looks of her, Rhonda was too.

After we introduced Chloe to Jean-Luc, I turned to Rhonda. "I'm going home. I'll see you here tomorrow morning." It would be a long day. Our four Thanksgiving meal serving times started at 11 AM and went through 6 PM.

"I'm outta here too," said Rhonda. "I'm relieved we're waiting to put on high teas in December."

I let out a long sigh. There was so much I could say.

Rhonda put her arm around me. "Don't worry so, Annie. What could go wrong? Hilda Hassel is someone who wants to have a lovely place to stay. The Beach House Hotel is perfect for her."

"You're right," I said reluctantly. "Having high teas will give us the practice we need for her visit."

"That's my girl," said Rhonda. "Now let's go home."

CHAPTER TEN

ALL STAFF MEMBERS WERE CALLED TO DUTY ON Thanksgiving Day. Sometimes, housekeepers were used to clear the tables between courses as kitchen staff served up more and more food.

Bernie was amidst those serving food, replenishing the buffet that held much more than turkey and stuffing. Ham and roast beef were offered along with mashed potatoes, roasted potatoes, sweet potato casserole, an array of vegetables, a table of seafood selections and the most popular of all, the dessert table. The men carving the meat were kept busy as serving pieces were constantly replenished.

My family was arriving for the four o'clock seating, and I could hardly wait to have the chance to sit and join them. Seeing the food, inhaling the delicious aromas for most of the day had whetted my appetite. The air of contentment in the dining room was one I enjoyed every year as those fortunate enough to have made reservations were enjoying their meals. Best of all, a portion of the sales was given to our local food bank for Christmas distributions. It made the food taste even better.

Seeing my family enter the dining room, I was filled with love. Liz and Chad were having Thanksgiving at home, giving Sydney the opportunity to join Vaughn and me and the rest of the family.

Bailey waved. "Hi, GeeGee."

She looked adorable. Nell had put an orange ribbon in Bailey's hair, and she was wearing a white smocked dress with a pumpkin design across the chest.

I took her from Clint's arms and hugged her. "Ready to eat?"

"Turkey."

I put my arm around Robbie. "Hope you have a healthy appetite. There's plenty of food."

We were seated at a table in the corner where I could keep an eye on things.

Vaughn sat next to me. "Relax and enjoy the meal. Everything is going smoothly."

"You're right. I should," I said smiling at him.

I'd just taken a bite of turkey when a commotion at the other side of the room caught my attention. I went over to see what was going on.

"It's okay," said Bernie. "A little choking incident." He spoke to the small crowd that had gathered around an elderly man. "Please go back to your seats. Fortunately, our staff was able to help."

I turned to him. "What happened?

"The gentleman choked on some food and the waiter performed the Heimlich maneuver and just like that, he's fine. I don't want to cause people to worry. Best if we all go on our way."

"Of course. Thanks for handling this."

"You're welcome, Ann. It's been quite a day but nothing we couldn't handle," he said with a smile.

I squeezed his arm. "That's why Rhonda and I are lucky to have you." Bernie had turned down other management offers from time to time to stay with us.

"Everything okay?" Vaughn asked as I slid into my chair.

"Fine," I said and filled him in on the situation.

"You're lucky to have the staff you do," said Nell. "Everyone here is being very pleasant. Especially with the little kids."

"Thanks. I'll be sure to let them know at our next staff meeting."

The rest of the meal went smoothly. Then I left them enjoying dessert to go back and greet people at the door. Annette needed a break.

The next morning, as we did every year, we put up Christmas decorations all over the hotel, including a large, freshly cut Douglas Fir tree in the lobby. I didn't care how many years we made it happen, I knew I'd never get over the excitement of seeing the bright colors and lights, inhaling the holiday scents. Fresh greens and candles and other decorations began to fill spaces in the lobby and on the dining room tables. Two staff members decorated the tree with tiny white lights that were reflected in the over-sized colored glass balls hanging from and in between the branches.

That afternoon, standing back to admire the tree, I turned to Rhonda. "Do you remember our first Christmas tree at the hotel? It was magical then, and it's magical now."

"It certainly dresses up the place. Our guests love it too. I guess we'd better go talk to Jean-Luc about high teas."

"It will mean keeping the kitchen staff busier than usual, but we all can pitch in," I said. "Bernie is already on board with it."

We walked together to Jean-Luc's office. He looked up at us and shook his head. "I got the memo. You want to put on high teas. Now, you want me to say okay, *oui?*"

"Yes," said Rhonda. "We were thinking of Sundays at three o'clock to start."

"In the month of December," I added. "If it goes well, we want to continue serving them through the high season. What do you think?"

"As long as I don't have to oversee it, I'm fine with it," said Jean-Luc. "Emilie, my pastry chef, is thrilled to have this opportunity."

"Thank you. We'll talk to her about it, but we wanted your approval first," I said. Jean-Luc was a valued member of the staff, but he, like most chefs, he could be prickly about protocol.

"Good thing Jean-Luc is on board," said Rhonda as we returned to our office. "Now, we need to make sure we have all the supplies we need for the high teas. I think we should have special teacups, plates, and serving pieces for them, something different from our standard supply."

"Maybe something with flowers," I said, excited by the idea. "Maybe we can serve the high tea in the library instead of trying to fill the lobby or change around the dining room."

Rhonda's eyes sparkled. "I love that. It's time we did something new like this."

After meeting with Emilie, Rhonda and I went online and chose what we wanted from our hotel dishware wholesaler in Atlanta and placed an emergency order.

After that was done, Rhonda turned to me. "Guess we're about to learn a little bit more about different varieties of tea. Let's have some fun and go to my favorite gourmet store and talk to the people there."

"Another day," I said. "I want to spend time with Nell and her family."

"Deal." Rhonda checked her watch. "I had no idea it was this late. Thank goodness, we have no weddings this weekend, though the way Arthur and Lorraine were falling all over each other at Thanksgiving dinner, I'm surprised they didn't decide to get married now." She wiggled her eyebrows and gave me an impish grin. "I knew it. Those two were made for each other."

Laughing, I left the office and hurried to my car. Nell and Clint were driving back to D.C. tomorrow afternoon. Nell had spent time with Liz earlier, but while Bailey was napping, I hoped to have some time alone with her.

At home, I found Nell on the lanai sipping a cup of tea.

I sat beside her on the couch, leaving room for Trudy and Cindy on the other side of her, and told her about our plans for high tea. "What is your favorite tea and why?"

"Of course, I like tea by Earl Grey and Twining, but there are a lot of other teas out there. Like Rhonda says, you can have some fun learning about them. My neighbor is sort of an expert. I'll send you information and some samples," said Nell. "I'm proud of you and the work you and Rhonda have done with the hotel."

"Thanks. That means a lot coming from you." I smiled at her. "You've been such a blessing in my life. I'll never forget how you supported a growing relationship between Vaughn and me. And now you're like a daughter to me."

"At the risk of sounding like Rhonda, I knew you two were meant for each other," said Nell with a twinkle of humor in her eyes.

I laughed and then hugged her. "I think so too. Now, what can I do for you during this last day here in Sabal?"

"I can't think of anything I'd like more than relaxing like this and talking. I haven't told Dad, but Clint and I have decided on a name for this little one," Nell said, caressing her round stomach. "How do you like Edward Vaughn Dawson. Ned for short?"

"I love it," I said. "Your father will be proud." I gazed around. "Are Vaughn and Clint sailing?"

"Yes. I encouraged it," Nell said. "I've been thinking about how we could move here. It would take some work and would mean traveling, but we might be able to do it. I don't want to push Clint too hard on the issue. We're going to have several talks about a move this big."

I chuckled and gave her a thumbs up. "I hope he sees the value of being close to family."

"It's very satisfying to see Bailey playing happily with her cousins and Angela's babies. Not many people get to have an extended family like ours."

"That's very true. I hope you enjoyed meeting Bobby Bailey. He and Sydney are new members of my hotel family." They'd stopped by the house to wish everyone a Happy Thanksgiving.

"He wasn't the jerk I thought he was," Nell said with her usual honesty. "And Sydney is a great person. Together, they're very appealing."

"I agree," I said and looked over to the doorway where Bailey was making her way toward us.

"Hi, sweetie. You're awake I see," I said, going to her and picking her up. She nestled her head against my shoulder, and I melted inside. She was an inquisitive, sensitive child who was easy to love.

She patted my cheek. "GeeGee."

"Yes?"

She said nothing but snuggled closer.

"I think when we go home this time, she'll remember much more about you," said Nell.

"We'll do more and more facetime," I said. "You're always good about that."

"That's a promise," said Nell. "Clint's parents are often busy with other things, and we sometimes miss out on sharing Bailey with them. It's sad really."

"Maybe that will change when your little boy gets here," I said, trying to comfort her.

"Maybe not," Nell answered with a tone of resignation.

I shook my head. Families were complicated.

The next morning, the family ate breakfast together before Nell and Clint did a few last-minute things before packing for their trip home.

Liz appeared just before they left. As I watched the sisters hug, tears stung my eyes.

Vaughn, standing next to me, squeezed my hand and I knew he was as sad as I to have Nell and her family leave.

We stood in the driveway and waved until the car was out of sight.

Liz came over to me. "Do you have time to help me? Chad is busy with a client, and Sydney is off. I want to do a little window shopping for a dress for a Christmas gala we've been invited to. I thought I'd put the Ts in their triple stroller and walk through downtown with them while I shop. But I can't do that alone."

"I'm happy to help. I need your advice on tea. I'll explain later as we walk through town."

Liz grinned. "Okay. Deal."

As we made our way along the sidewalks, people stopped to fuss over the babies. Olivia seemed to love it most, but Noah and Emma often responded too.

"I think you might find something at Styles. I was there recently, and they had a new shipment of holiday things," I said. "Let this be my treat."

"No, Mom, you do so much for us ..." Liz began.

"Please," I said. "You can call it a Christmas present, if you'd like."

Liz sighed. "Thanks, Mom. The problem will be finding a dress that looks good on me. I still haven't got my figure back."

"You look fine," I said, annoyed by the pressure young mothers felt to erase the signs they'd been pregnant.

After sharing this special time with Liz and the babies, the sadness I'd felt with Nell and her family leaving us dissipated. I liked being with the Ts away from Liz's house. It gave Liz and me a chance to share conversation while giving the little ones a new experience.

Still, by the time I went home I was tired and a little out of sorts. The pull from the hotel and my work there meant I had little time of my own. The hotel was, in many respects, my most demanding baby.

That evening, I got dressed to go to the hotel. Annette was having a day off and I'd promised to host a special private dinner in her place.

Sabal's mayor was having a dinner for five other mayors in the state and their wives. Though it was for only twelve people, it was treated as a special event where a staff member, Rhonda, or I provided personal attention.

"Sorry, I have to leave," I said to Vaughn. "I shouldn't be too late. Maybe we can share a cup of coffee or tea after I get home."

"Or something else," said Vaughn, wiggling his eyebrows to tease me.

I laughed. "That's even better."

As I drove up to the hotel, I stopped and stared at the effect of twinkling white lights wound into the branches of the landscaping at the front of the building. Two large Christmas wreaths hung on the double doors of the front entrance. Nearby, the trunks of palm trees glowed from the small white lights wrapped around them.

I let out a sigh of happiness. In its own way, the hotel looked every bit as holiday beautiful as any top hotel in New York City or any other northern location.

I left my car with the valet and climbed the front steps to get a true appreciation of our decorations at night. Inside, everywhere I looked there were tasteful reminders of the holidays—candles glowing, fresh greenery, and the aroma of evergreens.

"Gorgeous, huh?" I turned to face Helena Naylor, the mayor of Sabal, someone I counted as a friend.

"Good evening," I said, exchanging a quick hug with her. "I believe we have everything set for your dinner. I gather this is a very special occasion."

"Yes," she said, lowering her voice. "The Mayor of Jacksonville is planning a run for state senator, and I'm supporting him. But nothing has been announced yet. It's all very quiet. That's why we're having the dinner here."

"I see. We'll make sure you have privacy. Congratulations, by the way, on your re-election. I'm pleased we could be of help."

"You and Rhonda are such a boon to this community. I told that to Brock Goodwin the other day when he mentioned he didn't like the idea of two private homes on your land."

I gritted my teeth. Brock Goodwin had been like a snapping alligator to us from the beginning. He thought as president of the neighborhood association (a position no one else wanted) entitled him to be treated as someone important. Rhonda and I were forced to fight him over almost everything we did at the hotel.

Helena placed a hand on my shoulder. "Don't worry. I put him in his place. He is ...what does Rhonda call him?

"A rat bastard," I said primly, and we both laughed.

Later, after a small cocktail reception in the private dining room, people settled at the table for their meal. Helena had chosen sea bass with a ginger butter cream sauce drizzled with an Asian glaze as the main course. It was one of my favorite dishes. First course was a clear soup with mushrooms, perfect for preparing for the richness of the fish. A fresh green salad with a vinegar and oil dressing followed and then the staff discreetly served individual chocolate mousse cakes and coffee.

Standing by, making sure all was done well, I was proud of the compliments I overheard about the food. Jean-Luc did a magnificent job for us, making our efforts to be the best often come true.

After the meal was cleared, I watched as the staff left, and then after making sure all was in order, I closed the door behind me, leaving our guests to their privacy. In the beginning of running the hotel, I'd done this for every special meeting. Now I was more than content to turn the task over to Annette. But it was helpful for me to see the entire process again, to make sure that our specially selected waitstaff honored our policy of privacy.

At home, the house seemed especially quiet. Robbie was in bed with the dogs, and Vaughn had fallen asleep over an open book when I walked into the living room. A fire burned in the fireplace, a rare treat on a cool night.

I walked over to him and trailed a finger down his cheek.

His eyes flashed open and then a smile spread across face. He took hold of my hand and pulled me down into his lap. "Hey, there. We finally have some time alone."

I wrapped my arms around his neck and sighed as his lips met mine.

"I need to get out of this dress," I said when we pulled apart.

"Music to my ears," said Vaughn, giving me a wink. "I'm ready for bed if you are."

"Yes, it's been a long day."

While he turned off the lights and the gas fireplace, I headed to our bedroom. Vaughn might have a lot more planned, but I couldn't help wondering if he'd settle for a cuddle.

Later, after delicious lovemaking, I decided more than a cuddle was just fine.

CHAPTER ELEVEN

RHONDA AND I AWAITED OUR FIRST HIGH TEA ARRIVALS
with anticipation. We'd advertised in the local paper and
social media and had been thrilled by the response. As Sadie
had mentioned, it was a holiday treat for many. We'd also
advertised special discount Christmas tickets to high tea in
January, February, and March, and those sales were going
well too.

The library turned out to be a wonderful room for the
event. We were able to fit in seating for fifty and seeing the
tables, both two-and four-tops, covered with starched pink
tablecloths and little creamer pitchers and sugar bowls with a
floral design, along with crystal stemware and sparkling
silverware, it looked as lovely as I'd hoped. Wine and
champagne would be offered in addition to a selection of tea
and water. Though it wasn't on the menu, coffee would be
offered to those who asked.

I glanced at our special hostess, Loretta Kapp. She was a
friend of Sadie's. She was dressed for the occasion in a lovely
regency gown borrowed from a member of the Historical
Society. Though Lauren had agreed to handle high teas for us,
we liked the idea of having someone like Loretta add a touch
of distinction to them.

As guests arrived, Loretta played the part of genial hostess
perfectly, another reason for me to thank Chad's mother. The
waitstaff did not dress up, but Annette, as head of the dining
staff, had talked to them about proper decorum.

"Good afternoon, ladies," came a familiar voice and we

turned to see Terri Thomas walk toward us. "Thank you for the opportunity to report on High Tea at The Beach House Hotel to the Sabal *Daily News*. I appreciate being invited to partake."

Rhonda and I grinned at one another. Terri loved our food. Getting her to report on our high tea was easy. We'd shamelessly bribed her for news coverage with the cinnamon rolls she loved.

The cameraman who'd accompanied Terri took pictures of Rhonda and me, the dining room, and Loretta.

"Would you care to stay?" I asked him.

He shook his head. "No, thanks. There's a football game on that I want to see. I'll leave you ladies to the tea."

"I think things are in order here," I said to Rhonda after Lauren showed up. "I'm going to leave now, so I can come back early for our employee Christmas party." We'd scheduled it for five o'clock in the dining room, which was closed temporarily to guests.

"Me, too. First, let's check with Consuela to make sure the Christmas cookies are all set for the party," said Rhonda.

We went into the kitchen. Consuela and one of the kitchen staff were placing cookies on several trays.

"This looks delicious," said Rhonda, hovering over a tray. "May I?"

Beaming at us, Consuela said, "Of course. They need a proper tasting. *Si*?

Chuckling, I lifted a star-shaped, sugar cookie coated with white icing and took a bite.

"Hmmm," I said, enjoying every buttery morsel. My grandmother always had insisted that butter cookies have a lot of butter in them, and I felt the same.

"Is everything ready?" Consuela asked.

"I think so," I said. "A Christmas Tree is set up in the dining room and the presents placed underneath. Vaughn is going to be Santa Claus."

"The buffet table is ready for the food to be loaded onto it and the bar set up," added Rhonda. "Bernie, Annette, and I will be keeping the food going at the buffet." We made it a point of having members of the executive staff serve others at the Christmas party. The head of housekeeping and I would help bus tables.

Rhonda and I double-checked the dining room, and then I left the hotel for home.

When I pulled into the driveway, Vaughn was finishing putting up small white lights in the bushes by the house. We had professionals install lights on the roof and on the palm trees, but Vaughn liked to do this task.

I parked the car and got out. "They look so pretty."

"Thanks. It adds to what we already have," he said, grinning. He liked Christmas lights as much as I did.

I walked over to him and gave him a hug. "Are you ready to be Santa Claus?"

"Ho, Ho, Ho," Vaughn said, sounding like an excellent Santa. Though I'd had to talk him into doing it, he loved being amused by the kids and fell into the role easily.

He put his arm around me. "If you can wait on tables at the hotel, I can be Santa. But let's relax before we have to get ready. How about a swim? The pool is heated, and it's a pleasant day."

"Okay. We'll have time for a short swim."

Minutes later, my muscles were relaxed after swimming a few lengths of the pool. I got out, wrapped a towel around me and hurried inside to shower.

The stream of water sluicing over my body felt delicious,

and when I felt Vaughn's hands on me, it felt even better.

I turned to him, and hugged him to me, sharing the warm water. I loved that our attraction hadn't dimmed and hoped that would never change.

When we both stepped out of the shower, we grinned at one another. It was a perfect start to an evening of festivities.

I'd just finished putting on my makeup when Liz called. "Hi. I'm just checking in to make sure you'll phone me when it's almost time to hand out the presents at the hotel. Chad and I will join you with Robbie and the Ts."

"Yes, I'll definitely call you a few minutes before we start," I said, grateful she'd understood that the entire party would be too much for the triplets to handle.

"Okay, see you later." As Liz hung up, I heard a toddler fussing in the background.

At five o'clock, Rhonda and I greeted our staff and their families at the door to the dining room. Most of them were well-known to us. Observing them arrive in their best finery, I was touched by how carefully everyone had dressed up for the occasion. Little girls wore Christmas outfits—dresses, blouses, or sweaters especially chosen for the occasion. One three-year-old girl sported a sparkly tiara, and a young boy was wearing a white shirt and a red tie.

For me, our employee Christmas party marked the official beginning of the holidays.

I glanced at Rhonda. Dressed in a red caftan and wearing her usual diamonds, she looked the part of fairy godmother. She noticed me looking at her and grinned.

After greeting everyone, Rhonda and I went to our tasks. Everyone would be fed before Christmas presents were handed out. We'd worked out the timing that way, aware that as the kids began to get restless, Santa would appear.

After meals were finished, I cleared dinner dishes from the tables with other staff members so that everyone had room to open their gifts. Rhonda was working with a crew to replenish the dessert table, which included coffee and tea for those who wanted it.

I paused, taking it all in—the contagious excitement of the children, the smell of the food, the shimmering lights on the Christmas tree, the buzz of easy conversations, and staff helping staff. Unexpectedly, tears filled my eyes as I recalled the lonely holidays I'd endured as a child.

The arrival of Santa Claus jarred me out of my thoughts. Vaughn's "Ho, ho, ho!" filled the room and caused the children to rush toward him.

"Well, now," he said, carefully masked behind his costume and full white beard. "I heard we have some good children here. Am I right?"

A chorus of "Yeses" filled the air.

We'd set up a throne of sorts by the Christmas tree and Vaughn, like the pied piper, led the children there.

"Okay, children, take a seat on the floor. And when your name is called, come up and see me."

Liz and Chad arrived with Robbie and the Ts, quickly followed by Angela and Reggie and their three kids, and Will with Willow and Drew. Rhonda and I had discussed whether it was right for our own families to be present and decided they needed as much attention as any other child in the hotel family.

"You're just in time," I said softly. "Take seats up by Santa. Staff bonuses have already been given out."

Bernie, wearing a Santa hat, was acting as an elf, handing presents to Santa for names to be called. When Rhonda and I had first met Bernie with his proper, cold German accent, I never would've imagined he'd wear a Santa hat one day.

With forty-seven children to get through, Vaughn and Bernie kept a steady pace, leaving my family and Rhonda's to last.

Even though Robbie was the oldest and didn't really believe in Santa anymore, he went along with the idea, so that the other kids wouldn't suspect anything different.

Wearing a big grin, he brought his present over to me.

"Open it," I said, returning his smile.

He ripped off the paper. "Yay! Gift cards! Just what I wanted."

The Ts each carried a stuffed animal toward me, their eyes shiny with excitement. Noah carried a monkey, Olivia had a rag doll, and Emma hugged a white, fluffy lamb.

"Hi," I said to them. "Merry Christmas!"

"Mine," said Olivia clearly, clutching her doll.

I laughed. "Okay. She's yours."

"Cookie," said Noah.

I glanced at Liz.

"Okay, they can have cookies," she said. "But please, let's take pictures of them before they make a mess all over themselves." I snapped a few photos on my phone. The girls wore the dark-green smocked dresses I'd ordered for them. Noah wore a pair of khaki pants and a polo-style shirt in green. They were as excited as the other kids.

Several staff members came over to Liz and me to talk about the triplets. Out of the corner of my eye, I saw Vaughn make an exit, waving goodbye to the children who'd noticed. He'd done another excellent job.

Bernie spoke to the crowd. "Thank you all for coming. We wish a Merry Christmas to you and your family. See you back here at the hotel at your regular time and on your regular schedule."

Someone started clapping and soon the whole room reverberated with the sound. Even little children who had no idea of what was happening, joined in.

Looking at the smiling faces all around me, I glanced at Rhonda. Holding Bella, she was as proud as I was at what we'd brought together. Without them, the hotel would fail.

CHAPTER TWELVE

WITH THE STAFF PARTY BEHIND US, WE CONCENTRATED on the holiday itself.

"I'm excited by the response to Christmas Eve bookings. We're sold out," I said, looking up from our reservations list.

"Dorothy's suggestion is working," said Rhonda. "And, surprisingly, our staff hasn't complained about the extra time required to pull it off."

Dorothy had suggested offering a Christmas Eve package for families. Following a festive dinner, Santa would appear at each guest room that requested it, talking to children, and offering cups of cocoa to the kids and peppermint martinis to those adults who wanted it.

When our guests awoke, presents would be waiting for them outside their door—one from the hotel and any others that guests arranged with the housekeeping department to deliver. We advertised it as a family celebration, a first Christmas for newly married couples, and a last peaceful Christmas for expectant parents. The response had surprised us.

"What plans do you have for Christmas?" Rhonda asked me, leaning back in her chair.

"Vaughn and I have decided to have a little private celebration with Robbie on Christmas Eve and then we'll spend the day with Liz and Chad and the kids. Following brunch at Liz's house, I'll come to the hotel to help act as hostess for dinner groups."

"Thanks, Annie, for taking care of the dinner groups. I'll

make it up to you on New Year's Eve," said Rhonda. "Will and I will come to that party to make sure we're represented, but we won't stay too long." Hosting the New Year's Eve party at the hotel was something Rhonda and I shared by alternating each year.

I checked the reservations chart again. The first week of the year was usually slow with guests recovering at home from the holidays. This year was no exception, which worked out well because Bernie and Annette were taking that week off. Then the high season would start and there wouldn't be any rest for anybody until after Spring.

Rhonda looked up from the reservations sheet I handed her. "Seems like we're doing a good job. It's busier than ever."

"Along with some new people, our regulars are coming back. That's what satisfies me. It's those loyal people who help spread the word."

Rhonda and I worked a while longer, checking reservations both for rooms and for holiday meals. I made a few notes for Bernie regarding various guests' requests, and then before I could be stuck doing more, I left the office to go home.

Vaughn's movie had been pushed back until after the New Year, which suited me fine. Robbie was out of school for the holidays, and he and Vaughn were in San Francisco visiting Vaughn's son Ty, his wife, June, and their two-year-old boy, Bo. Ty and June were a darling couple who got a lot of attention from June's large Chinese family. I hated missing out, but Ty and June understood that it was a busy time of year for me and accepted my promise to visit in the summer, as usual.

I walked into the house and stood a moment in the quiet before Cindy and Trudy raced into the kitchen greeting me with enthusiastic barks. I reached down to pat them, grateful for their company.

I headed into my bedroom to change my clothes, thinking I might fix myself some popcorn, pour a glass of red wine and read a book, which was as decadent as I ever got when I had some time alone. I was delighted not to have to cook dinner.

After feeding the dogs and spending some time with them, they joined me on the lanai. I turned on the Christmas tree lights and sat on the couch, thinking of how fortunate I was as I stared at the handmade ornaments I'd collected for years.

My cell phone rang, and I knew who it was before I even checked. "Hi, Vaughn. How are you? And Robbie?"

"We're fine. Little Bo is a real cute boy and smart. June and Ty are doing great. I'm calling because I miss you. I'm setting up Facetime now so you can talk to Bo and Robbie."

"Okay. I'll answer."

A little boy's face appeared, and when I said, "Hi, Bo!" his grin lit his face. My heart filled with love. It was such a shame that Ty and June lived far away.

Guided by Vaughn, Bo said, "GeeGee", and tears stung my eyes. At moments like this, I was frustrated by having to work at the hotel.

Vaughn and I talked for a few minutes, I spoke to Robbie, and then I clicked off the call, wishing I could be with them.

Trudy sensed my sadness and climbed into my lap. I patted her and decided to go to Liz's house to see the Ts. They never failed to cheer me up.

I called Liz to tell her I'd like to come for a visit and suggested that she and Chad go out while I stayed with them.

Delighted, Liz quickly agreed.

The Ts were in their pajamas when I arrived. I sat on the

floor in the playroom and allowed them to climb over me. They reminded me of puppies as they both crawled and ran about. It was fascinating to watch them in action. As soon as one found something of interest, the other two went after it, keeping each one busy.

When it was time to put them to bed, I took Noah out of the playroom, changed his diaper, and put him into his crib. Olivia was next, and then Emma.

"Time for bed," I said quietly to all three of them. I played their favorite lullabies on the I-pod Chad had hooked up to speakers in the hallway to allow songs to be heard from both rooms.

Noah started to fuss.

I went into his room and rubbed his back. He settled down, and I left him and sat for a while in the hallway to make sure they all were quieting down. Now that they were more active, it usually didn't take them long to go to sleep.

Satisfied that all was quiet, I went into the living room and sat, deep in thought. Maybe the best Christmas present Vaughn and I could give Liz and Chad was a long weekend away. Maybe they'd like the Palm Island Club as much as Vaughn and I did. It was an idea.

I leaned back and rested my eyes.

I don't know how long I'd slept before I heard Liz and Chad return. I jumped to my feet. "Hi, how was it?"

"Delightful," said Liz. "The movie was great. But best of all was having some time alone afterwards."

"I'm glad, honey." I gathered my purse and prepared to go home. Having Liz and her family close by made it much easier for me after missing Vaughn and Robbie.

The next morning, I was awakened by the dogs barking. I

heard someone at the kitchen door, and wondering who it could be, I rose then stopped in surprise when I saw Vaughn and Robbie walk inside.

"What are you doing here? I thought you weren't coming home until later today," I asked as I hugged them both to me, thrilled to see them.

"Daddy said you were sad," said Robbie. "Do you feel better now?"

"Oh, yes. My boys are home," I said, hugging him tightly before he moved away. He was a loving boy but was growing into the stage where he didn't want to be hugged as much.

Vaughn wrapped his arms around me. "You sounded forlorn on the phone. Ty and June had no further plans, so I thought Robbie and I would surprise you."

"You took a red-eye flight to do that? That's so touching, Vaughn."

"I was missing you, too," he murmured, lowering his lips to mine as the two dogs jumped around us with excitement.

Robbie said, "Ugh. Kissing."

Vaughn and I laughed and pulled apart.

"When you're grown up, I hope you find someone you want to kiss as much as I want to kiss your mom," Vaughn told him.

I glanced at Robbie and wished with all my heart that Vaughn's words would come true for him.

CHAPTER THIRTEEN

ON CHRISTMAS EVE IN THE LATE AFTERNOON, I WALKED through the lobby, delighted by the buzz of excitement. It was such a joyous time for our guests, and I reveled in the idea that Rhonda and I and our staff were making it happen for them.

Bernie crossed the lobby toward me, wearing a look of concern.

"What is it?" I asked, approaching him.

"Stephanie and Randolph Willis are here insisting they made a reservation for tonight," said Bernie.

"Oh, but they usually don't come until January 3rd," I said. "I don't recall seeing a reservation for them for this time."

"I checked and there's nothing on the books," said Bernie. "When I explained that to them, they got very upset. Knowing how valuable they are as guests who usually stay for three months, I thought you should know. What would you like me to do?"

"The rooms are booked and in use, right?"

"Everything. The Presidential Suite, the two houses, all the rooms. We won't have anything available until tomorrow."

From Connecticut, Stephanie and Randolph were a delightful older couple who had no children of their own. I knew how important this change in plans must be for them, and I didn't want to do anything to ruin our relationship with them.

"Well?" asked Bernie, glancing over at them with a look of apprehension.

"I'm going to invite them to come home with me," I said,

suddenly excited about the idea. "They've come to my home for dinner, so they're aware of the comfortable space I have for guests. I was feeling a little let down by the fact that Vaughn's children wouldn't be with us.

"Are you sure? Stephanie and Randolph might want their privacy," said Bernie.

"Any other time but Christmas," I said. "I'm sure of it. They spend so much time here because they have no place else to go. Let me at least try."

"I'll wait here. If there's a problem, signal me, and I'll come right over," said Bernie.

Randolph lifted himself off the couch as I approached them. "Hello. Welcome," I said, giving them both a hug. "Bernie tells me there's a problem with your reservation. I'm sorry, but I have a suggestion that I hope will please you. I'd love it if you'd agree to spend the night with Vaughn and me and our son, Robbie. It would be a treat to have you stay with us."

The minute I saw Stephanie's face light up, I knew I'd made the right decision.

"But this is a time for family," said Randolph.

"But I feel like you are family," I said honestly. "You have supported Rhonda and me every year we've been open. You've met both our families, had dinners with us. Besides, I know one little boy who'd be thrilled to have you with us, like grandparents are for other kids."

"Oh, my!" said Stephanie blinking rapidly. "You got me there. Randolph, we must go."

A tall, stately man with gray hair and blue eyes that softened when he looked at his wife, he wrapped his arm around Stephanie. "Okay, darling. We'll do that." He turned and faced me. "Thank you, Ann. Inviting us into your home means a great deal to Stephanie and me. An even better

Christmas than we'd hoped for."

"That's so nice to hear." I gave them each another hug. "I suppose you drove as usual?"

Randolph nodded. "We'll follow you to your house."

I signaled Bernie and he walked over. "Stephanie and Randolph will be spending the night with me. Can you see that their luggage is returned to their car? I'll meet them out front, and they can follow me home."

"Wonderful," said Bernie, giving them a little bow. "Delighted to hear that."

I left them to go to my office to pick up my purse and a little present I'd bought for Vaughn. It would make a suitable small gift for Randolph. I had a gift at home that was going to be for Liz but would be perfect for Stephanie. Satisfied that my plan would work, I called Vaughn and gave him the news.

"Oh, okay. I like Randolph and Stephanie, and we've both been feeling a little down that my children won't be here."

"Have I told you lately how much I love you, Vaughn?" I asked.

"Well, not since this morning," he said, laughing. "There's plenty of cheese fondue for all of us."

"And I have enough fresh greens to make a large salad," I said. "I remember how easy Stephanie and Randolph were to have for dinner. I don't think it'll be a problem. Just do me a favor and tell Robbie what's going on. I told the Willises that it would be like Robbie having grandparents for Christmas."

"Okay. Will do," said Vaughn. "See you shortly."

I pulled into the garage, got out of the car, and waited while Randolph parked on the apron of the driveway.

As they got out of the car, Vaughn, Robbie, and the dogs came out of the house. The dogs barked with excitement as

Vaughn and Randolph shook hands and Robbie approached Stephanie.

"Dad said you're going to be like my grandparents for Christmas," he said studying Stephanie.

"How lovely," said she, beaming at him. "That's a gift, you know, because we have no grandchildren of our own. So, if you'll allow us to be that for you, it'll make this the most special Christmas of all."

Robbie bobbed his head. "Okay. What do I call you?" He looked from her to me.

"I think it's okay to address Mr. and Mrs. Willis any way that's comfortable for you, as long as it's respectful," I said quietly.

"I've never had a grandma or grandpa like Brett has," said Robbie, "and I think that's what I should call you."

"That'll be something very special for Randolph and me," said Stephanie, placing a hand on Robbie's shoulder. Her eyes were shiny with tears.

Robbie, bless his heart, said, "Awesome."

Vaughn and Randolph walked over to us. "Everything set?"

"Robbie is going to call us Grandma and Grandpa for this holiday stay," Stephanie told Randolph, her voice shaking with emotion.

Vaughn and I exchanged glances, and then Vaughn said, "That's really nice. We've wanted more family around."

"Very well then," said Randolph, smiling.

"Come inside," I said. "The guest suite is ready."

"Randolph and I will take care of the luggage," said Vaughn. "Robbie, you can help too."

I led Stephanie inside. She turned and hugged me tightly. "You have no idea how much this means to Randolph and me. We'd decided to come early to The Beach House Hotel because we have no family to share the holiday with. We thought it would be less noticeable away. But now, we have time with you and yours. I'll never forget your kindness, Ann."

"I have what I call my hotel family," I said. "And, Stephanie, you've always been part of that."

Stephanie dabbed at her eyes with a tissue. "I'm an emotional mess but very grateful to you."

"Let's get you settled and then have some fun. We'd planned cheese fondue for dinner. Will that be alright for you and Randolph?"

Stephanie's eyes lit. "Oh, yes! As you know from our time spent at the hotel, we're foodies, which is why we love the food there. Jean-Luc is marvelous."

I laughed. "Okay, We're off to a great beginning. By the time Christmas is over, you may have some regrets. Liz, Chad, and their triplets are waiting to see us tomorrow."

Stephanie clasped her hands. "That makes it even better. Liz is such a doll, and those children are adorable."

"See? You're already part of the family." I gave her a smile of approval and led her to their bedroom.

While Stephanie and Randolph were getting settled, I called Rhonda to tell her what had happened.

"Thank God they're thrilled to be staying with you. It's very kind of you to ask them. But then, that's how you are, Annie. It's a rat race here with Angela, Reggie, Arthur, and all the kids. Lorraine is joining us later. Angie is going to put her children down to sleep here so she and Reggie can put together some big toys at their house without being seen."

"It sounds like fun," I said, remembering that Rhonda had, like me, wanted a lot of children. "Enjoy it."

"I will. You too," said Rhonda.

I hung up pleased with how things were going for each of us.

Vaughn served cocktails in the living room. We sat in front of the gas-lit fireplace in a comfortable circle enjoying it and the lights on the Christmas tree. Gazing around, I thought this could be a typical holiday scene in most parts of the country except for the palm trees outside the window.

I listened as Robbie sat between Stephanie and Randolph on the couch and did his best to explain the video games he liked to play with Brett. Stephanie and Randolph, bless their hearts, were thrilled with the interchange, and Robbie was loving their attention.

I glanced at Vaughn, and he winked at me. We'd often bemoaned the fact that Robbie had no grandparents, making this scene especially touching.

While they talked, I got the fondue ready. I'd bought frozen packages of it, but knew from previous recipes I'd prepared that I should include a little bit of Kirsch and a sprinkle of nutmeg. In addition to chunks of bread to dip into the cheesy mixture, we offered sliced apples, chunks of sausage, boiled potatoes, and cornichons. Dried cherries and sliced pears were part of the green salad I made with a French vinegarette dressing to temper the richness of the fondue.

As we took our places at the dining room table, Stephanie said, "This is such a treat. When we were in Switzerland, Randolph and I enjoyed fondue. It brings back many fond memories."

"Indeed, it does," said Randolph giving his wife a loving look that touched me.

Talk of their travels made conversation pleasant while we ate. Stephanie thoughtfully mentioned tidbits that they thought Robbie would enjoy hearing about. I could almost sense what it would be like for him to have real grandparents.

After dinner, we returned to the living room.

"This year we're doing things a little differently," I said. "We're going to exchange gifts this evening. Tomorrow morning, Robbie will have his stocking gifts and then we're going to Liz's house to celebrate with her family there."

"Do I get to open all my gifts tonight?" asked Robbie, his eyes alight.

"Yes, but you might have a few to open at Liz's tomorrow." I replied.

"What about Grandma and Grandpa?" Robbie asked, and I could've kissed him for his concern.

"As a matter of fact, a certain elf has seen to it that they each have a gift," I said.

"An elf? Do you mean you?" asked Robbie.

"I like to think of surprise gifts as the magic of Christmas, like elves," I said, ruffling his hair.

"Okay," he said. "I get to hand them out."

"Deal." I turned to the adults. "Anyone want coffee or tea or something else?"

Vaughn asked for a cup of decaf coffee, and Randolph and Stephanie each requested water.

Then, with everyone comfortable in the living room, we began the gift exchange.

Vaughn and I didn't usually exchange a lot of presents, mutually agreeing that we had pretty much anything we wanted. Instead, we opted to give each other just one gift, in addition to small items in our stockings. Robbie was like any other kid making a list for Christmas seeing and wanting everything. But we emphasized the idea of just a few special gifts, and he was content with that.

Now, we watched as he opened a big box holding a guitar. "Yay! Now Brett and I can have a band," he explained. "He plays the keyboard, and I can do this." He picked it up and strummed a few notes, causing Cindy's and Trudy's ears to perk up.

"We've got you signed up for lessons," said Vaughn. "You'll be playing well in no time."

"Can I play any kind of music?" Robbie asked.

"As long as you learn how to read music and use the guitar properly, I don't see why not," I said.

"I hope you learn classical music, too," said Randolph.

"What's that?" asked Robbie.

"You could say classical music is the basis for all music," Randolph said.

While Robbie played with his guitar, I handed Vaughn his present.

He held up the box and shook it. "Can I guess what it is?"

I laughed. "Sure, but I bet you'll be surprised." At the suggestion of a fellow sailor, I'd bought Vaughn a Cordless Winch Handle. It would make sailing alone much easier. Besides, like any other guy, it was something new, a toy of sorts.

When Vaughn opened the box, he laughed. "I know exactly what this is. I've had my eye on one. Thank you."

"Can I give Grandma and Grandpa their gifts now?" asked Robbie.

"Sure," I said, relieved I'd had time to change nametags on a couple of gifts I'd already purchased.

Stephanie looked excited as Robbie handed her a sterling silver necklace I'd intended to give to Liz. The chain held a simple heart pendant.

"Do you like it?" Robbie asked, as Stephanie lifted it out of its box.

"Oh, yes, I do. I'm going to put it on right away," said Stephanie. "Thank you all."

Randolph struggled a bit with the wrapping on his box. But then, he opened it and said, "This is great. Every man can use a jacknife." He bobbed his head. "Thank you."

The doorbell rang.

I jumped up to get it.

A young man from Tropical Fleurs held an arrangement of pine branches, red roses, canella berries, bay leaves, holly, and mistletoe in a lovely wooden box. "For you. Merry Christmas."

"Thanks. You're running awfully late," I said, realizing it was almost nine o'clock.

"Yes, ma'am, but it's Christmas Eve and it's important to get every arrangement delivered," he said proudly.

"Hold on." I came back with his tip. "You have a Merry Christmas too."

I carried the flowers into the living room and read the note: "Thank you for making our Christmas special. Grandma and Grandpa Willis."

Suddenly, I was in tears. "What is it?" Vaughn asked gently, putting his arm around me.

"It's this Christmas. I'd have given anything to have one like it as a child. And now our child has the best holiday family ever." Sniffling, I went to Stephanie and Randolph and gave them each a hug. "You're the ones we need to thank. The flowers are gorgeous, but having you here is what is making this holiday special."

"Why is everyone crying?" asked Robbie.

"These are tears of joy," I said. "Having new people help us celebrate is the biggest gift of all."

Robbie studied me and remained quiet.

Later, lying in bed with Vaughn, my new sexy nightgown tossed on the floor, I cuddled up to him, thinking how lucky I was.

CHAPTER FOURTEEN

CHRISTMAS MORNING WAS A BLUR AS WE OPENED stocking gifts, had a quick breakfast, and then we all headed to Liz's house to celebrate with her family.

The Ts were excited about the lights on the tree and the bright-colored wrapping on the gifts more than the presents. They crinkled the paper, stomped on it, and squealed with laughter at the sounds it made. With the three toddlers going in different directions, it was hard to keep track of them. Their interest turned to the boxes which had held the presents, and they settled down. Liz served coffee and a Christmas stollen that a friend had sent her.

After getting up extra early for a light breakfast, we all dug into the treat.

When the triplets started to fuss, Vaughn and I headed home with Robbie and the Willises.

On the way back to my house, I checked with the reservations department and was told that they had a room for Stephanie and Randolph on the first floor like they usually requested. I turned to Stephanie. "I'm not pushing you out, by any means, but the hotel has a room for you anytime you're ready."

"That's perfect. It'll give me a chance to get unpacked before taking a walk on the beach and then having an early dinner." She turned to Randolph.

"That will be good," he said.

"Does that mean that you're not going to be my grandma and my grandpa anymore?" asked Robbie.

Stephanie glanced at me and back to him. "Well, if it's alright with your parents, we can still be your grandparents whenever you need us to be. How's that?"

"That's okay," Robbie said in his usual fashion but there was a lilt of happiness to his words that we all noticed.

"That's a lovely idea," I told them. I loved that a simple gesture of inviting Stephanie and Randolph to stay with us had turned out to be such a beautiful thing for Robbie.

At home, Stephanie and Randolph packed, and after thanking us profusely, hugged and kissed us goodbye.

After seeing them off, Vaughn wrapped an arm around me. "I have one more present to give you. I wasn't sure what I wanted it to be until last night when we had our fondue. My gift to you is a trip to Switzerland sometime this summer after things slow down for you. Just you and me. All first class. What do you think?"

"I think you're the best Santa Claus ever," I said, hugging him and then laughing when he nuzzled my neck with a growl.

"Are you two kissing again?" Robbie asked. "Can I go next door to Brett's house? I want to show him my guitar."

"Yes, you may go. But come right back if they're busy." We were close enough as families that if it wasn't convenient, Brett's parents would send him home.

"Guess that leaves us to clean up," I said after Robbie went on his way.

"Or we could just take a nap," said Vaughn giving me a sexy smile. We both knew he had no intention of sleeping.

"Later," I said. "I want to get things in order here."

When Brett's mother called and asked if Robbie could have dinner with them, I quickly agreed. I could still take a nap at close to five, couldn't I?

###

The next morning, Rhonda and I met for coffee at the hotel. I was eager to catch up on her news.

Sitting in our office we shared photos and talked about our Christmas celebrations.

"It was special that Robbie had time with Stephanie and Randolph," Rhonda said. "I know how much they enjoyed it because I saw them when I came to check on the dinner service at the hotel last night. It was another successful day for us."

"Hopefully we can catch our breaths before New Year's and Lorraine's wedding. How were Lorraine and Arthur through Christmas?"

"So in love it was disgusting," Rhonda said with a triumphant smile. "I'm telling ya, if Will and I hadn't had that trip to Tahiti, I don't know how we'd be as a couple. Just seeing reserved old Arthur swooning over Lorraine is enough to remind me what Will and I have been able to keep alive."

"Vaughn is taking me to Switzerland this summer, just the two of us. I can't wait. It'll be our chance to add a little zip to things."

"I can give you a few pointers about what to take with you," said Rhonda. "Will and I ..."

Knowing exactly where she was going with this, I raised my hand. "TMI."

"But, Annie, you can never have too much information, can you?" said Rhonda letting out a raucous laugh.

I couldn't help laughing but quickly changed the subject. "What do we need to think about for the New Year's Eve party?"

"Aw, Annie, you're no fun," complained Rhonda. She pulled out the folder we'd put together for the event, and we began to go over it. Even though Lauren and Annette would be working the party, Rhonda and I knew how important it was to be part of the planning, especially with Lorraine busy with her own wedding.

We arranged a meeting with Bernie, Annette, and Lauren to discuss the upcoming high tea, New Year's Eve function, and then the wedding. Thankfully, we had flexible wait staff willing to handle a lot of events, one right after another.

By the time I went home, I was ready to relax for a couple of days before the New Year's Eve party, which had become "the" place to be seen that evening. With a small jazz group, plenty of champagne and an elegant meal, people dressed up for the occasion, making it even more festive.

Vaughn met me at the kitchen door with a kiss. When we pulled apart, he said, "Just wanted to warn you that Robbie had his first guitar lesson and he's practicing with Brett. A lot. Loudly. And the dogs are going crazy."

I laughed. "They're that good, huh?"

"I have earphones. It helps."

As I changed my clothes, I thought about Robbie and how fast he was growing up. Though his past was complicated, he was such a blessing to me. But my time with him was going too quickly. Before we knew it, he'd be on his own, following his dreams. But I wouldn't hold him back. He deserved his chance for happiness.

With Christmas behind us, the one special event we all were waiting for was the wedding of Lorraine Grace and Angela's father-in-law, Arthur Smythe. Lorraine, who was exceptionally talented as the head of Wedding Perfection, had chosen to have a small, intimate wedding with her close friends, just a few of her hotel friends, and Arthur's friends and family. They'd chosen to be married on New Year's Day because New Year's Eve at the hotel was a busy, hectic time with guests celebrating in style.

Lorraine was keeping the details of her wedding secret, saying she wanted to surprise all of us. In her mid-fifties, Lorraine exuded an air of elegance and good taste in both her appearance and manner. A widow for a couple of years, she'd resisted the idea of getting married again until she met Arthur. As Rhonda had thought, social, friendly Lorraine was perfect for Arthur, who was a quiet and dignified, wealthy man who handled large accounts for his financial management company in New York.

During the week before the wedding, Annette arranged a small shower and luncheon for Lorraine at André's restaurant. Rhonda and I headed to the shower together.

"I hope Lorraine likes the peignoir I'm giving her," I said. "It's both sexy and sweet."

Rhonda laughed. "I have to admit it felt a little funny buying that sheer black so-called "Naughty Nightie' for Lorraine when I knew it was Arthur who was going to see her in it. I thought of Katherine and knew she'd never wear anything like it."

"The two women couldn't be more different," I said. Arthur's first wife had died of cancer. It wasn't until she was ill that Katherine and Rhonda became friends after not liking one another."

As we entered André's, Margot Durand greeted us. "Right this way. The other women are already here."

We walked into a small room, and Lorraine stood to greet us. "Hi."

After introductions were made, the twelve of us sat as a waiter poured champagne for each of us.

"This is the time for Lorraine to open her gifts," said Annette.

Lorraine started with my gift and then Rhonda's. When she

realized it was a lingerie party, she laughed. "Oh, my! Am I going to have fun with these."

By the time she'd opened the last gift, all of us were laughing at some of the outrageous things she'd been given.

I glanced around the room, loving this group of women who were enjoying one another and realized I needed to do something like this more often.

The pre-ordered luncheon consisted of Quiche Lorraine, which we all declared a cute idea, a green salad with a simple French vinaigrette, and assorted fruit tarts for dessert. As usual, the food was delicious.

As we prepared to leave, Lorraine came over to us. "Thank you for coming. I know this is a busy time at the hotel with holiday parties and dinners."

I hugged her. "You know we wouldn't miss this. I can't wait for the wedding."

"Are you sure you're not going to tell us about the plans?" said Rhonda. It had been killing her not to know the details. But Lorraine had sworn Lauren to secrecy and would tell no one about any of it.

Lorraine laughed. "Not even you, Rhonda."

"Don't you mean *especially* you, Rhonda?" I teased. Rhonda had been known to unwittingly expose a secret or two.

The three of us laughed, and Rhonda and I went on our way, anxious to check in at the hotel and then have a bit of family time.

Back at our desks, I checked messages. Hilda Hassel had left one stating that she'd be traveling with her husband's nephew, and he would need to be put up in the Presidential Suite.

I turned to Rhonda. "Why do I get the feeling that this woman is going to cause us all sorts of trouble?"

"I don't know," said Rhonda. "It's not like you at all. But no matter how you feel, we can't mess up this reservation. We've already mentioned royal visitors in our latest publicity."

"I wish we hadn't," I said, feeling uneasy.

"We can't worry about it now," said Rhonda. "We've got to get through New Year's Eve, and Lorraine's wedding. I don't know about you, but that's enough for me without thinking about what may or may not happen later."

At home, Robbie and Brett were practicing music.

Vaughn met me at the door. "Glad you're here."

"I'm ready to relax with a glass of wine. Let's retreat to our bedroom and let the boys have fun."

"Sounds peaceful to me," said Vaughn.

While I was changing clothes, Vaughn walked into the room with a tray holding two wine glasses and a bowl of peanuts. The dogs followed him.

He set down the tray on the table between the two soft-cushioned chairs by the sliding door to the private patio off the master bedroom. "There. This is better."

We lifted our glasses to toast one another and had just started to talk about the day when my cell phone rang. *Stephanie Willis.*

"Hi, Stephanie. How are you?"

"We're fine, thank you. I wanted to tell you once again how much we enjoyed Christmas and wanted to offer to babysit Robbie New Year's Eve, if you and Vaughn want to go out. We've missed that sweet face of his."

I chuckled. "It's such a lovely offer. Robbie has already had his first guitar lesson and is driving the dogs crazy practicing at home. Vaughn is right here with me. Let me ask him."

I covered my cell with my hand and told him what Stephanie had in mind. "We could go to the party at the hotel, get out of the house, and enjoy some time alone."

"A very good idea. I admit I'm going a bit stir-crazy," said Vaughn.

I turned back to my conversation with Stephanie. "That would be fantastic. Vaughn and I could go to the party at the hotel. But wouldn't we be denying you that pleasure?"

"The party is lovely, but we'd rather spend more time with Robbie, if you're agreeable."

"Vaughn and I both are *very* agreeable to that. The party starts at six o'clock."

"See you then," said Stephanie, sounding excited.

I ended the call and faced Vaughn. "It's great how everything with them has turned out."

"It's real nice of them to do it," said Vaughn. He smiled at me. "I haven't been on a date with you in a long time."

"A date? Okay, then." Maybe like Rhonda said, a trip for just Vaughn and me was in order. In the meantime, I'd make the most of New Year's Eve with him.

Even though I already knew every facet of the preparations for the evening ahead, I got ready for the New Year's Eve party feeling as if it was the first time Vaughn and I would attend. I wore a simple, floor-length, blue-silk dress that matched my eyes, with long sleeves and a deep V in the neckline. Around my neck I wore both the small necklace Vaughn had given me for Christmas as well as the heart pendant with five diamonds he'd given me after we'd made a vow to bring our two families together. I studied myself in the mirror. I'd styled my hair and did my makeup. Dangling diamond earrings completed the glam look.

Vaughn walked into the room and let out a whistle. "You look gorgeous."

I felt heat rush to my cheeks. "Thanks. You don't look bad yourself."

Seeing him in a tux looking like the famous star he was, I was startled to think the man other women swooned over was mine. I couldn't help smiling back.

Stephanie and Randolph were sitting in the kitchen with Robbie when I emerged from the bedroom with Vaughn.

Acknowledging me, Randolph stood.

"Well, don't the two of you look handsome," said Stephanie.

"Yeah, Mom. You look beautiful," Robbie said, grinning at me.

In that moment, I did feel beautiful. But it was more than being admired for what I was wearing, but a feeling that I was loved.

Vaughn wrapped a black velvet shawl around my shoulders. "Ready?"

I nodded, needing this evening more than ever.

When we drove up to the hotel, I gave it a critical glance. Extra sparkling lights had been added to the entrance, making it look like a fairyland leading to the doors where two staff members were serving as doormen.

Proudly, I climbed the steps thinking back to the first time I entered Rhonda's home. As she would say, 'We've come a long way, baby.'

Inside, the dining room was set up with a small stage and tables of eight strategically placed around a dance floor. Rotating crystal lights were hanging from the ceiling above the dancing area, adding light and shadows to it. The white tablecloths on the tables were scattered with bits of multi-colored confetti between crystal glasses and sparkling silverware.

Even though I'd helped to plan the space, the effect was very pleasing. Or maybe having Vaughn at my side made it seem glamorous.

We sat at a table with Bernie and Annette, the only other staff members attending the party.

"Ann, you look lovely," said Annette as we joined them.

"Thank you. So do you," I said. With her silvery hair, fine features and trim figure, Annette was stunning in a simple black dress. Bernie looked especially dashing in his tuxedo, his mustache adding a nice feature to his face.

Vaughn and Bernie shook hands and then Vaughn greeted Annette with a kiss on the cheek. "Happy New Year."

"It's been a good year," said Bernie. "Let's hope the next one does as well."

We lifted our water goblets in a salute just as a waiter approached us with a tray loaded with tulip glasses filled with champagne.

"Let's salute the New Year with both glasses," I said. "I think we're going to need it."

Surprised at myself for allowing such negative thoughts, I vowed to stop worrying about the upcoming year and the royal guest that made me feel uneasy.

The food, the company, the music were everything I hoped for. Dancing with Vaughn to a romantic song, I lifted my face to his, filled with love for him.

He leaned down and placed his lips on mine.

I responded, not caring who saw. This was a moment I'd remember. A moment we needed.

"Switzerland is going to be good for us," I said.

Vaughn smiled down at me. "Yes, it is. But until then, we have each day. I love you, Ann."

"I love you, too," I said, meaning it with my whole heart. He was the person who'd made me believe that true love did exist, that it was more than a broken dream of mine. I'd be forever grateful to have him in my life.

We stayed on our feet waiting for the next song. When the band played a tango, Vaughn took my elbow. "Let's sit."

We sat at the table and looked on as two couples who obviously had taken lessons did an outstanding job of it, bringing a round of applause from those of us who watched.

We were about to get up to enjoy another dance when my cell phone rang. *Stephanie.* My heart lurched. I clicked on the call. "Hi, Stephanie. What's up?"

"It's Randolph. He's having trouble breathing. I've called 911."

"Omigod! We'll come right home."

I clicked off the call and turned to Vaughn with the news.

We made our excuses to everyone at the table and dashed out.

CHAPTER FIFTEEN

WE ARRIVED HOME TO FIND AN AMBULANCE IN OUR driveway. Vaughn pulled to a stop and turned off the engine.

We both got out of the car and dashed inside. Two EMTs were standing talking to Randolph and Stephanie who were sitting on a couch in the living room. Trudy and Cindy were sitting on the floor nearby. I saw no sign of Robbie.

"What happened?" I said, hurrying to Stephanie's side. I glanced at Randolph. He looked fine.

"I'm okay. I fainted. That's all," said Randolph, but I could tell he was shaken.

Stephanie shook her head. "He fell face down on the carpet. Scared me to death."

"We're going to take him to the hospital to be checked," said one of the EMTs. "I suspect he's had a drop in his blood pressure."

"I don't want to go to the hospital," said Randolph.

"Darling, you are going. We need to find out what happened," said Stephanie, taking hold of one of his hands.

"Where's Robbie?" I asked.

"He's still asleep. Or was the last time I checked with him. We asked for no sirens for the ambulance."

"I'll check him now. He's a sound sleeper, but I want to make sure he's okay." I left them and went to Robbie's room. As Stephanie had said, he was sound asleep, sprawled across his bed, hugging his pillow.

When I went back to the living room, Randolph was fussing about having to lie down on the gurney the EMTs had brought.

"I'll meet you at the hospital," said Stephanie quietly but firmly to Randolph.

"I'm going to change my clothes, and then I'll take you," I said, aware she shouldn't drive under stress or be left alone.

At the hospital, Stephanie and I waited for Randolph to be checked by a physician. When the doctor spoke to us, he explained Randolph needed to have a test done in the morning.

"We've already done an ECG and will do another, more in-depth one tomorrow," the doctor told Stephanie. "Your husband can go home tonight, but we've scheduled further testing at eleven o'clock in the morning."

"And what will that test do?" I asked.

"That will determine if the patient should have a pacemaker as we suspect. It seems complicated, but it's a common occurrence and an easy resolution for most people."

Stephanie looked at me. "It seems like a reasonable plan."

"Why don't you spend the night at my house?" I suggested.

Stephanie shook her head. "Thanks, but it's easier to go to the hotel where we have all our things. Besides, I know you have an important wedding tomorrow. We'll be fine."

"No matter what plans are in place, I'll check on you tomorrow and stay with you at the hospital should you need me to."

Stephanie's eyes welled with tears. "That's very kind of you. Now, let's get you home. We've ruined your night out."

"It's more important for us to be here for you," I said. Smiling, trying to inject a little humor into the situation, I added, "Grandma and Grandpa."

At that, Stephanie's tears overflowed.

I put my arm around her. "It's going to be fine."

That night, as Vaughn and I snuggled in bed, I told him about Stephanie's tears and the need for me to help them.

"I suppose you consider them part of your hotel family," he said, smiling and rubbing my back. "It's growing by leaps and bounds."

I looked up at him. "It makes me feel very fulfilled."

"I know," he said, which was just one reason I loved him.

"I'll check up on them in the morning and tell Rhonda what's happened. She'll be at the hotel to make sure things are set for the wedding. After all she's done to make sure this was going to happen, she's not going to allow this event to be less than it can be."

Vaughn chuckled. "The two of you are sometimes hard to keep up with, but everything seems to turn out just fine in the end. I'm sure this wedding will too."

"I hope so. Arthur and Lorraine seem hopelessly in love," I said.

Vaughn turned to me and swept hair away from my cheek. "Like us?"

"Maybe. Maybe not as much," I said, smiling as his lips met mine.

"Happy New Year!" I said to Rhonda the next morning. "How did the family dinner go last night?"

"It was lovely," Rhonda said. "Very rewarding to see how connected Lorraine and Arthur are. Reggie really likes Lorraine. She's the type of person who'll make sure their relationship will continue to grow. Not to speak ill of Katherine, but Lorraine's a much warmer, more secure person, and that, alone, will make things easier."

"That's nice," I said. "Let me tell you what happened last night." I filled her in on the incident with Randolph. "I'm going to take Randolph and Stephanie to the hospital this morning. We'll see if the doctor is going to go ahead with implanting a pacemaker. He said it's a common and easy procedure to do."

"The wedding isn't until four. I'll call Stephanie and ask her how I can help," said Rhonda. "How was the party at the hotel?"

"It was lovely. The setting, the food, and the music were all great. And now that people have been coming back to it for several years, they seem to have a better time as a group."

"It's a lot of work but a great moneymaker," said Rhonda. "Think of how far we've come, Annie. Let's hope the New Year will be a good one for us. We'll be starting off with some profitable events. And a royal visitor."

A shudder shook my shoulders. I still was uneasy about that reservation. But Rhonda wouldn't give up the chance to say we had royalty at our hotel.

"See you later," I said. "Unless there's an emergency, Vaughn and I will be at the wedding and reception."

'I'm calling Stephanie right now," said Rhonda.

We ended the call, and a few moments later, I sat with Robbie in the living room, playing a board game with him. His favorite game was Clue, and he always chose Colonel Mustard.

At the hospital, I once again sat with Stephanie while Randolph was having a test done. If the test revealed a need for a pacemaker, they'd go ahead and do it then. It was a far better way of handling it, making it less stressful for Stephanie.

As we waited in our chairs, I read a book and Stephanie pretended to do the same.

I rose. "Can I get you water or coffee or tea?"

She shook her head. "No, thanks. But, Ann, I want to talk to you about something, and I need your honest answer."

"Of course. What is it?" I studied the concern in her eyes.

"Randolph and I were talking last night and again this morning about you and your family's kindness to us. With no living relatives, we're thinking we might move to Sabal. But, and this is a big but, we won't do it if you think we'd be intruding in your life in any way."

"Why would I or any of my family mind?" I said, gripping her hand and smiling at her. "I already told you that you and Randolph are part of my family. You wouldn't be taking away from anything in my life, you'd be adding to it. And I know one little boy who'd love the idea of having his 'grandparents' living nearby."

Stephanie bowed her head, and I heard a soft sob. When she lifted it, she said, "You have no idea what that means to me, to us. Last night was a scare for us, making us realize our vulnerability at this age. I promise we wouldn't be a burden to you. Just someone I could talk to once in a while."

I hugged her. "It's going to be a lot more than that. I promise."

The doctor, a specialist dealing with electricity of the heart, appeared. "Mrs. Willis?"

Stephanie stood and I rose next to her.

The doctor smiled at us. "Everything went very well. The test proved my suspicion that a pacemaker was needed, and it's all been done. Randolph is in the recovery room now. We'll let him rest for a few hours and then he can go home."

"Anything special I should know about?" Stephanie asked.

The doctor shook his head. "It's all very simple. The

discharge nurse will hand you some papers about treating the small incision and that's it. I'll want to see Randolph in a week. At the time of checkout, you can make your appointment."

"Great news," I said to Stephanie. "Shall I take you back to the hotel to rest a bit or are you going to stay here?"

"Thanks, but I'll wait here. I may be able to visit him in the recovery room."

"Well, then, I'm going to go. Call when you're ready, and I'll pick you up."

Stephanie shook her head emphatically. "We'll call a cab or Uber. I know you have a wedding this afternoon, and I don't want to interfere with that. But thank you for the offer."

Her voice softened. "More than that, thanks for understanding about our moving to this area. Because of you and Rhonda, this feels much more like home."

I hugged her. "It'll be lovely to have you here."

I left for home, thinking the New Year was off to an exciting start.

CHAPTER SIXTEEN

WHEN VAUGHN AND I WALKED INTO THE LIBRARY FOR Lorraine's wedding, I paused to take in every detail. With only forty guests, the room had been set up to look like an outdoor garden. Trellises lining the walls on either side of the altar held fresh flowers in every soft hue imaginable – whites, pinks, creams, peach, and lavender. Interspersed between the flowers was greenery adding a lush feel to them. On this cold, gray day it was a remarkable change from the outdoors and a relief from holiday decorations. I'd heard Lorraine had been given a tremendous deal by Tropical Fleurs, but even then, I couldn't get over the abundance of flowers.

On the small altar, a basket held white roses, freesia, orchids, and lilies. White candles mounted in brass holders sat on either side of the basket. Chairs in front of the altar were arranged in two semi-circles with a path between them. Off to the side, in a corner beside the altar, a guitar player sent musical notes in the air.

After we were all seated by Reggie and a male friend of Lorraine's, we listened to music as the minister walked into the room. Then Reggie and Arthur stepped inside. Wearing dark suits, white shirts, and pale-pink ties, both men looked dapper. The happiness radiating from Arthur's smile brought an unexpected sting to my eyes. I glanced at Rhonda sitting beside me and saw that she'd had the same reaction.

The music changed to Cole Porter's *I Love You*, and we turned to the doorway.

Angela entered the room wearing a tea-length pink silk

dress with a scoop neck and long sleeves. My breath caught at the sight of her. Angela and Liz thought their hectic lives with children had taken away their beauty. But seeing Angela now and observing my daughter sitting beside Vaughn, I knew that wasn't true. Motherhood agreed with them both.

Following Angela, wearing a similar dress in lavender, was a friend of Lorraine's, a pretty woman who often came for Sunday brunch at the hotel.

We waited for Lorraine's arrival.

She appeared in a cream silk suit that was just as lovely as the setting. Lorraine was a striking woman, but the look of love she gave Arthur made her beautiful.

I didn't have to glance at Rhonda to know she was quietly sobbing beside me. I suspected that in addition to her happiness for the bride and groom, Rhonda was remembering Katherine and their growing relationship.

I gave Rhonda a comforting pat on the shoulder and watched as Arthur took hold of Lorraine's hand.

Listening to the words being said by the minister, and then hearing the exchange of vows, I thought of the promises Vaughn and I had shared at our wedding. I hoped Lorraine and Arthur would be as happy as we were.

Sensing my emotions, Vaughn turned to me and winked.

I squeezed his hand, and we continued to sit holding hands. His strong fingers braided through mine, and I held onto them.

When the minister announced that the groom could kiss the bride, we all clapped and chuckled at the way Arthur was all but sweeping Lorraine off her feet.

Rather than make a quick exit, Lorraine and Arthur stood in front of the altar and thanked us individually for being part of the ceremony.

I couldn't wait to see the way Lorraine had designed the

private section of the dining room for their reception.

When we walked into the room, I let out a sigh of satisfaction. Pale lavender, almost-white linen cloths covered the tables. Small arrangements of orchids sat in the middle of each table, offset by sparkling crystal and gleaming silverware.

Servers holding trays of tulip glasses filled with champagne greeted guests as they entered the room for the reception. A bar had been set up in the room as well. There was plenty of space for people to stand and talk before being asked to sit down for dinner. Servers walked through the gathering offering smoked salmon appetizers, Cheese Toast, Goat cheese and jelly crackers, and other tasty tidbits, making it easy to continue conversations while they waited for the meal.

I spoke to several of Lorraine's friends, some of whom had been widowed like her. They spoke highly of Arthur and confided they hoped a couple of his older, single friends would consider a move to Florida.

"Don't mention that to Rhonda," I said, half-joking.

"Mention what to me?" Rhonda said, joining us.

"We need you to convince some of Arthur's friends to move here," one of the women said.

"Ah, you need my matchmaking skills. Is that it?" said Rhonda, her eyes lighting with pleasure. "Give me some time. I'll work on it. Two of the men are semi-retired. There's no reason they can't work from here."

I held in a groan. Rhonda would not give up her matchmaking after a request like this.

"Hello, ladies, why is everyone grinning like cats who swallowed canaries?" asked Lorraine.

"Just a little matchmaking talk," said Rhonda. "You know how clever I am."

"I certainly do," Lorraine said, giving her a kiss on the

cheek. "Let's all of us enjoy this time. Jean-Luc has outdone himself with his individual beef wellingtons and the rest of the meal.

My mouth watered. Jean-Luc's prime beef tenderloin cooked to perfection, seasonings, and crispy crust was a delicacy not to be missed. Though Jean-Luc wasn't able to accept the wedding invitation, his wife, Lindsay, was here for the reception and dinner. I was delighted to see Bernie and Annette in the crowd too. It pleased me that our top staff members had become friends.

I walked over to Arthur. "It was a lovely ceremony. Small and intimate."

Arthur beamed at me. "Lorraine has good taste and knew what she wanted. I didn't worry about a thing. I just want her happy, you know?"

"Oh, yes. And it's nice to see your happiness, too."

"Katherine would've understood today. She told me before she died that she wanted me to find someone else. That's a relief to me."

I squeezed his arm. "It was lovely to see Reggie and Angela take part in the wedding. That's a lovely way to start the marriage off."

"I'm thankful to them both for their support. Look, here comes my bride now." I turned to see Lorraine approaching. They were spending the night at her house and leaving on their honeymoon tomorrow.

We spoke for a minute or two, and then Annette announced that it was time for everyone to be seated for dinner.

I sat next to Lindsay. I didn't have the chance to see Lindsay very often, and this would give me some time to catch up with her. Studying her now, I could barely see the crook in her nose from a beating she'd taken from her ex, the brother of the president of the United States. Hers had been such a sad situation made better by her meeting and marrying Jean-Luc, who treated her like a queen. Some media reporters called their marriage a match made in heaven, and I thought it suited them.

Tonight, Lindsay looked lovely in a rich-brown silk dress perfect for a Florida winter day. Her shiny chestnut brown hair and twinkling blue eyes gave evidence to her health and happiness.

"How are you, Lindsay? We haven't talked in some time. Hopefully, before the high season takes off, we can have lunch."

"Thanks, Ann. I'd love that." She leaned closer. "I haven't mentioned it to others yet, but I want you and Rhonda to be among the first to know that I'm pregnant. Jean-Luc is beside himself with joy and has become a total nuisance about making sure I'm alright and not overdoing anything. He and Sabine never had children, so this is a big deal. For me too. Thankfully, Thomas and I never had children. It would've made a difficult problem worse, and I didn't want to bring a child into an abusive home."

"Yours was a terrible situation. Abuse can take place in any home no matter how small or grand."

"Amelia wants me to work on a special project with her. I want you and Rhonda to help too. I'll let you know more about it as plans take shape."

"You know how we feel about helping other women," I said. "Just let us know what we can do."

"I will. I promise." Lindsay turned to the man on her left and I faced one of Lorraine's friends. Lorraine knew everyone there and had purposely mixed up the group to keep conversation going. Vaughn was sitting at another table and Rhonda at still another. It gave me a chance to reconnect with people I didn't see on a regular basis.

While we were still eating our lemon tarts for dessert, Arthur rose. "Thank you, everyone, for sharing this day with Lorraine and me. It has made this occasion special on many levels. We look forward to spending lots of time here with our friends, new and old. When we return from our honeymoon, we plan to have everyone come to our new house. The negotiations for it are still taking place, but we hope to have details for you at a later time."

As everyone clapped, Reggie got to his feet. "I know I've already toasted the wedding couple, but I wanted to thank you all for being here too. I realize that Angela and I have added many new friends to our family and want you to know how grateful I am."

Rhonda caught my eye, and I could tell how close she was to tears. She hadn't been sure of Reggie at first but had grown to love him like a devoted mother. She and his mother had fought over where the kids should live. Seeing them settled here, we all knew Sabal was the right choice.

Later, after dinner, Rhonda and I made sure things were in order, and then we bid each other good night.

I walked down to Stephanie's room to check on Randolph and see if they needed anything.

Stephanie answered my knock on their door. Seeing me, she stood back and waved me inside the room. Randolph was stretched out on the couch, but sat up and smiled at me.

"Thank you for all you did to help us. I'm a little bit robot now with my pacemaker," he teased.

"How do you feel?"

He gave me a thumbs up. "Great. Better than ever. Guess it took a scare to make things right."

"I won't keep you. I just wanted to say, 'Happy New Year' again."

"Thank you. We'll talk in the coming days about what I mentioned earlier," said Stephanie. "Right now, we're about to get ready for dinner. How was the wedding?"

"Beautiful. But then Lorraine has a talent for making things lovely. She outdid herself with this one."

"Wonderful to hear," said Stephanie giving me a kiss on the cheek and hugging me. "Give Vaughn and Robbie our love."

"Will do," I said, and waved goodbye. I hoped the next few days would give me some time to get rested before "The Royal Visit" as Rhonda called it.

CHAPTER SEVENTEEN

ON THIS EARLY JANUARY DAY, RHONDA AND I CHECKED the reservations list for the week.

"Look, here, Annie. Vivian Forrest," said Rhonda.

"Yes, but no Gregory, just a reservation for her. How odd," I responded.

"Let's be sure to be here to greet her. I have an idea there's a story behind this. A story I want to hear," said Rhonda. "You know how I have a certain sense of these things."

"What? You're a matchmaker and now you can sense happenings in other people's lives?"

"Trust me. I know something's up. When her son married the governor's daughter last summer there were all kinds of undercurrents."

"I remember. The bride and groom almost eloped," I said. It was another Beach House Hotel wedding Rhonda and I had to help save. "Anyone else of interest?"

"A U.S. Senator and his wife will spend a long weekend here. Otherwise, some repeats and some new guests," said Rhonda.

As I looked over the list, I was keeping numbers in mind, not stories. We had to do well during high season to carry us through the slower months.

On the day of Vivian's arrival, Rhonda and I kept an eye on the clock. Curiosity was eating us alive. Was this visit just a getaway for Vivian or an escape from her controlling, demanding husband? A man who was never satisfied with what his wife did for him and who spent more time with his mother at social events than with his wife. While we tried not to judge our guests, the last time we'd seen Vivian, she seemed a woman under the soul crushing control of her husband, Gregory.

"Okay. The guessing's over. Here she is," said Rhonda, getting a head start on me.

I followed her down the stairs and waited for the driver to open the passenger door.

A woman we hardly recognized emerged from the car.

As I walked forward to give her an embrace, I took in the changes. Her slumped posture of the past was replaced by a woman standing erect, her trim body filled out and exposing muscle in the comfortable wrap skirt and sleeveless top she wore. Her hair was cut in a short carefree style. But it was the way her blue eyes lit with happiness that caught my attention. If I wasn't mistaken, this was a woman who was taking her life back. I checked the ring finger of her left hand and spied a turquoise stone instead of the diamond I'd noticed before.

"Welcome back to The Beach House Hotel," I said again to her, giving her a hug. "It's great to see you. You're traveling alone?"

"Definitely," Vivian said with a satisfied smile. "I'll have to tell you all about it since my stay here at the hotel helped me decide to leave Gregory."

"Yes, when you're ready to talk, give us a call. Annie and I have a secret little place we go to for privacy. We can take coffee or cocktails there and relax."

"I can order a bottle of champagne. The best, of course. Gregory's paying." Her laugh was contagious.

I gazed at her, still surprised by the change in her. "'How are the kids?"

"Brandon and Carolina are fine. They encouraged me to talk to a professional about my unhappiness, and I'm very glad they did. I feel as if I've been given a new life."

"I couldn't be happier for you," I said, thinking about how my life had changed after Robert left me.

"Well, come inside, and let's get you registered and settled," said Rhonda.

We walked Vivian into the hotel, left her at the front desk, and returned to our office.

"Hot Damn!" said Rhonda. "Vivian is a different person, and I say good for her."

"Me, too. It's nice when you see something work out like that."

A few days later, Rhonda and I waited at the top of the stairs to greet Hilda Hassel. As requested, we'd alerted our staff to prepare a high tea for her even though it was mid-week and not our usual Sunday high tea.

Rhonda elbowed me. "Here she comes!"

A white limousine pulled into the front circle, and Rhonda and I headed down the stairs. I hoped all my niggling worries about her had been foolish. A woman married into a royal family certainly would have class, wouldn't she?

As we reached the pavement, the limo driver opened the passenger door and a long, bare leg and a foot encased in stiletto red heels emerged, followed by a tall blond woman wearing a rather short skirt whose color matched her heels. A white, lacy, V-neck top showed off her breasts and completed her outfit. Her hair was pulled back into a knot behind her head. I thought of Kirsten Dunst, but when I looked closer, I saw the features of her face seemed harsh in comparison. I glanced at Rhonda and knew she was as surprised as I to see how young Hilda was. Henrick had died in his late seventies which should've made Hilda in her fifties.

"Welcome to The Beach House Hotel," said Rhonda shaking Hilda's hand politely.

I followed suit. "It's a pleasure to have you here."

"I get the Presidential Suite, right?" Hilda said, letting go of my hand. She turned as a man with long brown hair emerged from the other side of the limo. "Ah, here's my nephew, Kurt Bauer." Like Hilda, Kurt had a healthy, young appearance. His brown eyes swept over Rhonda and me.

"Welcome to The Beach House Hotel," I said smiling at him though I'd expected an older woman and her nephew to be older and wasn't sure how to handle it.

"How are you related to Hilda?" Rhonda asked him bluntly. "We're always excited to learn something about our guests."

Hilda and Kurt glanced at one another, and then Kurt said, "It's a long story involving my mother's family."

"Royal families can be complicated," said Hilda, her mouth curving into a smile that was a bit smug.

"Let's get you inside to register properly," I said. "We'll have a bellman handle your luggage."

"Do you mean I'm not pre-registered?" Hilda said, her eyebrows lifting.

"We ask all our guests to sign a Non-Disclosure Agreement about our others at the hotel. You'll need to sign that in addition to filling out regular check-in information. Kurt, too," I said smoothly.

Kurt shrugged. "I can do that."

"I'll get someone to handle your luggage," I said.

Rhonda led them inside while one of the bellmen brought a luggage cart to the limousine. I stood by as he hefted two large and one small Louis Vuitton suitcases onto the cart, along with two brown leather suitcases. I wasn't surprised by the number of pieces of luggage. I'd figured from the type of clothing she was wearing that Hilda had brought an extensive wardrobe with her. The bellman headed inside, and I climbed the stairs to the lobby. Hilda and Kurt were just finishing with their registration.

Rhonda and I led them to the Presidential Suite which had, at one time, been part of Rhonda's private living area. The five rooms were kept in immaculate condition and were lovely.

I unlocked the door and held it open for Hilda and Kurt to enter.

From the entry you could see across the living room to the sliding doors and balcony overlooking the side garden. An Oriental rug in shades of blue enhanced the wooden floor in the living room.

Hilda looked around. "This will do. Thank you. You have, I presume, arranged for high tea to be delivered here."

"Yes, we'll be ready anytime you are," said Rhonda.

"I want to get unpacked and then I'll call down to the front desk to let you know when to deliver it," said Hilda.

"All right. Let us show you around the suite, and you can relax on your own," I said.

Rhonda and I gave them a quick overview of the suite including the luxurious bathroom with gold plated fixtures at the double sinks, and then left.

We remained quiet until we reached our office. Then, taking seats in our chairs, we faced one another.

"How do you like them apples? Kurt Bauer as Hilda's nephew? No fuckin' way. They were all but making love with their eyes. I smell a rat bastard."

"Hilda is not how I imagined her," I said, disturbed. "Something is wrong. The ages don't match up, but I don't know what we can do about it. She's paid a healthy deposit for the room.

"Yeah, let me guess. She was a playmate for old Henrick before he died," said Rhonda. Her eyes widened. "Oh my God, Annie. Do you think his death was like that of Wilkins Jones? He and Hilda weren't married long before he died."

"I hope not," I said, unable to stop a shudder. Wilkins Jones was a food editor doing a report on The Beach House Hotel not long after we opened. He and a woman he called his wife, which we knew wasn't true, had come to the hotel for a few days of eating our food and playing around. He'd died during sex. That was our first encounter with a death at the hotel. Even now, I remembered every detail of it.

"We'll never know," I said. "Let's hope that her visit isn't going to be as horrible as I think. I agree with you. Hilda and Kurt are much more than aunt and nephew, and that's not all. We're going to have to watch them carefully."

"Yeah, it makes me wonder what the fuck they're up to," said Rhonda.

"Remember, our guests have a right to their privacy," I said. "We've seen some things I wished I hadn't. But it all worked out. And until we have cause to kick them out, we have to treat them like every other guest."

"You're right. We'll deal with them. They can't be worse than the rock star who brought his family here and demanded one thing after another," Rhonda said. "I probably should've listened to you and agreed to turn down their request. But I still think having celebrities and members of a royal family could be good for us, Annie. Word spreads and grows in the community."

I hope you're right,' I said, not believing it for a minute. I called the front desk.

"When you get a request from the Presidential Suite for high tea to be brought to their room, please let me know. Rhonda and I will deliver it in person." After I hung up, I turned to Rhonda. "Like you, I want to know what these two are up to."

Restless, I decided to walk around the hotel to check on things. Sometimes seeing our guests enjoying themselves gave me a sense that things were going well and a sign for me not to worry.

I walked out to the pool deck. Though the temperature had lost its summer heat, it was still pleasant and in the 70s. People were lounging by the pool. I stepped outside to join them and was surprised to see Kurt stretched out in a chair typing into his phone.

I approached him. "You're not going to participate in high tea?"

He shook his head. "Naw, that's Hilda's idea of a classy thing, something every member of that family does, but I'd prefer a beer anytime."

"I see. Well, enjoy yourself." I walked over to the small bar set up at the corner of the lanai and spoke to the bartender. "Busy afternoon?"

"Not really. One guest likes his beer, but others must be waiting for cocktail time."

"Okay, thanks." In the slower summer months, we often cut hours at the pool bar, but in high season, the guests tended to like having a Bloody Mary or Mimosas in the mornings. The pool was close enough to our inside bar that drinks could be delivered from there.

My cell buzzed.

"Ms. Sanders, it's Michael from the front desk. High tea has been ordered for two."

"Thank you." I ended the call and sent a text to Rhonda to meet me in the kitchen.

###

A short while later, Rhonda and I took the service elevator with a waiter who was wheeling a service cart carrying a small, three-tier plate holder with sandwiches, scones, and cakes. A teapot, cream, sugar, and lemon wedges sat atop the service cart as well.

"It looks delicious," said Rhonda. "I hope she enjoys it."

The small, crustless sandwiches that we normally served – cucumber with cream cheese, smoked salmon and cream cheese and egg and cress looked both dainty and delectable. We sometimes served roast beef sandwiches, but Hilda had requested that they not be included. Blueberry scones, slices of chocolate cake, and lemon tarts comprised the sweets.

The waiter knocked on the door of the suite.

At a voice calling, "Please come in," the waiter opened the door to wheel the cart inside and backed away.

Hilda was approaching us wearing a see-through silk robe with nothing on beneath it.

"Wait here. We'll call you in a minute," I told the waiter quietly.

"Oh, I'm sorry," said Hilda clasping the robe tight around her and looking at the waiter, a young man who was definitely uncomfortable. "I thought you were someone else."

"I saw Kurt by the pool," I said.

"Yes, he doesn't like high tea, says it's too fancy for him." Hilda shook her head. "It's such a normal thing in Bavaria. A very nice touch to any afternoon, sitting by the fire sipping tea like other family members."

"We wanted to make sure that everything was to your satisfaction," I said.

"Are you going to be having it here in the room or would you prefer to have it downstairs?" asked Rhonda.

"On Sundays, we offer high tea in our library. It's been quite a hit," I added.

Hilda shook her head. "No, I shall always want it served up here. I'll be receiving quite a few guests."

"Others from the royal family?" asked Rhonda with a hopeful note.

Hilda gave her a sad look. "Unfortunately, Henrik's family doesn't approve of me. Never did. But no matter."

I described what was on the serving table. "The waiter is available to serve you when you're presentable," I said giving her a meaningful look.

"Oh, right. Let me get the robe from the closet and I'll be right back."

Hilda returned wearing the white robe with the hotel logo we placed in guests' closets, and Rhonda asked the waiter to go ahead and serve.

"As long as you're satisfied with the offerings, we'll leave you to it," I said.

We left the suite as an older gentleman headed our way.

"Afternoon," said Rhonda. "Can we help you with anything?"

The man shook his head. "No. I'm here to see a friend. But thanks."

We waited in the hall while the man knocked on the door to the Presidential Suite.

The door opened and we could hear Hilda say, "Come in. They're just serving tea now."

The door closed and Rhonda and I stared at one another.

"What the fuck was that all about?" Rhonda asked.

I shrugged. "Your guess is as good as mine."

"Looked like a lot of what my mother used to call 'hanky panky' going on, if you ask me," huffed Rhonda.

"We'll see," I said.

CHAPTER EIGHTEEN

THAT NIGHT, I LAY IN BED TALKING ON THE PHONE WITH Vaughn. He was doing a movie in L.A., and I wanted to hear his reaction to my meeting Hilda and Kurt.

"Have someone keep an eye on them and the number of visitors Hilda gets. You don't want the reputation of the hotel to be marred by a guest acting as a hooker."

"Rhonda was really upset by it. We know some of our guests have clandestine meetings for a variety of reasons, but we've never faced something like this. It's bad enough that Hilda might be a royal bimbo, but her so-called nephew gives out even worse vibes. He lacks social graces and seems like a self-centered man along for the ride."

"I know you're concerned, but try not to obsess over it. Be watchful, but don't let your worries about Hilda's behavior ruin your contact with other guests," Vaughn said calmly.

"Thanks. I feel better about it already. We've had very unusual guests. Maybe that's all this is about. Heaven knows Hilda must have had a lot of interesting experiences while she was married to Henrick Hassel."

"Right," said Vaughn. "How's everything else going? Robbie has a swim meet tomorrow, right?"

"Yes, I told him I'd be there. Afterwards, we'll call you together."

"That would be nice. I love having a movie project to work on, but I miss being home too."

"We miss you like crazy. Cindy keeps looking for you."

Vaughn laughed. "How about you?"

"You know I miss you. The bed is empty without you. The whole house, in fact."

"I'll make it up to you when I get back," Vaughn said. "Gotta go. I'll call tomorrow."

"Love you," I said, already feeling even more alone.

"Love you too. Always," said Vaughn and the silence in the room after I ended the call was depressing. Tomorrow, before I went to Robbie's swim meet, I'd stop off to see the Ts. They always gave me joy.

The next morning, after dropping Robbie off at school, I headed into the hotel. I knew Vaughn was right and I shouldn't worry but simply be aware of Hilda Hassel's activities. For January, it was an unseasonably warm day, and the bright skies boosted my spirits.

When I entered the hotel, the smell of cinnamon rolls baking filled the kitchen with a delicious aroma. I said good morning to Consuela, and we hugged one another.

"Looks like it's going to be a beautiful day," I said, helping myself to a cup of coffee.

"How did high tea go yesterday?" Consuela asked. She worked an early morning shift and left right after lunch.

"I'm not sure. Rhonda and I made sure Hilda liked what we had to offer and then left, just as a gentleman caller arrived."

Consuela's eyebrows rose. "What do you mean 'gentleman caller'?"

I set down my coffee cup and faced her. "Something seems off about both Hilda and Kurt Bauer, her so-called nephew. They're much younger than we'd thought, they lack social graces, and we're pretty sure Kurt isn't just a nephew. But for now, there's nothing we can do about it." I shook my head. "If you weren't like a mother to me, I wouldn't discuss a guest like this."

"I know," said Consuela. "But you're usually right about people. I'll keep my eyes and ears open to any comments I might hear."

"Thanks," I said, picking up my coffee and heading into the office. I'd get a cinnamon roll after Rhonda arrived.

A few minutes later, Rhonda burst into the office. "Annie, let's talk. I think we should ask Hilda and Kurt to leave. I've thought about it, and I don't like what I see."

"Hold on," I said, rising. "As much as we can't hurt the hotel's reputation by having certain guests here, we can't simply accuse people of doing something we don't like. We need to have sufficient evidence before asking them to leave."

"You're right, I suppose. But when we have proof, I'm doing it."

"Come on. Let's get a cinnamon roll and take a break in the kitchen. I've already told Consuela about my concerns. She'll let us know if she hears anything. But we owe it to Bernie to tell him our thoughts."

Rhonda let out a sigh. "Let's see him now and then have our treat."

I called Bernie and we arranged a quick meeting in his office now.

Bernie listened carefully to what we had to say. "We'll assign a trusted housekeeper to the room and ask for pertinent information. But you're right. We must be careful."

Rhonda and I exchanged glances.

"I guess that's the best we can do," I said. "Guests have a right to their privacy. That's always been our policy. We need to honor it."

"Indeed," said Bernie. "It may simply be a case of false assumptions. Now, how are we doing with our scheduled weddings. Lorraine is back and Lauren has held her own handling a small wedding and Sunday High Teas. I think we should make a commitment to Lauren for her good work by giving her a raise and a new title."

"I like it," said Rhonda. "Lorraine and Arthur were very happy with the way their wedding was overseen. Even if Lorraine did the planning, it was executed perfectly."

"It's going to be a busy winter and a hectic spring wedding period," I said. "We have an outstanding staff, but I feel more comfortable knowing we have competent people to take over important positions when necessary."

"Agreed," said Bernie. "I'll speak to Lorraine today."

"Thanks for your time, Bernie," said Rhonda, rising to her feet. "How's the planning going for the Hotel Association Dinner tonight?"

"It's looking like we'll have about sixteen top hotel people in the area here. It'll be served in the private dining room. Jean-Luc is going all out with a small, but elegant seafood buffet."

"Great. It's a great chance for him to show off his cooking skills to people who will appreciate them," I said.

"I'll stop by to say hello before I leave," said Rhonda.

"Rhonda will represent both of us. Robbie has a swim meet, so I won't be able to make it. I know you understand."

Bernie bobbed his head. "No problem. Both of you have earned time for your families as you've requested." He gave us a teasing smile and a wink. "That's why you pay me so well."

"See you later," I said, and followed Rhonda out of the office.

After the door closed behind us, Rhonda grabbed my arm. "Holy Shit! Did Bernie just make a joke? He's come a long way since he told me he didn't want to be called anything but Bernhard."

Remembering how stiff and formal Bernie had been when we first met him, I laughed. Only Rhonda could get someone to let loose. I remembered how she'd helped me win back my confidence when I was shattered after Robert left me.

I gave myself time to visit Liz's triplets before Robbie's swim meet. It was always such fun to see their progress. In a few months they'd be two. It hardly seemed possible. But then Robbie was growing fast too.

At Liz's house, I parked the car and hurried to the front door anxious to see Emma, Noah, and Olivia. The sound of crying met me as I knocked and then opened the door.

Liz met me holding Olivia. "Come on in. We've had a little accident. Olivia fell and bumped her lip. When she started crying, the other two began. Syd is getting them calmed. It's cute the way they empathize with one another."

"Want to see GeeGee?" I asked holding out my arms to Olivia.

She reached for me, and I hugged her to me. "There, there. Feel better?"

Olivia's big blue eyes looked up at me and I saw that her lip was swollen. "All better."

I chuckled softly and squeezed her. Growing up as one of three, each child had to be a little independent because she or he couldn't have the complete attention of the person caring for them.

"I'm glad you're better. Let's go see your brother and sister," I said, heading to the kitchen where Liz and Syd were hoisting the toddlers into highchairs for an after-nap treat.

"Hi, Syd. How are you?" I asked.

"Fine, thanks. Things are going well. Bobby is well and will have no problem participating in the play-offs. So, he's a happy man."

"Are his parents going to be able to attend the game on Saturday?"

"Yes, they're here now, staying at the house with us. It's been fun to be with them. They're very thoughtful."

"It's a nice family. We love having Rick working for us. He's bright and eager." Bobby's brother was learning the hotel business from bottom to top, and Bernie was pleased with his enthusiasm and willingness to learn.

"Bobby likes having his brother around. They're good together. Rick doesn't let him get away with anything," said Sydney smiling.

"No sign of an engagement yet?" I asked, and then realized I was beginning to sound like Rhonda. "Sorry, I didn't mean to intrude."

Syd's eyes sparkled. "I have a feeling Bobby's going to ask me on Valentine's Day. We have talked about not wanting to wait. Even though we haven't known each other for long, we're sure about it."

"I've seen how you've grown together," I said. "It seems very natural."

Noah pounded on his tray, and laughing, Syd turned to him. "All right, little guy. Juice coming up."

I kissed the top of his head and went over to Emma. "Hi, little girl."

"Hi," she said clearly.

I kissed her on the cheek and said, "Who loves you and your brother and sister?"

She grinned and pointed a finger at me. "GeeGee."

"That's right." Liz handed me a sippy cup with juice and a graham cracker which I promptly gave to Emma.

"What do you say?" prompted Liz.

"Tank you," Emma said proudly.

"How are you, darling?" I asked Liz. "You look tired but happy."

"That's about it. Tired as usual but content. It's just a rat race around here. Thank God for Syd." She turned to her.

"It's my pleasure," said Syd. "Before I worked for Tina Marks, I worked for a family with one child who was more work than these three together."

"I think keeping to a routine helps. Angela warned me about that," said Liz. "In another couple of years, the kids will be in pre-school, and I'll have some time to myself. Chad keeps reminding me of that."

"Take every moment you can with them because they'll grow fast. Just think of how fast the years have gone by since we got Robbie. He was a toddler not much older than the Ts."

"I think Dad would be pleased at how well he's growing. You and Vaughn have been excellent parents for him." Liz threw her arms around me. "Love you, Mom."

"Love you too," I said, pleased we'd become adult friends.

After spending a few minutes chatting with the kids and singing their favorite song, I left them to go to Robbie's swim meet, which was being held at the local high school pool.

At the meet, I found a seat on the bleachers beside the pool and sat next to Cindy Brigham, Brett's mother.

"Hi," she said. "As usual, our boys are together. It's great that they're such close friends."

"And good neighbors. It's been a joy to have Brett living next door." Brett was an only child too, and he and Robbie had formed a deep friendship.

Cindy gave me a teasing smile. "I hear you've named a pup after me."

I laughed. "She's a sweetie, like you. Robbie thought her

black coat was like cinders from coal and that's where the name came from. The name suits her."

"I've told Charlie it's time for us to get another dog, but he's still not ready after our lab, Duke, died."

"I love seeing Trudy and Cindy curled up with Robbie at night. It's very cute."

We stopped chatting as the swim team entered in a line and then took a moment to get wet before being paired off with members of an opposing swim team for races.

I studied Robbie's long legs and arms. He was at such an awkward age. But he had the build of a swimmer with those long limbs and broad shoulders and chest and was already filling out some.

Standing beside him, Brett was a bit taller.

The moist, chlorine-tainted air swirled around us as one race followed another. When it came time for Robbie to race, doing a crawl, I got my cell phone ready to record a video for Vaughn.

Robbie was one of six boys lined up at one end of the pool. At the sound of a whistle, they all dove into the water and began stroking. In no time, the race ended with Brett in first, and Robbie in second place.

Cindy and I yelled and clapped.

Robbie looked over at me, grinned, and bobbed his head in acknowledgement.

I wanted to give him a hug but knew enough not to embarrass him that way. Still, the feeling was there.

After the swim meet ended, Cindy suggested going to dinner at the boys' favorite burger restaurant, and I quickly agreed.

That night, as Vaughn and I talked, I thought back to the

time when he'd done a lot of traveling and I realized how spoiled I'd become after he left the soap opera in New York. Later in the year, he'd do a few appearances on the show, but it was just a temporary arrangement.

"Have a good night," I said to him, blowing him a kiss through the phone.

"You, too, hon. Miss you," he replied, and we ended the short call.

Leaning back against the pillow, I sighed and turned on the television. It was a relaxing way to eventually fall asleep without the heat of Vaughn's body to keep me warm.

CHAPTER NINETEEN

THE NEXT MORNING, I SAT IN THE OFFICE GOING over financials when Rhonda appeared, looking like the early bird who'd swallowed a worm.

Suspicion rose within me. "What's going on?"

"I was talking to Bernie. It seems one of the gentlemen from last night's dinner stayed later than the others and ended up in the Presidential Suite."

"Whoa! How did he get there? Invitation?"

"I think Kurt is the one who invited him. Bernie asked Rick Bailey, who was working as bartender, if he'd heard or seen anything." Rhonda leaned toward me with a smirk. "Kurt mentioned something about a cure for loneliness to this man sitting alone, and though Rick couldn't hear everything that was being said, the man left soon afterwards, and then Rick heard him in the hall ask someone for directions to the Presidential Suite." Rhonda shook her head. "How do you like them apples?"

"It's a start for making our case against Hilda. But we need more proof than that," I said.

"Why don't we get one of our trusted friends to play the part of lonely man?" Rhonda said.

"I know someone who doesn't have to play the part," I said grinning.

"Oh, my God, Annie! Do you mean Brock?"

"Maybe," I said smugly. "But we can't let him in on it. We have to suggest that at the hotel meeting last night, someone mentioned what an excellent job he was doing as president of the neighborhood association and we wanted to offer him a complimentary drink in the bar. We'll clue Rick into our game."

Rhonda looked at me and we both laughed. Tricking Brock was such a satisfying thought.

We met with Bernie, who was not a fan of Brock's. He laughed at the idea. "Okay," he said. "I'll approach Brock the next time I see him. He usually drops by for a drink a couple times a week. It gives him a chance to tell guests how important he is."

"If we see him on the beach, we'll tell him you want to meet with him," said Rhonda, rubbing her hands together in anticipation.

"I'll speak to Rick and ask if he'd be willing to extend his time as bartender to help us carry out this plan," said Bernie with a gleam in his eye.

I couldn't help but wonder if Brock realized how many people he'd annoyed. Constantly.

A couple of days later, Rhonda and I were going over an advertising campaign we wanted to put together for summer weddings. Our present campaign was perfect for spring, but we wanted to change it up for summer with suggestions for different times of days for ceremonies, refreshing menus, and other things we offered to make it special. Once we got our ideas down, we'd confer with Lorraine and Lauren for their input. It was satisfying work for Rhonda and me to remain creative, searching for new ideas to keep the hotel in the news.

My cell phone rang, and I checked Caller ID. *Vivian Forrest*.

"Good afternoon, Vivian."

"Hi, Ann. I was wondering if you and Rhonda were free to

sit and share some champagne and news with me."

I checked my watch. Four o'clock wasn't too soon. I spoke to Rhonda and then said, "Rhonda says she's more than ready. I am too. We'll meet you in the bar."

"Okay, I'll pick up the bottle and glasses there. Will that be all right?" Vivian asked.

"Perfect," I said. "Meet you there in a few minutes."

After I ended the call, Rhonda smiled. "This day is getting better and better. Before we meet her, let's check to see how high tea is going with Hilda."

When we walked into the kitchen, Emelie Francis, our pastry chef, was about to slide a small tray of mini tarts into one of the refrigerators.

"Hold on," said Rhonda. "Can we each taste one?"

Emelie laughed. "Sure, why not. I'm keeping a supply on hand for high tea each day."

"How is that going? Is Ms. Hassel enjoying it?" I asked.

"The waiter told me she's been satisfied with them. No complaints have been made. Most everything is eaten or stored in her mini refrigerator in her room."

"That's good," I said, but I wondered why Hilda kept leftovers. She made a big deal about coming to our cocktail hour and dinner, wearing her finest outfits and glittering with jewels. Were those tiny morsels she saved used to treat the visitors she received on a daily basis?

As we walked away, I told Rhonda my suspicions about her serving the food to her guests.

"Could be. We have to entice Brock to go to her room. He could be a witness, willing or not," said Rhonda grinning.

When we walked into the bar, Vivian was there talking to the bartender. Rick would not come on duty for another hour or so. Dressed in a wrap skirt and a knit top, she looked adorable.

"We'll take all of this with us," said Rhonda, picking up the ice bucket holding the bottle of champagne.

"I've got the glasses and napkins," said Vivian.

I led the way to the second floor. Down the hall from the Presidential Suite, I opened the door to what appeared to be a maid's closet and walked to the far end to unlock a door that led to a balcony that Rhonda and I used for privacy.

"Oh, this really is a hideaway," exclaimed Vivian stepping onto the balcony and looking out at the Gulf.

"A very private place," said Rhonda setting down the bucket. Once we were seated, Rhonda lifted out the bottle and deftly opened the champagne, which emitted a soft pop when the cork was withdrawn.

"Nicely done," I said, smiling at Rhonda.

"Thanks." She poured some of the bubbly liquid into the three tulip glasses and handed them out.

Vivian straightened in her chair and lifted her glass. "I'd like to thank you for helping me realize what women can do either alone or together to gain control of their lives. Having the wedding here and the talks I've had with both my daughter-in-law and my therapist have made me understand why I was in such an unhappy place. You two, without knowing it, gave me a reason to think that just because I'm older I didn't have to remain as I was. Thank you, Ann and Rhonda."

"Hear! Hear!" said Rhonda, clicking her glass against Vivian's.

"I'm glad we could be a help, if only by example," I said. "Meeting Rhonda, deciding to go into business with her, was the best decision I could ever have made."

"Yeah, if Annie hadn't agreed to go into business with me, I don't know where I'd be today," said Rhonda. "My life was empty."

Vivian glanced from Rhonda to me. "I have a close friend in New York, but she's happily married and never saw Gregory at his worst, so she didn't understand why I'd give up the so-called glamorous life I had there. Now she understands. Her own husband doesn't belittle her or yell at her. He's simply having an affair with a younger woman. And yes, before you ask, Gregory was doing that too."

Rhonda lifted her glass of champagne. "You say Gregory is paying for this?"

Vivian grinned and bobbed her head. "Drink up."

"Are you divorced?" I asked, practical as always.

"I've filed for divorce, but it hasn't been finalized. Gregory thinks I'll come to my senses, as he says, but I won't. While I'm down here enjoying myself, my lawyer is working up an agreement that will be fair to both of us. Luckily both my children, Brandon and Hazel, understand why I'm going through with a divorce from their father."

"I love that you've gained such strength," I said.

"Me, too," said Vivian. "I feel as if a thousand pounds has been lifted off my shoulders. I was so weighed down by all my supposed faults." She gave us a sheepish look. "I apologize for how difficult I was at the wedding."

"No need," said Rhonda firmly. "Are you having a good time here?"

"The best. You have many interesting guests. I met Hilda Hassel, and we talked quite a bit about being single. She was married to someone in the Bavarian royal family and now that she's on her own, she says she's having a lot of fun."

I leaned closer. "Was Kurt Bauer with her?"

"Yes, but he pretty much stayed with the men at the bar, and then he left before dinner. A handsome man but not my type. He seemed, let's say ... well-satisfied with himself," said Vivian.

Rhonda and I glanced at one another and then I couldn't hold in my laughter. "Well-satisfied with himself? What a marvelous term. Sounds like someone we all know."

"Do you mean Brock Goodwin?" said Vivian. "He met up with me on the beach this morning and offered once more to show me around. I quickly turned him down, which surprised him."

My heart swelled with affection for her. "I'm glad you decided to come back to the hotel. If we can do anything to help you have a delightful stay, you need to simply ask."

"Thanks," she said. "I'm pleased to be here."

"Perhaps you can do us a favor," I said. "Keep an eye on Hilda and Kurt. We want them to have a nice time too."

"Yes," said Rhonda. "That might be helpful to us."

"I'd be delighted to do that for you. After I leave here, I plan on going to Tallahassee to look for an apartment there. Carolina is eager for me to do that. And her mother agrees, which is such a blessing. But then as the governor's wife, Carlotta is a very generous woman."

"It seems as if your life has taken a wonderful turn. I'm very excited for you," I said sincerely.

We finished our champagne while chatting about events in town. Though Sabal was a resort town, many of its residents lived year-'round and were kept busy by an assortment of activities.

"Thanks for meeting with me," said Vivian. "I wanted this opportunity to thank you."

"We're delighted to be invited," said Rhonda. "I've got to get home to my kids, but I hope to see you around the hotel."

"Deal," said Vivian. She winked. "I'll keep an eye out for Hilda. She's pretty hard to miss."

###

That night as I talked to Vaughn on my cell, I told him about what a surprise Vivian had turned out to be.

"People can change given the right circumstances. Guess who I ran into today? Lily Dorio was in the same restaurant for lunch. She came right over to the table I shared with Nick Swain and was very pleasant as she explained she was trying to build a business representing actors in the business."

"Interesting. Is she succeeding?"

"Who knows? She talks a good game. She brings a lot of unnecessary drama with her, She's not someone I admire."

"You're right about her. When are you coming home?" I asked. "We all miss you here."

"Within a couple of days. Nick has been diverted. We're not shooting as many segments as we'd thought. But we have enough for a test period. I hope the streaming audience loves it. We have a talented crew working on it."

We talked some more, and after Vaughn said goodbye to Robbie, we said our own.

Once Robbie was settled for the night, I went to bed with a book. I'd loved to read since I was a child, and without Vaughn sharing my bed, reading filled the time. Still, I missed him.

My cell rang, startling me. *Rhonda.*

I answered. "Hi, what's up?"

"I just got a call from Rick at the bar. Brock took the bait. After talking to Kurt, he headed up to the Presidential Suite."

"Let's see where that leads us."

"Talk to you tomorrow," said Rhonda. "Thought you should know."

"Thanks," I said, unable to stop smiling. I had a feeling that Brock's involvement would prove to be important to us.

CHAPTER TWENTY

THE NEXT MORNING, I WAS SERVING BREAKFAST TO Robbie when I got a call from Bernie. Surprised to see his name on Caller ID, I answered. "Hi, Bernie. What's up?"

"I need to meet with you and Rhonda first thing. There's something important that we need to discuss right away."

"Okay. I can be there in a half hour after I drop Robbie off to school."

"Okay. Please come directly to my office."

"No coffee?" I teased.

"Not unless you bring me a cinnamon roll," he answered, with an unexpected retort. He really was loosening up and developing a cute sense of humor.

I laughed. "Deal."

"Who was that, Mom?" asked Robbie after I slid my phone into my pocket.

"Mr. Bernhard. I have a meeting with him," I answered, a bit unsettled.

My cell rang again. *Rhonda.*

"What the freak is going on?" Rhonda asked me. "Bernie called sounding like someone in a spy movie."

"All I know is that he wants us to meet with him right away. And I've agreed to bring him a cinnamon roll."

"Sorry, if I sound grumpy. Drew wasn't feeling well, and I was up with him in the middle of the night."

"I'm sorry." I ended the call and sat back in my chair. Bernie was acting in an unusual manner but that shouldn't mean trouble, should it?

I entered Bernie's office carrying a tray holding a coffee pot, three cups, and a plate of cinnamon rolls. Rhonda had called to say she was running late but would be there soon.

Bernie took the tray out of my hands. "You weren't kidding when you said you'd bring cinnamon rolls."

"You sounded as if we all might need one," I said.

Becoming serious, he said, "I'll wait to discuss it until Rhonda is here, but it's concerning."

We sat and chatted about our dogs and Bernie's new grandbaby. It was nice to see him so vivacious. When he first came to The Beach House Hotel to interview for the job of general manager, he seemed aloof and alone, except for his dog, Trudy, who'd become a member of my own family.

Rhonda arrived out of breath. "Sorry I'm late. It's been a crazy morning." She spied the tray. "Coffee. Thank God. I need it."

"Relax and enjoy it. Bernie and I have been discussing family, waiting for you."

"You sounded unusually serious, Bernie," said Rhonda after taking a sip of coffee.

"When you're ready, I'll begin," said Bernie. He pulled a sheet of paper in front of him and picked up his reading glasses.

"What's going on?" I asked. "You said it was very concerning."

"I got a call from the FBI early this morning. It seems our Hilda Hassel and her friend, Kurt Bauer, are known to them. Within the past year, two upscale hotels in New York City have filed reports indicating their suspicion that these two are involved in stealing jewelry and, perhaps, other things as well."

"Did they mention our suspicions about prostitution?"

Rhonda asked.

"I mentioned it to them first. That really caught their attention. It was something that one of the other hotels mentioned in passing, but that's much harder to track in a large, metropolitan hotel."

"How did they know that Hilda and Kurt were here?" I asked, not liking the idea of people's activities being attached to our hotel.

"They've been tracking their expenses. That's all they're going to divulge to us. Remember, this is very secret. I told them we could have a witness for the prostitution aspect of their dealings, and they were interested in that."

"Are you talking about Brock Goodwin?" asked Rhonda, her eyes rounded with surprise.

"We know he visited the Presidential Suite in the evening quite recently. He could be a credible witness."

Rhonda and I looked at each other aghast. We wanted to best Brock for his constant harassment of us, but this was a bigger trick than even we'd imagined.

"It would serve Brock right to be pulled into something like this," said Bernie. "He's been obnoxious, blatantly interfering with the ongoing business of the hotel whenever and however he can."

Rhonda straightened. "You're right. Too bad if Brock is embarrassed to be caught up in this scandal. He's been overly aggressive to a few of our female guests, telling them he's the president of the neighborhood association and can give them a special tour. Vivian Forrest is just one woman he's approached."

Bernie held up his hand. "Remember, we are to take no action or give any indication we are aware of their illegal activities. The FBI will send someone here as a guest. Only I will know who that is, so no mistakes are made. The FBI insisted on that."

"This is really unnerving," I said, feeling a little sick. "We must keep the reputation of the hotel intact. This puts us in an awkward position. There can be no idea that guests and their jewelry are unsafe here."

"I totally agree," said Bernie. "Have you seen or heard of any incidents involving jewelry being lost?"

"No," I said, "but Vivian mentioned meeting Hilda at our cocktail and dinner hours and had admired all her jewelry. I didn't think anything at the time, but what if Hilda's jewelry is stolen?"

"Pretty damn brazen of her, if it is," said Rhonda.

"Both Hilda and Kurt are pretty self-confident, which is where they might have made some mistakes," said Bernie.

"What are we supposed to do now?" I asked. "I want to get this situation resolved as soon as possible. We're starting the high season, and we count on a busy one to carry us through the down times."

"Yeah, are we supposed to spy on them?" asked Rhonda. "I'm pretty talented at that. Remember when we hid in the bushes, Annie?"

I chuckled. Rhonda and I were trying to figure out what was happening inside the house on the hotel property when it was rented to someone we didn't trust. She'd thrown herself into the role of detective and came dressed all in black for her skulking.

Bernie was not amused. "We must be careful not to let on to anyone that we have concerns about Hilda and Kurt. The FBI is counting on us to be discreet."

"We understand," I said quietly. "We're just letting off steam because the thought of the hotel's reputation being ruined is horrifying."

"Okay," said Bernie getting to his feet. "I'll speak to Rick about being eyes and ears in the bar, and I'll call in the department heads and speak quietly to them about what they might see or hear. The housekeeping department could be very useful."

"Thanks for taking care of this, Bernie," said Rhonda contritely. "We're here to help in whatever way we can."

"Of course," said Bernie. "I'll keep you updated as much as I'm able."

As we left Bernie's office, Rhonda and I were unusually quiet. Walking through the lobby to our offices in the back of the hotel, I studied our guests. A lot of the women wore expensive jewelry—diamond earrings, small diamond pendants that weren't too flashy but were fine pieces. The Beach House Hotel attracted guests who were used to dressing up and wearing valuable jewelry. Rhonda, herself, was a prime example of a woman who loved her "sparkles."

"Let's head out to the beach," I said, needing to gain some perspective on what the hotel was being asked to do.

"Good idea," said Rhonda. "I'm worried, Annie."

"Me, too," I said, anxious to feel the sand on my feet and fresh air on my face.

On the shore, I stood and looked back at the hotel. It was much more than an upscale property. It represented all Rhonda and I had worked for—our freedom, our hopes and dreams, the ability to prove to others that we could pull off a successful business in the hospitality industry.

"The Beach House Hotel is really special," said Rhonda placing a hand on my shoulder. "Our baby."

I nodded, too emotional to speak. Hilda and Kurt's use of the hotel was everything I abhorred about greed at the expense of others. I prayed they'd soon be caught.

I glanced at a figure in the distance heading toward us and gasped. Brock Goodwin had no idea what was coming. Rhonda and I had planned to take advantage of his ego but having to confess to the FBI was something we'd never envisioned.

"Let's go. I don't want to speak to Brock," I said.

We headed inside, and continued as if we didn't hear him call our names.

Reviewing the wedding plans for the weekend, my worries grew. Stanley Horwath, the president of the state-wide hospitality association, was being married for the second time. His bride, Melanie Morgan, was a model from Miami, who ran an on-line jewelry business and loved wearing some of her jewelry in public. While her pieces weren't priceless, some sold for thousands of dollars.

"Even though it's a small, intimate one, Stanley and Melanie's wedding might be a problem for us," I said to Rhonda. "She's going to flaunt her jewelry line."

"That could be too tempting to resist to someone like Kurt Bauer," she responded. "Gawd! If anything happened to Melanie, think of the bad press that would create."

"But if we try to interfere, that will be a giveaway to Kurt and Hilda and will make Stanley suspicious that something improper is going on at our hotel."

"Okay, let's speak to Bernie about it."

"But we can't say anything to Lorraine or Lauren," I warned her. "That will have to come from him."

Rhonda called him, and on a conference line, we aired our concerns.

"Noted," Bernie said. "Thanks. I'll take care of everything."

After we ended the call, Rhonda sighed. "Guess we're not

going to be part of this intrigue."

"No, we're not," I said firmly. "We've already been shot at, pistol whipped, driven in near hurricane conditions, and took part in a kidnapping recovery. We've done enough."

"You're right. But I feel helpless just waiting to see what happens."

"Bernie's already hired extra security for the weekend. Only a handful of wedding guests are staying here, but we'll have to be watchful. As we've always said, weddings bring out the best and worst in people."

"How does the rest of the month look? Rhonda asked.

"Busy. A convenient way for Hilda to do her thing and for Kurt to peruse the crowd. Like you, I feel bad sitting and doing nothing while some of our guests could be victims. It's frustrating."

That evening when I drove into my driveway, I was surprised to see the lights in the house welcoming me. These dark evenings were sometimes depressing when Vaughn was away. Elena's cousin, Liana Sousa, who now worked for me, was as conscientious as Elena had always been.

Inside, the dogs rushed to greet me and then ran back to the lanai. I heard a deep voice coming from there and paused, wondering who Liana might be entertaining.

Before I could follow the dogs, Vaughn walked toward me with a big smile. "Surprise!"

I dropped my purse on the kitchen counter and ran to him.

Vaughn kissed me and hugged me tight. I nestled against him feeling protected, unleashing the unexpected sting of tears, and I realized I was more upset about what was going on at the hotel than I'd thought. The idea of the hotel's reputation being ruined was enough to set me on edge.

"What's going on?" Vaughn said, giving me a look of concern.

"It's the hotel and the idea of the FBI making arrests there, and worse yet, guests having things stolen from them. The head of the state's hospitality association is the groom in our next wedding." I filled him in on the situation with Hilda and Kurt.

"Hey, slow down. I'm sure it's something that Bernie and the staff can handle. You say the FBI will be there?"

Feeling sick to my stomach, I nodded. "At least one of our guests will be from there. No one will know who it is except Bernie."

"Shouldn't you and Rhonda know too?" Vaughn asked.

"No, it's safest that way, keeping us from slipping up and saying something."

"Well, then, if there's nothing else you can do about it, let's relax and enjoy being together while we can. There's talk of more filming."

"Oh? Are you happy about that?"

Vaughn nodded and smiled. "Very much so. Working for Nick Swain is the best."

"Nothing like a sleezy producer at the soap?" I teased.

He laughed. "Not at all."

"Mom!" Robbie came into the room. His headphones around his neck rested on his shoulders. "I didn't hear you come in."

"I'm sure you couldn't with your ears blocked like that." I gave him a kiss and hugged him.

"What's for dinner? Liana made cookies for me, but I'm hungry," said Robbie.

"What would you like?" I asked. I tended not to fuss when Vaughn was away and hadn't planned anything special.

"Can we make this a pizza night?" Robbie asked.

I looked at Vaughn.

"Fine with me," he said. "Anything at home is better than eating out. After being away, I can't wait for a simple meal."

"Yay!" said Robbie.

"But you have to eat some salad too," I said. "Let's make a list of what everyone wants, then you can order."

While I set the table, Vaughn opened a bottle of wine and handed me a glass. "We can talk after dinner."

"Okay, I've pretty much filled you in on hotel news."

"I was thinking about my schedule. Maybe we can get away for a couple of days."

"I'm listening," I said, loving the idea while I put together a salad. "When the pizza comes, I'll toss the salad with dressing."

Vaughn and I took our wine into the living room. During winter months, I loved being able to sit in front of a gas fire.

Settled on the couch beside me, Vaughn said, "Can you get away next week?"

"Yes, if we get the jewelry thief investigation resolved. Where did you have in mind?"

"Probably someplace in the Virgin Islands, maybe do some sailing. How would you feel if you and I and Nick and Tina went cruising there for a week?"

"Staying on the boat for the whole week? I'd be comfortable sharing that space with them. After going through the trauma of their kidnapped child, we've all become close."

"I like Tina and Nick is a great guy," said Vaughn. "I don't know if he could take the time off soon, but it's something I'd like to do with them someday."

"Okay, we'll do it. I think of Tina as a daughter. In the meantime, should we try to take a trip to South Beach for something fun to do. Or a cruise?"

"No, to the cruise. Yes, to South Beach," said Vaughn. "I'd

feel trapped on a cruise ship with a boatload of people I don't know and who may know who I am. Does that sound bad on my part?"

"Not at all." I'd been places with Vaughn where fans had been over enthusiastic. It was very uncomfortable.

Our pizza came and conversation at the dinner table turned to Robbie's swim practice and his latest meet.

Robbie spoke with pride when he told Vaughn that his coach, Troy, thought he had potential to get college scholarships someday. "And the best thing is that Grandma and Grandpa came to see me practice one day."

"I'm proud of all the hard work you're doing, and I really like that you invited them to come watch you," Vaughn told him. They smiled at one another.

And later, lying next to Vaughn after making love, I curled up and had the best sleep I'd had in a long time.

CHAPTER TWENTY-ONE

WITH VAUGHN BACK HOME, THE TENSION I'D FELT OVER the FBI investigation eased. As we'd discussed, there was very little Rhonda or I could do about the situation. We had to let the Feds do their work.

I was sitting with Rhonda, Lorraine, and Lauren in Lorraine's office discussing the weekend wedding when my cell rang. Seeing Stephanie's number, I picked up the call and moved away from the circle of chairs for privacy.

"Hello, Stephanie. What's up?" I asked.

"This may sound silly, irresponsible even, but I was wondering if I somehow left my diamond bracelet at your house. It's missing, and with all the confusion over Randolph's illness, I think I may have dropped it somewhere or missed packing it up to move to the hotel."

My pulse raced, and for a moment, I couldn't breathe. Was this the type of thing we had to look forward to? One awkward security issue after another with our treasured guests?

I forced myself to speak calmly. "I have a very reliable woman clean my house. I'm certain if she'd found anything like that, she'd tell me. But I'll check the drawers in the guest suite and let you know."

"Thanks. I don't want Randolph to know, so we'll keep it quiet, okay?"

"Fine by me. Thanks again for attending one of Robbie's practice swim sessions. He was proud to tell Vaughn about it."

"You know how we feel about that boy," said Stephanie, her voice softening with affection. "We're attending the next meet."

"Lovely," I said. "Let's go out to supper afterward."

"Perfect," said Stephanie. "Let me know as soon as possible about the bracelet."

"I promise," I said and hung up.

When I returned to the group, Rhonda said, "What's up?"

"Just an issue at home. I'll tell you about it later," I said. "So, any other special plans for this wedding?"

"We'll be using the private dining room for both a reception and dinner, which will make it easy to provide excellent service. Melanie has asked for permission to film the room both before and during the activities, and that's been approved. Nothing else to comment on," said Lorraine.

"Okay. I know I can trust you to do a superb job. We're lucky to have the two of you."

"Amen," said Rhonda. "How are you newlyweds doing? Angela told me that you and Arthur are getting settled in your new home together."

Lorraine beamed. "It's working out nicely. I never thought I'd be married again, but Arthur was irresistible."

Rhonda shot me a triumphant look. "I knew it would be that way."

I smiled and shook my head as Rhonda and Lorraine embraced.

We left them, and as soon as we got to the office, Rhonda turned to me and said, "Okay, spill. For a moment back there, you looked white as a ghost. What's going on?"

"The call was from Stephanie Willis. She's missing her diamond bracelet."

"Oh, my God! I hope this isn't the beginning of a disaster. Did you tell Bernie?"

"Not yet. Stephanie asked me to be quiet about it. She doesn't want Randolph to know. But I thought I'd go home and look around for it. Phina, hasn't mentioned finding one." Seraphina, a cousin of Consuela's, was my cleaning woman and was as trustworthy as she.

"Okay, I'll stay here. I'm working on some Valentine's Day publicity for the newspaper," said Rhonda.

On my way home, I phoned Bernie and told him about the call.

He said. "Don't discuss this with anyone else, please. Only Rhonda."

When I drove into my driveway, I noticed Vaughn's car was gone and was relieved. As Bernie had stressed, no one else needed to know anything about what had happened.

The dogs greeted me at the door with their usual enthusiasm, barking and wiggling happily in welcome.

I walked through the house to the guest suite. Inside each of the rooms in that wing of the house, I searched the corners, looked under the beds, and scoured any area I could think of. I opened the drawers of each chest or bureau, looking inside, but though I found a couple of hair ribbons from Bailey's last visit, I didn't find the bracelet.

Disappointed, I got in my car and drove back to the hotel. In time, the FBI might need to talk to Stephanie. But for the moment, as Bernie had explained, everything would be kept quiet.

The two days leading up to the wedding were quiet. Though there'd been one report of a male visitor to the Presidential Suite, there hadn't been any others. Rick had turned into a useful informant on that score.

Whenever I had the opportunity, I studied my guests wondering if they were associated with the FBI, but no one stood out.

Bernie called Rhonda and me into the office. "The FBI has requested one of you invite Hilda and Kurt to dinner. Annette and I will attend along with a cousin of hers. Are you willing to do this?"

"Is this like a sting operation?" Rhonda asked, her eyes glowing with excitement. "If so, I'm happy to have you all for dinner."

"We'll just make it seem as if it's an honor to have Hilda here at the hotel, and this dinner is a way to have special time with them," said Bernie. "We'd like to do this right after the wedding, if that's possible."

Rhonda and I glanced at each other.

"I can do that," said Rhonda. "Do you want me to plan my usual Italian dinner or make it a little simpler?"

"Do what you want as long as a lot of wine is served. After the date and time are confirmed with Hilda's and Kurt's acceptance, I'll have a list of instructions for you," said Bernie.

"Okay," said Rhonda. "How do you want me to invite Hilda and Kurt? Telephone call? What?"

"It's already been taken care of." Bernie placed a printed invitation on the desk. The invitation read:

> **"In honor of your presence at the hotel, we invite you to a special evening with the owners and the manager of the hotel for cocktails and dinner at the home of _____ on _____at _____six o'clock. RSVP: Bernhard Bruner, General Manager."**

"We'll fill in the correct information and reprint it."

"Who is this cousin of Annette's?" I asked.

"A very interesting relative who happens to work for the FBI. She and her husband arrived a couple of days ago and are wedding guests. No doubt you've seen them around."

I wracked my brain trying to recall who was new to The Beach House Hotel. "Are you talking about Annabelle and David Duggan?" I said, shocked. Annabelle was an attractive brunette in what I guessed was her forties, David a non-descript-looking man with light brown hair. They seemed very quiet, very pleasant, not people used to intrigue and perhaps violence.

"Only Annabelle will attend the dinner," said Bernie. "David will be busy here."

"If they've been seen as a couple, what explanation will you give for David being absent?" I asked.

Bernie said, "Shall we leave that up to them?

"Of course."

Rhonda elbowed me. "It's all part of the sting we're planning."

"Okay," said Bernie. "Clear this date and time with your spouses and get back to me immediately. I'll take care of delivering the invitation."

After we left Bernie's office, Rhonda went to call Will. Instead of phoning Vaughn, I decided to go home to talk to him about the dinner. After having him away for a while, it felt wonderful to know I could see him in the middle of the day.

It might seem silly to others, but my pulse picked up at the sight of his car parked outside the garage. I always anticipated being with him, knowing he'd be happy to see me.

As usual, the dogs met me at the door, and Vaughn soon followed.

"Hi. What are you doing home?" he asked, grinning.

"Rather than call you, I decided to talk to you in person about the latest developments at the hotel."

"Mmm. Okay," he murmured wrapping his arms around me and drawing me close. "How does a "nooner" sound?"

I laughed. "I don't have time today but maybe another day."

"Oh, then I might not tell you about what I found," said Vaughn.

"What are you talking about?" I asked, seeing his teasing grin.

"Follow me," he said. "I left it in place."

I followed him into Robbie's room and over to Cindy's cage.

"What?" I asked.

"Look closely. It seems diamonds really are a girl's best friend even if you're a dog."

I peeked into the cage. Cindy's soft blanket was scrunched up in the middle of the cage floor, but a glimmer of something sparkly in the corner caught my attention.

"You're kidding me!" I cried, reaching inside the cage and pulling out a diamond bracelet. "How did Stephanie's bracelet get there?"

Chuckling, Vaughn shook his head. "Who knows? It must have caught her attention. She placed it right next to one of her favorite toys."

"I'll call Stephanie and meet her at the hotel to return it," I said, relieved and then wondered why other people hadn't reported stolen jewelry.

"Come sit for a minute and tell me why you're here," said Vaughn, leading me into the kitchen. He fixed some coffee for both of us and sat at the kitchen table near me.

"I need to make sure you can attend a dinner at Rhonda's house in a few days. Will you be in town?"

"Yes, I'll be here until sometime after Valentine's Day.

What's going on?"

I filled Vaugh in on the purpose of the dinner, who else would be attending, and the fact that the dinner was going to be some sort of sting operation.

"There's no chance of danger to either you or Rhonda, is there? After what the two of you have gone through in the past, I want to be sure."

"I trust Bernie to be honest about something like that. He would tell us if there was any real danger. Once everybody has agreed to come to the dinner, Rhonda will be given instructions."

"Okay, of course, I'll be there with you. I'm anxious to meet this *femme fatale* and her dishonorable crony."

"We'll see what happens. But I'm relieved you'll be with me. It's got to be a bigger situation if the FBI is going to all this trouble."

"No doubt about it," said Vaughn. "Are you sure you can't stay?"

"I wish I could, but I'm leaving the hotel early this afternoon so I can go with you to Robbie's swim meet."

"Right," said Vaughn. He hugged me and gazed down at me with the dark, sexy eyes his followers loved. "I'll meet you there. I have an appointment with the local theater group before then."

"Okay. See you then." I wrapped the treasured bracelet with soft tissues, tucked it into my purse, and headed back to the hotel.

Once there, I called Stephanie and asked her to join me in the lobby.

"Did you find it?" asked Stephanie, hurrying toward me.

I waited until she got closer and then held out the bracelet in my hand.

Stephanie clapped a hand to her chest. "Thank God!

Randolph would be upset to think I was careless with it. He gave me this bracelet to celebrate our fortieth wedding anniversary and was very proud to do so."

Stephanie hooked it around her wrist and beamed at me. "Where did you find it?"

"Vaughn found it in Cindy's dog cage. As he said, 'diamonds are even a dog's best friend.' Cindy had carefully placed it beside her favorite toy."

Stephanie laughed. "I'm relieved she was careful with it and very glad I didn't report it to the hotel. I would've felt foolish now that you've discovered it at your house."

"Thankfully, it's yours again. I'll see you later this afternoon at Robbie's swim meet, but I wanted you to have this back without Randolph knowing."

Stephanie leaned forward and kissed me on the cheek. "You're such a dear. Thank you."

I went to my office pleased I'd been able to assist Stephanie, but I couldn't help wondering if other female guests weren't telling the hotel about missing jewelry for fear of finding it later.

CHAPTER TWENTY-TWO

THAT AFTERNOON I SAT WITH VAUGHN, STEPHANIE, AND Randolph on the bleachers beside the pool area. The seats were uncomfortable. Observing Stephanie and Randolph shifting in their seats, I realized how pleased they must be to have been asked to come. On more than one occasion, they'd participated in a family event as Robbie's Grandma and Grandpa, and it was pleasing to see a warm relationship developing between them.

Robbie was aware of us and gave a little wave whenever he could.

He and Brett were both friends and competitors, urging each other to do the best they could. Seeing how both their bodies were growing, I could well remember the two of them as toddlers playing together.

A row below us, Brett's mother, Cindy, was taking photos of the two of them.

Stephanie turned to me. "Ann, I should've mentioned this to you before, but Madelyn Austin, a guest at the hotel, mentioned that she couldn't find her diamond earrings. I told her to simply wait. That, like me, they were probably misplaced, and she'll find them somewhere in the room on her own. Housekeeping hasn't found them."

"You're right. No doubt, they'll reappear later. Things have a habit of doing that. Once, right after the hotel first opened, two sisters from Miami were visiting and one misplaced some earrings. She'd already accused a maid of stealing them and then had to apologize when she found them among her things later. But I'll have a chat with Madelyn." Though I gave Stephanie a confident smile, my stomach filled with acid. Madelyn was a long-time guest, and I didn't want to destroy that relationship.

My attention was diverted by a relay race Robbie and Brett were in, and I rose on my feet to cheer their team on.

Stanley Horwath and Melanie Morgan had chosen to have a small wedding, but because Melanie was an online influencer, she saw to every detail large and small. And with Stanley being president of the state's hospitality association and knowing how hotels should be run, this wedding was extremely important to us. Even Lorraine, used to high-level weddings was anxious about this one.

Considering the care with which we wanted the wedding between Stanley and Morgan to be carried out, Rhonda and I would be present for the ceremony and the following reception and dinner.

Rhonda and I had regular outfits we wore to such occasions, dressing as if we were guests. And though I didn't always like the time allotted to seeing that some weddings were carried off beautifully, I was always intrigued by the differences in them.

On this January afternoon, outside winds tousled the fronds of palm trees as the gray skies began to unburden themselves of the rain stored in clouds that had threatened all day.

Inside, the library was bedecked with bright tropical flowers. White silken fabric formed an aisle between the rows of chairs on either side of it. Candles both real and battery-operated lined the aisle and filled nooks and crannies of the room. Other candles mounted on a white trellis-like construction against the back wall served as a flickering background to the small white table atop the dais at the back of the room. A basket of flowers sat between two thick candles on the table and the tropical color theme was carried out in the small bouquets that were attached to the white cloth-covered chairs that lined the aisle. The effect was lovely, almost ethereal, saved from being boring by the lovely pinks, reds, and oranges of the flowers.

In place of a minister, the couple had chosen a close friend to officiate at the wedding. Melanie's best friend was serving as matron of honor, while Stanley's grown son was serving as best man.

The intimacy of the room was inviting as Rhonda and I stood behind the rows of chairs watching people enter and then stop and gaze around the room with admiration. I straightened when I saw Annabelle and David Dugan enter the room and then take seats toward the back.

Rhonda and I exchanged glances. Who knew what they hoped to accomplish?

I noticed Annabelle wearing a gorgeous gold bead and diamond necklace. On her wrist she wore a gold and diamond bracelet. I wondered if they were supposed to be tempting pieces to someone like Kurt Bauer.

At the front of the room, Stanley stood with his son, Mark, waiting for the matron of honor and the bride to appear. We already knew that Melanie would walk herself down the aisle. Her father had recently died, and she couldn't bear the thought of anyone else taking on that duty. Her mother was too ill to attend the wedding.

After all the guests had arrived, the soft harp music that had been playing changed to classic love songs and my eyes smarted with tears when I realized the new song was "I Will Always Love You", a Whitney Houston/Dolly Parton favorite and a special song of Vaughn's and mine.

Wearing a bright green dress, Suzanne Hopkins, the matron of honor, made her way down the aisle. Obviously pregnant, her face glowed with health and happiness. Her blond hair hung at her shoulders in a simple bob and her eyes almost matched the color of the gown. Even though her husband was forced to stay at home with their two toddlers, she seemed ecstatic to be part of this celebration.

And then Melanie appeared. Wearing a white dress with long sleeves and a bodice cut low in the front, she looked stunning. The dress clung to her body without being overly tight and showed off her fit figure beautifully. Her dark hair fell just beyond her shoulders in soft curls and was held back from her striking face by diamond encrusted clips she'd designed herself. Her understated necklace contained a large diamond whose weight rested on her chest above the V of the neckline. Diamond and blue sapphire earrings matched her engagement ring.

As expected, she'd created a tasteful, beautiful image for her online business, showcasing some of her fine jewelry designs.

I turned to look at Stanley and was touched to see his eyes swimming with tears. He'd lost a wife to cancer but was excited to have a fresh start with Melanie. I glanced at Rhonda. She was as moved as I.

As I listened to them exchange vows, I thought of the wonder of love. It could fill someone's life with joy. And though it didn't happen to everyone, that joy was something most of us wished for, however it took shape.

I gazed around the room. People had come dressed up for this wedding, and I realized a lot of the women in the room were wearing jewelry designed by Melanie. The thought of having all of those pieces stolen made my heart clench. Would

Hilda and Kurt be that daring?

After the ceremony ended, Stanley and Melanie were taken to the small dining room where they could greet people attending the reception and dinner. Melanie had hired a photographer and he'd already taken photographs of the room, which was as stunning as the library. Starched white linen tablecloths covered the tables, along with sparkling crystal, gleaming silverware, and flickering candles. They were offset by the colorful flowers that matched those in the library with various shades of reds, pinks and a touch of orange. At one end of the room sat a bar. Waiters lined the walls of the room waiting to serve the wedding guests.

Lorraine and Lauren appeared and helped guests through the receiving line into the room, careful to see that the procedure wasn't delayed by people taking too much time.

Once everyone was in the room, cocktails and hors d'oeuvres were served while people found their way to their seats and then moved around as they wished.

With things going well, Rhonda and I left the dining room and headed to our office. As we were crossing the lobby, we heard our names being called and turned to find Brock waving to us.

"What does he want?" grumbled Rhonda under her breath.

"Hey, there. What's the best way to handle a lost credit card?" Brock asked. "I tried calling your hotel security about it, but they said they had no record of a credit card being found. I'm pretty sure I left it at the bar."

"We're very careful with found credit cards. It doesn't happen often, but sometimes guests forget to pick them up after paying. Whenever it does happen, we're very cautious about security, keeping the cards locked up at the front desk."

"Check with them there," said Rhonda. "Unless you were

using the card in another part of the hotel?" Her question hung in the air.

"Oh, yeah. Maybe that's the problem. Thanks. I'll check it out on my own," said Brock. "Besides, I've got other credit cards."

He walked away, and Rhonda turned to me. "Bets on this loss happening while he was in the Presidential Suite?"

I waved away her comment. "I don't even want to think about that. I'm worried all the women wearing Melanie's designs for the wedding might be targeted. Let's find out where Kurt and Hilda are. Hilda usually likes our cocktail hour."

We walked into the lobby where several of our guests were enjoying appetizers and free wine for a limited time. A bar was set up for those that wanted something more than wine. Though the evening reception didn't last long, it was worth the effort of work and money to run it. Guests loved the idea.

In the lobby, Hilda was surrounded by three men vying for her attention. I understood their attraction to her. The idea of her being royalty was almost as appealing as the sexy, low-cut dress she wore or the way she flirted with them. This was a woman who knew how to make men respond to her.

Off to the side, Kurt was talking to other gentlemen while women stood or sat together on the couches conversing with Lauren, who was acting as hostess.

"I'm about ready to go home," said Rhonda. "Everything seems fine here."

"Me, too. Vaughn is cooking, and I can't wait to have a glass of wine and enjoy some of his chicken piccata. During his time off, he's become a great cook."

"That will never happen with Will. He says I've spoiled him with my cooking." Rhonda grinned. "I make him help me with the dishes though."

As we left the lobby, Brock came over to us. "Look, I don't know what's happened, but my credit cards aren't working here at the hotel. Have you two closed down my account?"

"No, we wouldn't do that," I said. "Have you checked with your bank?"

"Not yet. I thought I'd come to the source first," said Brock. "I wouldn't put it past the two of you to make trouble for me."

"Like you do for us any chance you get?" sneered Rhonda.

I held up my hand to stop any argument. "Brock, I don't think you should hesitate to call the bank. What if someone has stolen your credit card?"

His face turned white. "I'd better check. That could be a disaster."

As he hurried off, Rhonda turned to me. "Doesn't Brock realize he's the one who makes trouble for us?"

"In this case, he might be right. Maybe using him for information for what's going on in the Presidential Suite is going to cost him a lot."

"Serves him right," said Rhonda, but I could see she was troubled.

CHAPTER TWENTY-THREE

WITH THE WEDDING BEHIND US AND NO REPORTS OF stolen jewelry, I was relieved when the last of the wedding guests departed. But I was a little confused. That wedding was the perfect opportunity for jewel thieves to do their thing.

Rhonda and I spoke to Bernie about it.

"We'd have known if anything went on here," he said. "We've had several new cameras installed in the hallways, and we actually had one installed in Melanie and Stanley's room, with their permission, explaining we wanted to provide them with extra security for Melanie's jewelry."

"Then what's all the fuss about if nothing is happening here with jewelry being stolen?" Rhonda asked.

"We do have a pair of diamond earrings missing," Bernie reminded us. "But this is much larger than a few punks stealing jewelry from hotel guests."

"What do you mean?" asked Rhonda.

"While hotels are concerned about guests and their belongings remaining safe, identity and confidential information is a matter of greater concern."

"Oh my God! Brock's identity may be stolen," said Rhonda.

"He asked us if the hotel had his credit card, then he asked us if the hotel was programmed not to accept his credit cards," I said. "I told him to get in touch with his bank right away."

"Another reason for the FBI to talk to him. But I'll want the two of you present when that happens."

Rhonda shot me a look that told me she was looking forward to that scene. Though I chuckled, I didn't want Brock to blame us for what was happening to him. No one but he had made the decision to visit the alluring woman in the Presidential Suite. His ego was the problem. Not us.

"What else?" said Rhonda.

"We suspect this theft ring is larger than originally thought. While male visitors are ... busy, shall we say? ...Kurt gathers information about them. Home address. Bank. Credit card numbers and the like. This information is sent to others who break into their houses knowing the owners are not at home. Others go to work emptying savings accounts, and the like." Bernie shook his head. "It's a pretty ugly business."

"I hate to think of them operating here," I said, and a wave of horror went through me. A lot of our guests had become friends over the years. The idea of thieves using their stay at The Beach House Hotel as an opportunity to steal was sickening.

"What can we do about it?" asked Rhonda.

"Having the dinner at your house tonight will be helpful, I'm told," said Bernie. "There's going to be a bit of subterfuge involved. Annabelle will explain to you." He looked up as a knock sounded at the door. "I believe she's here now."

He stood, answered the door, and then invited her inside.

"Good morning," Annabelle said cheerfully. "I trust the two of you are ready to help us this evening."

Rhonda clasped her hands together. "Oh, yes. I told Will all about being part of a sting."

Annabelle held up a warning finger. "I don't want you to think of this as anything more than inviting hotel guests to dinner. Thinking beyond that can make mistakes and create failures for us."

Rhonda and I exchanged solemn looks.

"Bernie is going to let it slip that you, Rhonda, won millions of dollars in the Florida Lottery. And we've had fake credit cards made for you. You need to empty your purse of anything valuable, insert the fake cards in your wallet and leave your purse vulnerable and in a spot where guests could easily swipe a card or two."

"I keep my purse on a chair in the hallway off the kitchen and by the guest bathroom," said Rhonda. "That should work, don't you think?"

"Perfect," said Annabelle. "Now, let's talk about me. I'm Annette's cousin through our mothers, who are not close, but Annette and I have always kept in touch. Our mother's maiden name is Conklin. Other than that, we have no connection. Recently, I got a call from Annette and we decided to stay for extra days after attending the wedding for Stanley and Melanie." She smiled at Rhonda. "After hearing about the connection and wanting to do something nice for Hilda, you invited us all for dinner."

"This all seems sensible to me," said Ann. "Is there anything else we're supposed to know?"

Annabelle shook her head. "The less you know the better. Then everything will seem more natural. Once the dinner is over, we'll want the two of you to be present when we talk to Brock Goodwin. I understand from a local bank manager, he's trying to put the blame on the hotel being lax in security for his identity being stolen for."

"That rat bastard," said Rhonda. "I knew he'd try something like that."

"We're going to start the investigation on a different note," said Annabelle. "But that can wait until later. Tonight, we have to see what we can do to get more information about all those involved."

"You may go," said Bernie. "But make sure to keep anyone from peering in when you open the door and leave. We don't want anyone to see Annabelle here in my office."

Rhonda and I left and automatically headed outside to the beach. I knew she was upset because she didn't say a word until we were both standing on the beach facing the Gulf waters.

"That Brock Goodwin. I could wring his fucking neck! He's always making trouble for us," said Rhonda.

"I think we'd better call the bank to see what information they'll share with us about what's happening. We can't afford to let anyone think the hotel is not secure for our guests," I said. It was amazing how fast rumors could destroy a business.

Rhonda let out a long sigh. "You're right. We've come too far to allow The Beach House Hotel's reputation to be ruined. Having VIPs here, protecting them and their interest is what makes our hotel a success."

I looked down at my toes covered with the foamy edges of the waves pulling back, then preparing to race to shore again. I drew a deep breath of tangy air, closed my eyes, and allowed my senses to fill with the smells and sounds around me. The raucous cries of seagulls and terns circling in the air above us sounded like sweet music with their familiarity. The lapping of the water meeting the sand with a moist kiss slowed my pulse and helped me gain perspective. We wouldn't, couldn't let a single man and his constant obsessing about our success in business destroy what we'd built.

I opened my eyes and smiled at Rhonda. "Feel better?"

She shrugged. "Not until we nail that bastard."

I laughed. "From the sound of things, I think Annabelle is pretty capable of that."

"We'll see," said Rhonda.

Together, we walked back to the hotel with every intention of keeping it safe.

That afternoon, I was sitting at my desk when the phone rang. "Hello? Ann Sanders here."

"Hi, Ann. Terri Thomas. I heard a rumor and thought I should come to the source."

Every nerve ending inside me quivered. "What rumor?"

"Something about hotel security being an issue," she said.

"Was your source someone named Brock Goodwin? Because if it is, you know that isn't true."

"Well, I never reveal my sources, but I'll listen to what you have to say," said Terri.

"And I never talk about guests," I retorted. "But I will say a certain someone was careless with his credit card and when it wasn't turned in, he's blamed the hotel when, in fact, we have a very secure system of keeping credit cards that patrons may lose in the bar or restaurants."

"So, it's just another of his gripes?" Terri asked, clarifying for both of us who we were talking about.

"Yes, the only problem is his. I'm not surprised he tried to make trouble for us. By now, you recognize that, I hope."

"Oh, yes," said Terri. "But I always follow a lead. By the way, I understand your royal visitor is a beautiful woman. I'd love to do an article for the Sabal *Daily News* covering her visit."

"You're welcome to leave a note at the front desk requesting an interview, but I have no idea how she may or may not respond."

"Thanks, Ann. That's what I'll do. And thanks for your honesty."

I ended the call and held in a scream of frustration. Thank goodness Rhonda had left the hotel to get ready for her dinner party. Brock's neck was already in trouble.

###

That night, Vaughn and I approached Rhonda's front door with every intention to relax and let the evening roll out as intended. But I couldn't stop a wave of anxiety from flowing through me. As Rhonda said, this was a sting operation.

Will greeted us at the door. "The others haven't arrived yet. Can I get you something to drink? We're serving cocktails in the living room."

Vaughn asked for bourbon, and I wanted a glass of red wine before walking into the spotless living room. With two young children in the house, I knew how hard they'd worked to make everything nice and orderly. Best of all, a lovely aroma of tomato and garlic wafted in the air.

Rhonda appeared wearing a lacy apron over her caftan. "Hi, there. I thought I'd keep things simple and offer lasagna and my usual antipasto and ..."

"Your tiramisu?" Vaughn said giving her a hopeful look.

Rhonda laughed. "I knew you'd want that. I made it just for you." She laughed when Vaughn gave her a kiss on each cheek.

"I'm going to check things out," I said, going to the guest bathroom off the back hallway. Sure enough, Rhonda's purse was there, along with her flip flops, looking as if she'd casually tossed the purse on the chair and slid the sandals off her feet. The purse was open enough to be an inviting target for a thief.

The sound of someone at the front door made me hurry back to the living room.

Bernie, Annette, and Annabelle followed Hilda and Kurt inside.

"How nice to greet you all together," said Will. Shaking hands with Bernie and listening as Bernie introduced Annabelle and Hilda and Kurt. "It's an honor to have royalty here."

Rhonda came into the living room, the apron missing, as

she approached Hilda and Kurt. Her jewelry sparkled at her ears, neck, and wrists. It was the one indulgence Rhonda allowed herself after winning the lottery.

As she exchanged greetings with Hilda, I noticed Hilda eying the jewelry, but Kurt seemed not to notice. He was busy gazing around and I had the eerie feeling he was casing the place.

After introductions were made and greetings exchanged, we all sat in the living room with our drinks.

"So, Annette, how are you related to Annabelle?" I asked, as if I didn't know.

Annabelle turned to Annette. "As young girls we used to play together at our grandmother's house. Our mothers were sisters but, sadly, were not that close. And then when Annette heard I'd be in town for a wedding, she urged us to stay longer to get reacquainted."

Annette smiled at her. "Our time together has been such a gift."

"I grew up an only child with no close relatives," I said. "I envy you that connection."

"How about you, Rhonda?" Annabelle asked. "Brothers or sisters?"

"One brother. He's the best. He took over the family butcher shop in New Jersey. I don't get to see him too often."

"And you?" Annabelle asked Hilda.

Hilda looked startled and said, "I have two sisters, but we're not close at all. I think they may be jealous of me."

Annette gave her a sympathetic look. "Yes, that can happen."

"For tonight, I've chosen to serve some family recipes," said Rhonda. "Coming from an Italian family, food was always important at any gatherings, and my mother was a fabulous cook. Hilda, I know you must be used to fancy meals, but I thought you'd enjoy this."

"Oh, I will," said Hilda politely.

"I understand you like high tea," said Vaughn. "When I'm in London, I like having that bit of refreshment in the afternoon."

"How is that going at the hotel?" Bernie asked Hilda. "I haven't heard of any complaints. In fact, I hardly know you're at the hotel except for the friends who come to visit."

Hilda glanced at Kurt and back to Bernie. "I'm enjoying having high tea in my suite. It was something we did every afternoon at home. An important part of every day. Your pastry chef does a marvelous job."

"She's very talented," I said. "Remember, you can order room service any time you want. One of the special privileges of being in the Presidential Suite."

"Yes, it's lovely and convenient." She smiled at Vaughn in a sexy way that caught my attention. "I couldn't wait to meet you. I've seen you in a recent movie—*Something Like Love*. You were fantastic."

"Thanks," said Vaughn. "It was a fun one to make."

Hilda turned to me. "Isn't it hard to be married to a famous actor? I can't be the only woman who's in love with your husband."

My breath caught. "Vaughn and I are very happy together."

"For sure," said Vaughn giving me a look of affection I knew well. "Ann is one of the best things to happen to me."

"Would you be interested in meeting for lunch one day?" asked Hilda in a throaty, German-accented voice. "I think I could help you by offering you tips for filming locations in Europe."

Vaughn, gracious as ever, shook his head. "That isn't my job, but thanks for the offer." He turned to Kurt. "What do you do in Germany?"

"I'm a computer programmer," said Kurt with a note of pride.

I quickly glanced at Annabelle, but she was talking quietly to Annette about family. I was thinking that Kurt might be more involved with identity theft than I'd thought.

As promised, Will and Rhonda kept cocktails and wine flowing. By the time we sat down to dinner, it was a congenial group, albeit a little loud. Rita, Rhonda's housekeeper, served the antipasto and we all dug into the offerings of olives, anchovies, assorted cheeses, marinated peppers, prosciutto, salami, pepperoni, grapes, bread sticks and crackers.

"Save room for Rhonda's lasagna," said Vaughn, helping himself to a fine array of items from the antipasto platter.

"I've been to Italy, of course," said Hilda, "but I've never seen anything quite like this."

"This is great," Kurt chimed in, more relaxed.

After we'd eaten, I excused myself from the dinner table to use the rest room.

"I'll follow you," said Kurt.

Feeling as if I was leading him to temptation, I headed down the hallway and then slipped inside the powder room. I'd give him enough time to take what he wanted or to film it with his phone, which I'd noticed he'd picked up.

I opened the door to leave and was surprised when Kurt blocked my way.

"It's yours. I'm through," I said.

"Look. I want to know what's going on," Kurt said.

I frowned, genuinely puzzled. "What do you mean?"

"I don't know. It sort of feels like a set-up," Kurt said, his voice soft and low but with a threat in it I couldn't ignore.

My pulse pounded. "I don't understand."

Annabelle entered the hallway. "Is this where the line starts?"

"Yes, I'm leaving," I said.

"Me, too," said Kurt.

"Great, thanks." Annabelle hurried by me, and I eased my way past Kurt, grateful for the interruption, relieved to have been spared from giving away any part of our plans.

Later as we ate dessert and sipped coffee, the soft buzz of conversation was relaxed. Even Kurt seemed mollified by the excellent food, many servings of wine, and lack of troubling conversation.

The limo that had delivered Bernie, Annette, and Annabelle, along with the royal couple, arrived with perfect timing, and we all said goodnight to Will and Rhonda, thanking them for a delightful evening.

As Vaughn and I drove home, my cell rang. *Rhonda.*

"Well? How do you think it went?" Rhonda asked.

"Very well. If Kurt wanted to get into your purse, I gave him plenty of time to do so. But I think it seemed so easy, it frightened him."

"Not that much," said Rhonda. "One of my credit cards is gone."

CHAPTER TWENTY-FOUR

VAUGHN AND I LAY IN BED REHASHING THE DINNER AND the guests. "Hilda is a very sexually aggressive woman," said Vaughn. "Sitting next to me, she tried more than once to place a hand on my thigh."

"Is that why you got up and stretched after dinner, before dessert was served?" I asked.

"Yes," said Vaughn.

I snuggled against Vaughn. "I appreciate how you handle people like Hilda."

"Because I let them know you're more than enough for me?" said Vaughn, cupping my cheeks in his broad hands. "You know you're all I want in a woman, a wife, a mother." Hie eyes twinkled with humor. "I meant to add grandmother too."

"You were doing fine up until that point," I teased. We both knew I loved being a grandmother to the Ts, Bailey, and Bo. And when Nell's little boy arrived, we'd all love him too.

The next morning, Rhonda and I were working in the office when I got a call from David.

"Thanks for everything last night. We've already got a trace on the credit card that was stolen from Rhonda's purse. Now, we're ready to interview Brock Goodwin to confirm how things went down for him. With Bernie's advice, I'll call him and tell him I'm from security at the hotel and we want to talk to him, be of help to him, as he's president of the neighborhood association."

"Perfect. The sooner the better," I said. "He's already saying bad things about the hotel, blaming us for the identity theft."

"We'll take care of that," said David in a pleasant but firm voice, and I realized how much I'd come to rely upon his professional confidence.

"Can we meet in your office?" David asked. "If so, I'll send a technician there to install a microphone and camera."

"Okay. We'll stay right here." I hung up the phone and turned to Rhonda with the news.

She rubbed her hands together. "I can't wait for this. Brock is going to be furious."

"If it stops his bad-mouthing the hotel, I don't care," I said.

A few minutes later, a young man arrived with equipment and quickly installed the camera and recorder. "We'll want the gentleman to sit in the chair against the wall," he said. "Our man will sit opposite him and the two of you will be at your desks. All right?"

"Yes," Rhonda and I said together.

About twenty minutes later, Rhonda received a phone call from David and put the call on speaker phone. "We'll be there in a few minutes. He's more than anxious to blame you for his mess."

"Okay, we're ready," said Rhonda.

We were working at our desks when a knock sounded at the door. I got up to answer it.

"Hello, David, Brock. You're here to discuss the break-down of security here at the hotel?"

A smug expression crossed Brock's face. "Yes, we are."

I stood back and allowed them to enter the room.

David led Brock over to the designated seat. "I wanted to

meet you here to have a clear understanding about what was going on with your security issues."

"It's more than that. Ann and Rhonda don't like me. We've never gotten along. I believe I left my card at the bar, and someone took it," said Brock. "Maybe even one of their employees. Now, someone has charged several items to the credit card and even got into my savings account. Ann and Rhonda need to train their staff to be careful about cards accidentally left behind. I've never had this problem before."

Burning inside, I responded. "We've already told you that we take situations like this seriously. Any card left behind is immediately locked up and no one can retrieve it without proper notification."

"Let's talk about this. You think you left it in the bar?" said David.

"Yes," said Brock firmly.

"Is there any other place in the hotel besides the dining room where you might've used the credit card?

Brock frowned and then his cheeks grew pink. "I'm not sure what you mean."

"Well, as someone hired to ensure proper security at the hotel, I'm aware that you visited a certain lady at the Presidential Suite and paid for services with a credit card."

Brock straightened in his chair. "Are you accusing me of needing a prostitute?"

David studied him. "As a matter of fact, I am. Illegal as it may be, we know this situation exists and is about to be taken down. You might want to know that I'm from the FBI and we're obviously on the case."

"FBI?" Brock gasped, looking from David to us. "You knew about this?"

Rhonda and I remained silent.

"Oh my God! This can never get out. I might lose my

position as president of the neighborhood association. We can't let that happen!"

"It wouldn't bother us a bit, if it did," said Rhonda quietly.

"In exchange for the three of us keeping this situation quiet, we expect you to stop accusing the hotel of poor security. Understood?" David asked.

Brock bobbed his head so fast it was laughable.

"And now, I need you to tell us exactly how you ended up in the Presidential Suite. We'll start with you in the bar."

Brock glanced at Valentine'sus and turned to speak to David. "Do I have to talk about this in front of them?"

David nodded. "As they're the owners of the hotel, yes. Now, let's begin."

It was very interesting listening to Brock as he told how he'd been approached by Kurt, given a story about Hilda being royalty, how she was feeling lonely in the Presidential Suite, and needed to talk to someone important in the community.

Brock smiled at David. "As I'm president of the neighborhood association, I felt I could certainly be of service." In a way, it was pathetic that Brock's ego naturally led him to believe he could help her.

"And when you got there?" David asked.

Brock cleared his throat. "Hilda is attractive. A royal. She was very glad to see me. It's nothing new. I'm used to having women interested in me. When she came on to me, naturally I thought I'd be helping her out from feeling so lonely."

"So, you're a good lover?" asked David, and I swear he was enjoying every minute of this.

"I'd like to think so," Brock said. "I get asked to a lot of dinner parties."

I bit my lips to keep from letting out a snort.

Rhonda looked at me and rolled her eyes.

I'd share a hearty laugh with her later. Until then we had to remain serious. But really? Was Brock that dense?

"Am I right that you used a credit card to help Ms. Hassel … enjoy your company?" David asked Brock.

Brock gave him a sheepish look and nodded. "Once I realized money was involved, I had no choice but to pay." I realized how much it must have hurt his fragile ego to be forced to pay.

"Was there anyone else in the suite?" David asked.

"No, I don't think so," said Brock. "After we, uh, finished, Kurt showed up. But I left soon afterward."

David stood. "I think I have the information we need. Do we all agree that as long as Brock refrains from issuing any negative comments about security at the hotel, this information will go no further?"

Rhonda and I nodded.

David continued, "If you, Brock, should break your promise, the hotel has the right to respond in any way they see fit."

"As long as Brock sticks to his word, we won't say anything about this meeting," said Rhonda. "But if he doesn't, all agreements are off."

David shook hands with Brock. "The FBI may call upon you at another time, but for now, you're free to go."

Brock gave each of us a look of disgust and left.

As soon as the door closed behind him, I couldn't hold back the laughter I'd kept inside. David and Rhonda joined in.

Rhonda wiped tears of laughter from her face. "The only reason Brock is invited to dinner parties is because the ratio of men to women in this neighborhood is way off."

David cleared his throat, stopping another laugh. "I think it's fair to say that this has been a productive meeting. We can use Brock as a witness, if needed. But this theft ring goes far beyond prostitution. Still, after hearing about Brock and knowing what a pompous ass he is, I've enjoyed being part of this interview."

"Not as much as we have," I said. Thinking of Brock's shock and embarrassment at having to confess to being part of the story in the Presidential Suite, paying for the services Hilda provided, my lips curved. Even though I knew it wouldn't last, it felt great to have one up on Brock.

Our good humor ended when Rhonda received a telephone call from her bank telling her that her fake savings account had been wiped out. Even though the money wasn't hers, she still felt violated.

"I wonder what else they're doing?" said Rhonda. "All of my investments are secure, my real bank accounts too. But this proves to me how important it is to have tight security over financial information. The fact that the FBI is giving Kurt and Hilda room to act isn't much comfort."

Stephanie Willis came into the office.

"Hi. What's up?" I asked, concerned by her grim expression.

Her eyes filled. "I just got word from the chief of police in our small town. Our house has been broken into. The thieves took what jewelry they wanted from the safe, but worse, they took some confidential financial information. And then we got a call from our bank. The robbers tried to get into our bank accounts. Our town is small enough that the bank knows to call us about any unusual activity."

Stephanie covered her face with her hands. When she lifted her head, tears that had filled her eyes overflowed. "They must have known we were away. But then, we come here every year, so that wouldn't be hard to figure out. But something like this has never happened before."

I hugged her and said, "Come with Rhonda and me. We know someone who might be able to help you."

CHAPTER TWENTY-FIVE

SITTING IN BERNIE'S OFFICE WITH DAVID AND Annabelle, Stephanie tearfully told them of the situation she and Randolph faced.

"I don't know how we'll recover. We've lost our credit rating and had some of our savings taken away. And though I haven't seen it, I understand the house has been trashed."

"This is going to seem like an odd question, but I understand you were talking to Hilda Hassel about your love of the hotel and the fact that you stay for most of the season," said Annabelle. "Is that true?"

Stephanie blinked with surprise. "I only spoke to her at one cocktail party, but I did express my love of The Beach House Hotel." She looked at me. "I have a special reason to do so, as my husband and I have become particularly close to Ann and her family, and I hoped Hilda would spread the word among her royal friends."

I took hold of Stephanie's hand. "That's thoughtful of you."

"We believe the financial troubles you're facing might be part of a bigger operation," said David. "Annabelle and I are both with the FBI. We'd like your permission to go to Connecticut, inspect the house, and talk to both your financial advisor and the bank you use. Is that something you and your husband would be amenable to our doing?"

Stephanie looked to me.

"They believe it's part of a large theft ring," I said to her. "I would feel much more comfortable having you and Randolph stay with us while you're going through this difficult time.

With Randolph's recent health problems, he might worry less there."

"Oh, my! This is a lot to take in. But I trust you, Ann. If you think we should go ahead with letting the FBI take this on, and if you really want us to stay with you, I say yes." She closed her eyes, but tears beneath her eyelids escaped onto her cheeks.

I squeezed her hand.

"Let me get Randolph for you and ask him to join you here," said Rhonda, fighting tears of her own."

"Thank you," said Stephanie.

After getting Randolph comfortable with David and Annabelle, Rhonda and I went to our office.

Rhonda put an arm around me. "I know how upset you are by Stephanie and Randolph's troubles. I am, too. But the FBI will help them, and maybe by doing so, they'll break up the ring of these rat bastard thieves." She shook her head. "I was excited by the idea of a sting. But now, it feels creepy."

"Your accounts are as safe as any could be right now, but I know how you feel. The thieves were inside your home."

"Running a hotel can bring lots of surprises. You never know what guests will appear and what their stories are," said Rhonda. "But sometimes I wonder how some people can be so despicable."

"Overall, we have a nice crowd," I reminded her.

"You're right, Annie. But you never liked the idea of Hilda Hassel being here."

"That's true. Even before I met her. And we suspected from the moment we met her that she was a fraud. She and her so-called nephew. But we couldn't do anything about it. Hopefully Annabelle and David will see that this terrible business ends."

All the angst I'd been feeling about Stephanie and Randolph eased a bit when I saw the way Robbie's eyes lit at the sight of them.

Stephanie went over to him and gave him a tight hug, while Randolph gave him a pat on the back.

"You told me you had a surprise for me," said Robbie, smiling at them. He glanced at their suitcases. "Are you going to live with us?"

Stephanie shook her head. "We're just staying with you until we get things sorted out with a few problems."

"Okay," he said, picking up Cindy who was wiggling with excitement. Trudy, the lovely dog that she was sat patiently nearby, waiting for someone to pay attention to her. When no one did, she barked.

Vaughn came into the kitchen, his hair still wet from a shower. He shook hands with Randolph and gave Stephanie a kiss on the cheek. "Nice to have you. Ann gave me an update on your situation, and I think it's a wise idea for you to be here. We'll make it as relaxing for you as possible."

"Can we do more family puzzles?" asked Robbie.

Stephanie and Randolph smiled at him. The three of them had worked on jigsaw puzzles together over Christmas.

"How nice," I said, wanting to hug Robbie for his affection for his "grandparents". A simple idea of having temporary grandparents was turning into a very tender reality.

Vaughn picked up their suitcases and led Stephanie and Randolph to the guest suite. The dogs followed them all the way.

As I often did, I wondered if this was what having grandparents was like for everyone. Thinking back to my childhood, I knew how lucky I was to now have many people, related or not, in my growing family.

Later, when I received a phone call from Tina Marks telling me that she and Nicholas were coming for a long weekend and staying at one of the hotel's houses, I was reminded all over again.

"It's the sweetest story," said Tina. "Bobby Bailey called us, and not knowing who else to ask, he spoke to Nick and asked for Sydney's hand in marriage. I swear, both Nick and I teared up listening to him on the speaker phone. It's all very secret. Sydney thinks he's going to propose on Valentine's Day which is why he's doing it the weekend before. And here's the best part, I'm in charge of a surprise engagement party to be held at his house."

"How exciting," I said, able to brush aside my worries in my excitement.

"Again, Sydney knows nothing about this," said Tina. "He's taking her to the Sanderling Cove Inn for an overnight stay and will make some excuse to return early. His parents are coming into town for the party, and I'll handle all the arrangements."

"Wow! I never realized he was such a romantic, such a family man."

"Me either. I'm so pleased that Syd will have the loving support she's lacked in much of her life. I think of her as a daughter."

"The same way I think of you," I said, feeling a sting in my eyes. When Tina first came to the hotel as a starlet looking to hide out while she lost weight, she'd been as difficult as anyone I'd ever met.

"Yes, I remember how kind you were to me. That's why I was able to reach out to Syd when she was in trouble."

"Will you tell Rhonda, Liz, and Angela about what's going on so they can plan to be at the party? Is there anyone else who should be invited?"

"Not that I know of ... maybe Rick's friend here at the hotel, Lauren Fletcher. They've gone out a few times. Liz will know more about it. I'll ask her."

"Great. Having just the two boys, this gives me an opportunity to do something I might not get a chance to do otherwise. Oh, I know it's not a wedding, but it's pretty close to one," said Tina, and I smiled at her enthusiasm.

Our conversation went on to other things, and though I wanted to tell her about the theft ring, I knew I couldn't. But I did tell her that Stephanie and Randolph were staying with us for a few days, and by the time they were here, our royal guest would be gone.

She told me about the boys and their activities and mentioned again how disappointed she'd been not to be able to come for the Christmas holidays.

"We'll make each of your visits a holiday," I said.

"Okay, I've got to go," said Tina. "I wish Jean-Luc had a catering business. I'd hire him in a minute."

"Jean-Luc and Lindsay are going to have a baby, and right now, when he's not working, his attention is focused on her. It's very sweet. He and his first wife couldn't have children, and Jean-Luc didn't think he'd ever have a child of his own."

"For Lindsay, it might be another way to push aside memories of her abusive husband," said Tina. "The world is full of troubled people."

"Yes," I said, wishing I could ask her opinion about Hilda Hassel.

We ended the call, and I immediately phoned Rhonda with the news.

"How nice," said Rhonda. "I thought Bobby was such a prick when I met him. Underneath all that bravado and entitled bullshit, he was a nice guy all along. I'm thrilled for him and Sydney. It proves to me what love can do. And after our time with Hilda Hassel and her gang, I'll be relieved to focus on something nice."

"Me, too. I hope Hilda will pay her hotel bill and we can get her out of the Presidential Suite."

"Oh, my Gawd! I never thought of that. What if she decides not to leave?"

"I think a certain couple we know might help her decide her time at The Beach House Hotel is up," I said, hoping it wouldn't end in a big confrontation. Foremost in my mind was protecting the reputation of the hotel and keeping our guests protected.

"Will you do me a favor and ask Angela and Reggie to save the date for the engagement party. I'm going to call Liz now."

"Sure," said Rhonda. "I may even drive over to see Angela. I haven't talked to her in a couple of days, and it will be good to have some time with her."

"When did our girls get so busy with families of their own?" I asked. "It seems like yesterday they and we first met."

"Do you ever think about growing old, Annie? Some days I worry I'll be too old to enjoy my kids as adults. Ever since I had that scare with a lump in my breast, I wonder what would've happened if it'd turned out to be bad."

"I get it, but, Rhonda, the best we all can do is live each day well. It's one reason I love working at the hotel with you. Every day is full of surprises and challenges. Without them, we might be focusing on the downs in our lives, not celebrating the highs."

"Yeah," said Rhonda quietly. In a brighter tone, she said, "It sure makes life fun when we can outdo Brock Goodwin."

"Thatta girl," I said, happy to see the old Rhonda back.

We laughed together.

CHAPTER TWENTY-SIX

I HEADED TO LIZ'S TO TELL HER ABOUT THE PARTY. I KNEW it would be a busy time there, but Sydney would be gone for the day, and I wanted the opportunity to talk to Liz without her around. I'd also get to see the Ts. Now that they were walking and had begun saying a couple of words, they didn't seem like babies anymore, and I didn't want to miss spending time with them.

Chad met me at the front door, holding Emma.

"Hi, darling," I said, giving both of them kisses on the cheek. I'd always liked Chad. A strawberry-blonde with sparkling blue eyes, he was a quiet, somewhat nerdy man who loved technology in all its forms. He was also a great water-sports guy who looked as if he could be on a poster advertising Florida. Best of all, he was a good husband and father.

"Want to go to GeeGee?" he asked Emma, and she held out her arms to me.

I pressed her close to me and inhaled her fresh, clean baby smell. She patted my cheek. "Soff."

"Oh! She's learned a new word," I said surprised.

Chad laughed. "Between the three of them they're always saying something. The girls especially."

Liz emerged from a bedroom carrying Noah wrapped in a towel. Olivia ran toward us naked.

"Ready for me?" asked Chad.

"You can get Olivia dressed. I'll take care of Noah." She smiled at me. "Hi, Mom! Want to see your grandson?"

"Sure," I said, laughing when she handed me Noah in the

towel. With three children the same ages, Liz and Chad were used to handing one or two of them to family and friends.

As I got him dressed, I blew bubbles on Noah's stomach. He laughed and pinched my nose.

Squealing, I pulled away, and he laughed harder. My heart filled. Those musical notes were precious to me.

As soon as I'd finished dressing Noah, he wiggled to get down off the dressing table.

I set him on his feet, and he toddled away.

Liz appeared at the doorway. "Chad said he'd watch the kids. Let's go into his office and have a glass of wine. It's nice to see you."

"Thanks, sweetie. I'm always pleased to be here, but I don't want to intrude on your private time with Chad."

Liz laughed. "What private time? By the end of the evening, we're both exhausted. The only way we can have any private time is to get out of the house."

"Well, I may have some welcome news then."

In the kitchen, Liz poured us each a glass of red wine and we carried the glasses to Chad's office which was in a converted space above the garage.

We sat there, taking a moment to sip our wine as we faced one another with smiles.

"What's the news that couldn't wait?" Liz asked.

I told her about Tina's call and then said, "Can you think of people who'd want to be part of the surprise party?"

"You know Chad and I want to be there. And you already told me about Angela and Reggie. You're right about Bobby's brother, Rick, dating Lauren, so that's another one. But, Mom, Sydney's made a ton of friends in the neighborhood. Even the older couple next door to me would be devastated not to be invited."

"Just give me a list of names to send to Tina. She's making

all the arrangements and is thrilled to be doing so."

"I'll type a list for you later tonight—names and addresses. Sydney is going to be totally surprised. She's even picked out a restaurant for them to go to for Valentine's Day."

"This is going to be a lot of fun. I can't believe something that started out badly and then got worse with the kidnapping has turned out to be such a sweet story."

"All because of The Beach House Hotel," said Liz. "Another success."

"We've had a few," I admitted.

"And more to come," said Liz. "I hope they continue until Ange and I can take over."

"There are days when Rhonda and I can't wait, and then I sometimes wonder if I'll miss running it too much to let it go," I admitted.

"It's amazing what you two have done with the hotel, but Ange and I have some ideas, too." Liz shrugged. "But that's not going to happen for a while." She lifted her glass. "Here's to you. Our GeeGee."

"I have to admit I love that name," I said, growing teary. "I remember those dark days when we thought it might not happen."

We finished our wine, and then I explained that I had to get home to Vaughn and Robbie and our guests. "I can't share the details of the story just yet. When I can, both you and Angela should be told all about it."

Downstairs, I kissed each little one goodbye, thanked Chad for being a fantastic son-in-law and father, and hugged Liz. "Thanks for putting together a list. I don't believe there's any limit to the number of people who can be invited. Bobby's house is big enough to support a crowd."

I went back to my car looking forward to something pleasant happening in the future while still dealing with the reality of Hilda and Kurt.

As the time approached for Hilda's reservation to end, Rhonda and I became nervous about the hotel being scammed by them. I half expected Hilda and Kurt to disappear in the night. When we spoke to David and Annabelle about it, they told us not to worry. They were working on another plan. In the meantime, they were getting closer to identifying two men who were working with Hilda and Kurt by robbing houses up north.

One afternoon, Rhonda and I were standing in the lobby discussing decorations for our special Valentine's Day celebrations when I noticed a man heading for the private stairs to the Presidential Suite.

"Don't look now, but I think Hilda might be having a visitor."

Rhonda whipped around. "Yeah, I think you're right."

I took her arm. "Let's go see Bernie now."

We knocked on Bernie's office door, and when he called, "Come in."

We didn't hesitate.

"Hilda is having a visitor right now as we speak," I said.

"Do something," said Rhonda.

Bernie shook his head. "I don't have to. A friend of David's is involved. In fact, he promised to meet Kurt there."

"Is it safe for him to do this?" I asked.

"Absolutely. When Kurt asked Brock if he wanted to purchase his, Brock learned that the men Hilda was entertaining in bed were being filmed, and he told David about it."

"He must have been hysterical to think people in the neighborhood might find out about his time with her," I said.

"What a way to kick him out of office," Rhonda said gleefully.

Bernie raised a hand to stop her. "The FBI has promised to protect his name in exchange for the information he gave them."

My mind raced. "So, in addition to drawing men into having an encounter, Hilda and Kurt are blackmailing them with threats of releasing their videos?"

Bernie nodded. "Afraid so. Believe me, they and their friends are very nasty people."

"I hate the idea they're staying in our hotel," I said, rubbing my stomach as acid filled it.

"It's sickening," agreed Rhonda.

"They won't be here that much longer," said Bernie. "The FBI is going to arrest them this afternoon."

"What about their bill? We can't lose the money they owe us," I said.

Bernie's smile was triumphant. "I've already charged their credit card and it went through. Even if they complain to the credit card company, we'll win. The FBI will make sure of it."

"I want to see them before they leave to make certain they know what kind of rotten people they are," stormed Rhonda.

"There will be none of that. The gentleman working with David and Annabelle will make sure all goes smoothly. At the same time, they're arresting Hilda and Kurt, David's co-workers in New York are arresting the two men who've been assisting in these thefts, stealing documents, and breaking into homes. Even more people will be arrested in the days to come."

"What about Stephanie's house? Their accounts?" I asked.

"I don't know the status of that. But, hopefully, much of their stolen property can be returned."

"Stephanie and Randolph planned to sell their house and

move to Florida after their winter vacation. I can't imagine
Stephanie ever wanting to live there again."

"I understand," said Bernie. "As more information comes
to light, I hope it doesn't affect our guests. We can't control
who decides to visit Hilda, of course, but we hope to prevent
possible exposure and financial ruin to those who did."

I wrung my hands. "People could complain that we knew
about prostitution but did nothing about it."

"That is something the FBI will have to explain," said
Bernie. "Our job is to take care of our guests, and we do a
superb job of that."

"Stupid is as stupid does. We don't have to take the rap for
stupidity," said Rhonda.

"No, we don't," said Bernie. A knock sounded on the door.
Bernie stood and walked toward it.

"Hello, David. Ready to go?"

"Yes, Annabelle will meet us there shortly," said David.

"I want to come with you," said Rhonda.

David shook his head. "You can meet us behind the hotel
to see Hilda and Kurt taken off the property, but you can't join
us until then. It could be dangerous."

The men left, and deflated, Rhonda sank down in a chair.
"I wanted to see the surprise on Kurt's face when he realized
his game was over."

"I'd like to ask Hilda what in the world she was doing
mixed up in something like this," I said.

"I'm ecstatic we didn't lose thousands of dollars of fees for
renting the Presidential Suite to them," said Rhonda.

"Me, too." I went over rooms' revenues daily and the
thought of losing money to someone I hadn't trusted from the
beginning was a reminder for me in the future.

A short while later, Bernie texted us, and Rhonda and I took off for the back of the hotel. I was anxious to make sure that all had gone smoothly, and we'd never see Hilda or Kurt again.

We went through the back kitchen door and onto the receiving area. Two black SUVs were parked beyond it. David and Annabelle stood by with Bernie as two men loaded luggage into the backs of the cars. Hilda sat in the back seat of one SUV; Kurt, in the other. I walked over to where Hilda was and saw that her hands were handcuffed behind her back. The men who'd finished loading luggage in the cars approached Rhonda and me. With their suit jackets unbuttoned, I noticed their shoulder straps holding guns. It made the terrible situation seem real, even sinister.

One of the men said, "These two won't be doing any damage to anyone for a long time."

As the two SUVs drove away, David said, "Their mistake was being greedy and taking that extra step of extortion, blackmailing the men they'd entrapped." He turned to Rhonda. "Your friend's ego helped us make these arrests."

"You mean Brock Goodwin?" asked Rhonda, her eyes round with surprise.

"Yes," said Annabelle. "You can't imagine how frightened he was about losing his position as president of the neighborhood association." She coughed and then a soft laugh escaped her lips. "Apparently, it's a very important position."

I looked at Rhonda and we both began to laugh, helping to ease the tension of the day.

Still laughing, Rhonda said, "I refuse to think of Brock as a fuckin' hero. And if you make him think he was, he'll try even harder to make our lives difficult."

"I understand," said Annabelle.

"What happened to the film of Brock and Hilda?" I asked.

Bernie's lips curved. "Let's just say it's in a safe place."

"Very good," said Rhonda.

I nodded my approval, but I knew we'd never get rid of Brock Goodwin and his antics.

grown. It takes a grounded woman to handle Bobby," said Michelle, "and he adores her."

"He's a sweetheart," said Tina, and I glanced at Rhonda who'd just entered the kitchen. She hadn't liked Bobby at all when we'd first met him.

"I hope Bobby's coach is going to be here," I said. "He had enough faith in Bobby to send him to us at The Beach House Hotel."

Michelle smiled at me. "At the time, I wondered how that would help him, and then I met you and Rhonda."

"No one gets away with much with Rhonda around. She's not afraid to speak up."

"Who's not afraid to speak up?" asked Rhonda coming to stand beside me.

"You," I said.

"Honesty is the best policy," Rhonda said. "And when I meet a dickhead, I'm not afraid to tell him what I think."

"See?" I said, chuckling with the others.

The kitchen became fuller with guests. I was delighted but not surprised to see Consuela and Manny arrive. Bobby and Manny continued to be close. The idea of a continuing relationship between the two of them was another indication that life was full of circles.

"I see Bobby's car," cried one of Liz's neighbors who'd been standing guard by a living room window.

Everyone stopped talking and huddled together in the kitchen.

We heard Bobby park the car in the front circle. Then we heard car doors slamming.

In the kitchen, we held our collective breaths as we waited for the right moment to show ourselves.

A key sounded in the front door, and then light from the front entrance poured into the house.

When Bobby snapped on the lights in the living room, we all rushed toward them shouting, "Surprise!"

Stunned, Sydney stared at them, disbelief widening her eyes. She turned to Bobby. "What's this?"

"Happy Engagement Party, honey," said Bobby, wrapping an arm around her.

"Really?" Sydney burst into tears.

Michelle and Tina went to the couple together.

"We're all excited for the two of you," said Michelle, patting Sydney on the back.

Tina caressed Sydney's cheek and then pulled her close for a hug.

Between little sobs, Sydney said, "All these people are here for us?"

"Yes, silly," said Liz, beaming at her. "We all love you."

Sydney clapped a hand to her chest. "I can't believe it." She turned to Bobby. "And you arranged this?"

He shrugged shyly. "I asked Tina to put it together."

Sniffling, Sydney faced the crowd. "Okay, then. Let's party!"

Later, as Vaughn and I lay in bed and reminisced about our early love for one another, I fit my body to his. Sometimes people were brought together by unusual circumstances. It had happened for Vaughn and me.

"I believe they, like us, were fated to be together. Who knew that when Tina's little boy was taken and Bobby, one of the fastest football players, couldn't catch the kidnapper, he'd become a hero for being such a romantic.

The next morning, I was still feeling pleased to be part of

celebrating Bobby and Sydney's engagement with them.

I entered the hotel and went to get my cup of coffee in the kitchen. Rhonda was already there talking to Consuela about the party.

"It was beautiful, wasn't it?" I said, pouring myself a cup of coffee while Consuela handed me a warm cinnamon roll.

"A lovely party for a special couple," said Consuela. "Tina was as proud as any parent would be. She told me how much it meant to her to be asked to step in and help."

"I can only imagine what Sydney and Bobby's wedding will be like if Tina has any say in it," said Rhonda. "Thank goodness it will be here at the hotel."

"Sydney was adamant they wanted the wedding here on the beach, where Syd and Bobby first met," I added.

"Another opportunity for the two of you and the hotel," said Consuela.

"For the entire hotel family," I said, smiling at her. "Nothing could happen here at the hotel without the support you and everyone else gives us."

"I remember how thankful you were for us from the beginning," said Consuela. "A lot has happened since then."

"And will continue to do so," I said. "It's late. I'd better get to work."

"I'll be right there," said Rhonda.

Later, Rhonda and I were working in the office when Bernie called. "Ann? Can you and Rhonda please come to my office? There's someone I want you to meet."

Puzzled, I said, "Sure. We'll be right there."

"What's up?" Rhonda asked.

"Bernie wants us to meet someone. He sounded excited about it."

"I'm in the middle of a project. It'd better be good," grumbled Rhonda, getting to her feet.

As we walked through the lobby to Bernie's office, I looked around for any hints as to who Bernie might be with, but I noticed nothing.

We knocked on the door, and at Bernie's request to come in, we entered the room to find a very elegant-looking woman in her fifties sitting in a chair in front of Bernie's desk. Dressed in a pale green suit, she had silver hair pulled back in a stylish bun behind her head. Emerald earrings glittered at her ears. As I drew closer, I saw her features were refined and distinct with a patrician nose and brown eyes that sparkled. Her lips curved when she saw us.

Bernie stood. "Ann, Rhonda, I'd like you to meet Hilda Hassel."

I shook Hilda's hand. "I'm very pleased to meet you."

"The real you," said Rhonda, shaking Hilda's hand. "Welcome to The Beach House Hotel."

"Thank you." Hilda shook her head. "I can't believe my ex-housekeeper has done so many awful things using my name. I live a very quiet life. That's what Henrick and I chose to do when he was alive. I still miss him every day. He was such a lovely man."

"How did the two of you meet?" I asked.

"We met when I was doing some research. He and his family helped members of my own during terrible times in Germany. I knew he was the angel some had once called him. Even though he was much older than I, I believe we were meant to be together."

"That's such a touching story," I said realizing the terrible times she'd referred to were those in the Second World War when millions of people were ruthlessly murdered.

"You can imagine my distress when I learned what my

former housekeeper had done to destroy the Hassel name. I was most anxious to meet you, to explain that the real Hilda Hassel would never do anything to besmirch Henrick's reputation."

"I understand," I said. "It seems very unfair to have your identity used in such an awful way."

"Yes. It's horrifying. When I discovered that they'd used The Beach House Hotel as one of their chosen sites, I looked you up." Hilda's smile lit her eyes. "No wonder many people choose to come to such a beautiful place. I won't be able to stay here at this time, but I hope to be able to come back for a vacation. Perhaps, next year. I will certainly tell others about it."

"That's what we'd hoped when we saw your reservations request," said Rhonda.

"I understand High Tea has become a favorite event at The Beach House Hotel. I read all about it. I have brought a special gift for each of you."

Bernie lifted a silver box up onto his desk. Tied with a beautiful blue ribbon, it looked too nice to destroy.

"Please open it," said Hilda.

Together, Rhonda and I lifted the top and then ruffled through the tissue inside and lifted out four gifts wrapped in bubble wrap.

"Please be careful," warned Hilda.

A few minutes later, two saucers sat on Bernie's desk, each holding a lovely, paper-thin teacup. A coat of arms was painted on the side of the cup. Beautiful old-fashioned flowers were painted elsewhere on the cup and on the gold-rimmed saucer.

"How lovely," I said, realizing they were not only old, but valuable.

"They're antique family pieces. Since Henrick and I had no

children, I like to give them to people I admire," said Hilda. "I've read all about the two of you—two women who've worked together to prove they could survive after heartbreak." She beamed at us. "And survive you have! I hope you'll use these teacups to celebrate all you've accomplished."

Rhonda and I glanced at each other and back to her.

"I appreciate it. You must come and stay at the hotel," I said. "We'd love to have you here."

"We'd even serve you high tea every day if that's what you wanted," said Rhonda.

Hilda laughed. "Bernie told me that was my impostor's request. That part would be true. I love my tea in the afternoon. She used to serve it to me sometimes." She checked her watch and stood. "I'm sorry, but I can't stay. I have a flight to New York soon. But I couldn't come to the States without visiting you and your hotel."

"We'll see you out," I said.

After Hilda said goodbye to Bernie, she took my elbow, and Rhonda and I walked Hilda to the front of the hotel and down the stairs to where a black limousine waited.

We stood aside while Hilda got settled in the back seat. Then, just before the driver pulled away, Hilda leaned forward, looked out the window, and gave us a regal wave.

"Wow," said Rhonda. "She's definitely the real deal. What do you think? Will she come back to the hotel like she said?"

"I don't know," I said. "But if she does, I want to have high tea with her."

Rhonda laughed. "Who knows what's going to happen at The Beach House Hotel next?" She grabbed hold of my arm. "C'mon. Let's go in and find out."

CHAPTER TWENTY-EIGHT

A WEEK AFTER OUR VALENTINE'S DINNER DANCE, Rhonda and I sat with our daughters in the library of The Beach House Hotel to enjoy our first high tea together. Even though we were a little late to the event, due to illness among all six of our grandchildren, I was delighted to make this time together a late Valentine's Day gift for Liz and Angela. The idea of providing high tea on Sunday afternoons had caught on, and the room was crowded.

Behind the scenes, Lauren was doing a fabulous job of orchestrating the event, and Loretta Kapp from the local theater group was playing hostess dressed in appropriate costume. Sitting among our guests decked out in their finest, hearing their chatter, I let out a sigh of satisfaction. It seemed so festive inside on this cold February day.

As we were sipping our mimosas, Liz turned to me. "I had no idea what was going on behind the scenes nor that the fake Hilda Hassel and her accomplice, Kurt Bauer, would be that successful swindling people. I saw something on social media about the theft ring. Thank God, they didn't mention The Beach House Hotel."

"If Liz and I are to run the hotel one day, we don't want The Beach House Hotel's name to be tarnished. Right, Liz?" Angela asked her.

"Damn straight," said Liz, sounding more like Rhonda than her own daughter. Was that how it was going to be in the future?

I set down my glass and picked up the lovely but fragile

teacup the real Hilda had given me. I'd brought it with me to honor her. "We can survive most anything as long as our family ties remain strong. And I mean the hotel family as well as our own. It's growing in all kinds of interesting ways, but there's always room for more."

"Hear, hear!" said Rhonda, lifting her special teacup carefully, her crooked baby finger held away from the cup in a dainty fashion. "As we've done with high tea, we can work together on other new ideas, making them work for us. That's how we'll grow and keep up with the times."

"Yes, but we'll always make sure The Beach House Hotel remains the upscale place it is," I said.

Liz and Angela saluted us by raising their teacups. They, like Rhonda and I, knew that the hotel was unique, that guests came back year after year because we poured our love into keeping The Beach House Hotel a place where all were welcome. And if some of our hotel guests joined my hotel family, that made it even better.

# # #

Thank you for reading *High Tea at The Beach House Hotel*. If you enjoyed this book, please help other readers discover it by leaving a review on Amazon, Bookbub, Goodreads, or your favorite site. It's such a nice thing to do.

For your further enjoyment, the other books in The Beach House Hotel Series are available on all sites. Here are the Universal links:

Breakfast at The Beach House Hotel:
https://books2read.com/u/bpkoq4
Lunch at The Beach House Hotel:
https://books2read.com/u/3GWvp3
Dinner at The Beach House Hotel:
https://books2read.com/u/4N1yDW
Christmas at The Beach House Hotel:
https://books2read.com/u/38gZvd
Margaritas at The Beach House Hotel:
https://books2read.com/u/bMRrP7
Dessert at The Beach House Hotel:
ttps://books2read.com/u/mV6kX6
Coffee at The Beach House Hotel:
https://books2read.com/u/bOnE7A
High Tea at The Beach House Hotel:
https://books2read.com/u/mgN9AK
Nightcaps at The Beach Houise Hotel:
https://books2read.com/u/mBA2oy
Bubbles at The Beach House Hotel:
https://books2read.com/u/meGgRV

Sign up for my newsletter and get a free story. I keep my newsletters short and fun with giveaways, recipes, and the latest must-have news about me and my books. Welcome! Here's the link:

https://BookHip.com/RRGJKGN

Enjoy Chapter 1 of *Nightcaps at The Beach House Hotel,* Book 9 in The Beach House Hotel Series:

CHAPTER ONE

I SAT WITH MY BUSINESS PARTNER, RHONDA DELMONTE Grayson, in our office at The Beach House Hotel on the Gulf Coast in sunny Sable, Florida, wondering if we were facing another problem that we'd have trouble solving.

"Who is this nighttime talk show host anyway?" Rhonda asked. "I've never heard of him. Of course, I can't stay up beyond nine o'clock. Besides, who wants to see a program where every famous star is talking about who is dating whom or telling us what their favorite thing to wear is, or what they like to eat. Who the fuck cares? I'm too tired working here at the hotel and taking care of kids and grandkids to want to bother with stuff like that."

I knew enough to wait until Rhonda caught her breath. She and I were as different as two people could be. I'd grown up with a strict grandmother in Boston where proper language and decorum were everything. It still amazed me that Rhonda and I had become best friends and business partners. But Rhonda had a heart as big as the diamonds she wore in her ears, on her fingers, and at her neck and wrists. And I'd never forget all she'd done for me.

"Before we decide to honor his request to stay here for several weeks, we need to view at least a couple of his shows to help us decide for ourselves if it could work," I said. "C'mon, it won't be so bad. We'll have a couple of nightcaps and snacks while we watch the show."

"Humph. I suppose we need to know who we're dealing with, especially because he's requesting the same dates as Tina Marks," Rhonda said.

"The two of them would be staying in the hotel's two guesthouses apart from one another, so they should have the seclusion they require," I said. "But our loyalty goes to Tina." Tina Marks was like a daughter to us after we'd agreed to hide her at the hotel to lose some weight between movies. She'd been a tough brat when she'd first arrived but was now dear to us both.

"So, what's his name?" Rhonda asked me.

"Darryl Douglas," I replied. "He's fairly new in the business. He's had his own show for only a couple of years. I looked him up online. He's got a nice smile."

"Already I don't trust him. I hate a person who smiles while they're gossiping," said Rhonda, and I knew this was a piece of baggage from Rhonda's childhood. She grew up in New Jersey in a rough neighborhood and had been teased for her size.

Now that she was happily married and was financially secure after winning one hundred eighty-seven million dollars in the Florida lottery, people were much nicer to her. Still, Rhonda was a loyal person who saw through others who were not very kind. Maybe that's why our relationship worked. We'd both been betrayed by the men we'd first married.

"Let's look at a couple of his shows this week and see how we feel about his request after that," I said. "You can come to my house. Vaughn is away working on a movie in Canada, and Robbie will be in bed. We can enjoy our time together."

"Nightcaps, huh? With a few treats? Okay, but if I still don't like the guy, I don't care what kind of situation he's in, he's not staying at the hotel."

"As I understand it, Darryl's ex-wife is saying he owes her more money and there's some sort of problem at work. That's all his agent would tell me when he called to ask for the reservation. He did mention the vice-president had recommended the hotel."

Rhonda shook her head. "That does it. Every time Amelia Swanson recommends the hotel to someone, we get caught in a bad situation. I still haven't recovered from the kidnapping attempt."

"I admit that was scary, but it was a one-time thing. We've beefed up security at the hotel and have vetted our guests whenever we feel it's necessary."

"Let's take a walk on the beach. We do our best thinking there," said Rhonda.

I happily followed her through the back of the hotel, the pool area, and onto the sand. An onshore breeze ruffled the fronds of the palm trees on our property, and satisfied that all was well at the hotel, I took off my sandals and followed Rhonda onto the beach.

The smell of salt air loosened some of the tension in my body. I always felt more clearheaded watching the waves roll in, kiss the shore, and back away in a rhythm as old as time. I went to the water's frothy edge and dipped my toe into the cool wetness.

Seagulls and terns whirled in the air above us, their cries echoing against the moving water. Down the beach, sandpipers and sanderlings trotted along the water's edge looking for food, leaving tiny footprints behind.

I took in a deep breath of fresh air and let out a sigh of happiness. Then I turned and studied the hotel.

Like a lazy flamingo stretched along the sand, the front of it hugged a wide expanse of beach while the rest of the building's image was softened by palm trees and the immaculate landscaping surrounding it.

"Look what we've done," said Rhonda, throwing an arm around my shoulder. "Our own special baby."

I laughed. We were surrounded by babies. Rhonda had

three children and three grandchildren while I had my two kids and triplet grandchildren. But Rhonda was right. The Beach House Hotel was our special baby, born of the need to prove that two dumped women could make a new, better life on their own and with new men in their lives who truly loved them.

Rhonda and I took off, walking together on the sand, talking.

"We've always helped people," said Rhonda. "And I like that part of the business we've built. But we have to be careful. Remember, when we first started our privacy-for-guests policy, you worried we were going to be running a place where all kinds of hanky-panky would take place."

I couldn't help laughing. We'd started that policy when certain members of Congress had come to us needing an upscale place to meet in secret. Since then, the hotel had hosted numerous VIP guests and endured many unusual experiences. But we were known for being as upfront and straightforward as we could be. Our guests came back again and again.

"Has Tina decided to bring the kids when she comes to the hotel?" Rhonda asked me.

"She's leaving them at home with her nanny and bringing her personal trainer instead. She has to be ready to start filming in a month, and like her first time here, she needs to lose weight and get in shape. It must be hard to feel you have to be perfect to compete with younger actresses."

"It can be a nasty business." Rhonda grabbed my arm. "Speaking of nasty business, look who's headed our way. No chance I can run fast enough to get away."

"We'll say hi and keep walking," I said, hoping we could. Brock Goodwin was president of the neighborhood association and had been a thorn in our sides since the beginning when he'd tried to stop the hotel from opening. Though we'd succeeded in getting past those objections, he was always looking for a way to interfere. We detested him.

Tall, gray-haired, and in shape, Brock was sought-after by single women living in the area for his looks and suave manner which hid his true personality.

"Well, if it isn't the two biggest troublemakers in the neighborhood," said Brock.

"Hello, Brock," I said moving past him. "We can't stay to chat. We're talking business."

He ran to catch up to us. "Is there anything I should know about?"

"As you know, we keep business and our guests private," said Rhonda.

He studied her. "I can already tell you've got something going on, something you no doubt want to keep secret," he said in his presumptuous way. "You know I won't rest until I find out what it is. After all, as president of the neighborhood association, it's my duty to be well-informed."

"I hear someone is going to run against you for that position. Someone new in town," said Rhonda. "See ya later."

We kept on walking.

A few minutes later, I looked back. Brock was still standing there staring out at the water. I nudged Rhonda. "Good job. He's still wondering who might take his precious position away from him. You were kidding about it, right?"

"Yeah. Who wants to be president of a fuckin' neighborhood association? No one. That's who."

I started to chuckle, and soon we were both laughing hard. We'd do anything to get Brock off our backs. After tricking him into bidding on something he couldn't afford for a charity event, we'd made a special deal with him to stay away from the second guesthouse we were building on our property. It wasn't a bad idea. The house was constructed in record time with no problems from anyone. It was this house that Darryl wanted to stay in.

When we headed back to the hotel, Brock wasn't in sight. I decided to call our friend, Dorothy Stern, to tell her about Rhonda's remark to Brock. Dorothy was a retired businesswoman who'd help us out when we first opened the hotel by doing volunteer work sending out notices and invitations to our special events. At just over five feet tall, she was the one person who seemed able to stand up to Brock. She'd been known to put him in his place more than once. We adored her.

We headed into the kitchen for a morning cup of coffee and one of Consuela's cinnamon rolls. These treats had been helpful when trying to tempt early guests with reasons to stay at The Beach House Hotel. They had become a specialty of the hotel after a food critic from New York stayed at the hotel and mentioned it to all his fans.

Consuela greeted us with a smile. "*Buenos Dias!* You're just in time. A few minutes ago, I took a second batch of sweet rolls out of the oven."

"Good morning. Did you have a nice couple of days off?" I gave her a hug. Consuela and her husband, Manny, had been working for Rhonda before we opened the hotel. They stayed on and became the heart of the hotel family. The two of them were the parents I always wished I'd had.

"We did have a nice break, though you know Manny," said Consuela. "He doesn't like to leave the landscaping of the property in anyone else's hands for too long."

"Annie, I told you when we first met, he's my 'Manny around the house'," said Rhonda, giving me a wide grin.

Consuela and I glanced at one another and laughed.

At the time, Rhonda had also mentioned she had a beach

house. I had no idea it was a seaside estate that had once been a small hotel.

"It's nice to have you and Manny back with us," I said, placing a warm sweet roll onto a plate..

"We couldn't run the place without you," said Rhonda giving Consuela a bosomy hug. "I'm going to take one more cinnamon roll to the office. Annie and I have to talk about an upcoming guest."

We took coffee and our treats to the office we shared.

I no sooner sat down at my desk than my cell phone rang. *Amelia Swanson.*

"Hello, Madame Vice President. I'm going to put you on speaker phone in our office so Rhonda can hear too. Okay?"

"Yes. I just wanted to check to see if you're going to be able to handle Darryl Douglas's request. His agent is a friend of mine and the president's too."

"We have the request, but I'm not sure we can accommodate him. We'll know more tomorrow. It would mean moving someone out of the guesthouse and into a room."

"And after the last time we did you a favor ..." Rhonda began.

"We'll be sure to let you know," I interrupted. I knew Rhonda was going to mention the kidnapping that took place, and I didn't want to get her riled up and saying something we'd both regret. We'd survived a couple of tricky situations satisfying Amelia's requests, and the thought of being forced to face the possibility of another traumatic one was worrisome.

"I've got to go," said Amelia. "I hope you understand the political importance of this for me. I may be needing people in the media in the future."

"We understand," I said, "but we must be able to take care

of our guests properly."

"I'm aware," said Amelia. "You know how much I appreciate your help in the past. I can't think of a better place than your hotel to send people to."

I felt my lips curving. Amelia was an excellent politician.

"We'll have a decision tomorrow," I said.

"Okay, I'll hold you to it," said Amelia. "How's the weather? Any storms?"

"Nothing to report," I said, crossing my fingers. Early fall was a time for hurricanes to

visit.

"Nice to talk to you. I may be down to visit my sister soon and hope to stop in," said Amelia. "Thanks."

She ended the call, and Rhonda and I faced one another.

Rhonda made a face. "That woman always gets her way. No wonder she's close to the president. He couldn't do his job without her."

"That's not the way that position usually works, but I agree with you." I took a sip of coffee, my mind whirling. "Let's see what we can find out about Darryl online. First, I want to return these dishes to the kitchen and check the dining room. It's a bit of a slow time, and we need to know how the dining staff is doing."

We walked into the dining room and saw Dorothy Stern sitting at a table with three friends deep in conversation.

I waved, and Rhonda and I went over to her. "It's great to see you here. We have something to tell you in private. What are you ladies talking about?"

"Darryl Douglas. We think he's having some kind of breakdown and wants to leave the show," said Dorothy.

"It all started with that horrible ex-wife of his, Everly Jansen," said one of the other women. "She's greedy. She married him for his money."

"Yeah, it wasn't for his looks," said another woman. "I love the guy, but you have to admit he's not buff or drop-dead gorgeous like some of the stars he interviews."

"That's what makes him special. He has a quick wit, and the way he comes up with jokes is hilarious," said Dorothy. "We're all fans of his."

"And none of us wanted him to marry that woman. We knew she was bad news," said one of women.

"I'm curious," said Rhonda. "Why do you care so much about Darryl Douglas and his career?"

"I'll tell you. As funny as he is, he doesn't tear down other people to make us laugh like a lot of other comedians." Dorothy glanced at the others for their approval. "I don't know. He's kind. Heaven knows we could use a lot more people like that."

The other women at the table nodded their agreement.

"But shows like his seem meaningless," countered Rhonda.

"You have to see his shows to believe us," said Dorothy.

"Right. That's why we're watching one tonight," I said shooting a look of determination to Rhonda. "But if what you say is right, it makes me like him already."

"Let me know what you both think," said Dorothy.

I gave her a thumbs up. Rhonda and I had to make that decision quickly, though we might regret it.

# # # # #

About the Author

A *USA Today* **Best-Selling Author,** Judith Keim is a hybrid author who both has a publisher and self-publishes. Ms. Keim writes heart-warming novels about women who face unexpected challenges, meet them with strength, and find love and happiness along the way—stories with heart. Her best-selling books are based, in part, on many of the places she's lived or visited, and on the interesting people she's met, creating believable characters and realistic settings her many loyal readers love.

She enjoyed her childhood and young adult years in Elmira, New York, and now makes her home in Boise, Idaho, with her husband, Peter, and their lovable miniature Dachshund, Wally, and other members of her family.

While growing up, she was drawn to the idea of writing stories from a young age. Books were always present, being read, ready to go back to the library, or about to be discovered. All in her family shared information from the books in general conversation, giving them a wealth of knowledge and vivid imaginations.

Ms. Keim loves to hear from her readers and appreciates their enthusiasm for her stories.

"I hope you've enjoyed this book. If you have, please help other readers discover it by leaving a review on the site of your choice. And please check out my other books and series:

The Hartwell Women Series
The Beach House Hotel Series
The Fat Fridays Group
The Salty Key Inn Series
The Chandler Hill Inn Series
Seashell Cottage Books
The Desert Sage Inn Series
Soul Sisters at Cedar Mountain Lodge
The Sanderling Cove Inn Series
The Lilac Lake Inn Series

ALL THE BOOKS ARE NOW AVAILABLE IN AUDIO on Audible, iTunes, Findaway, Kobo, and Google Play! So fun to have these characters come alive!"

Ms. Keim can be reached at **www.judithkeim.com**

And to like my author page on Facebook and keep up with the news, go to: **http://bit.ly/2pZWDgA**

To receive notices about new books, follow me on Book Bub:

https://www.bookbub.com/authors/judith-keim

Sign up for my newsletter and get a free story. I keep my newsletters short and fun with giveaways, recipes, and the latest must-have news about me and my books. Welcome! Here's the link:

https://BookHip.com/RRGJKGN

I am also on Twitter @judithkeim, LinkedIn, and Goodreads. Come say hello!

Acknowledgements

As always, I am eternally grateful to my team of editors, Peter Keim and Lynn Mapp, my book cover designer, Lou Harper, and my narrator for Audible and iTunes, Angela Dawe. They are the people who take what I've written and help turn it into the book I proudly present to you, my readers! I also wish to thank my coffee group of writers who listen and encourage me to keep on going. Thank you, Peggy Staggs, Lynn Mapp, Cate Cobb, Nikki Jean Triska, Joanne Pence, Melanie Olsen, and Megan Bryce. And to you, my fabulous readers, I thank you for your continued support and encouragement. Without you, this book would not exist. You are the wind beneath my wings.

Printed in the USA
CPSIA information can be obtained
at www.ICGtesting.com
LVHW090354090924
790474LV00010B/592